PRISONERS
& OTHER STORIES

PRISONERS
& OTHER STORIES

ED GORMAN

CD PUBLICATIONS

Baltimore

❖ 1992 ❖

ACKNOWLEDGEMENTS

"The Reason Why" first appeared in *Criminal Elements*, edited by Bill Pronzini and Martin Greenberg, Copyright 1988 by Ed Gorman

"Mother Darkness" first appeared in *New Crimes 4*, edited by Maxim Jakubowski, Copyright 1992 by Ed Gorman

"Render Unto Caesar" first appeared in *Pulphouse Magazine*, Copyright 1992 by Ed Gorman

"Dancers" first appeared (in different form) in *The New Review*, Copyright 1978, 1992 by Gorman

"Duty" first appeared in *Under The Fang*, edited by Robert R. McCammon, Copyright 1991 by Ed Gorman

"Failed Prayers" first appeared in The *Mystery Scene Reader*, Copyright 1987 by Ed Gorman

"Layover" first appeared (in different form) in *Lonesome Roads*, Copyright 1977, 1992 by Ed Gorman

"Idol" first appeared in *The Further Adventures of Batman*, edited by Martin H. Greenberg, Copyright 1989 by DC Comics, reprinted here with permission

"The Jungle" first appeared in *Stalkers*, Copyright 1992 by Ed Gorman

"My Cousin Cal" first appeared in *Mr. President, Private Eye*, edited by Martin H. Greenberg, Copyright 1989 by Ed Gorman

"The Curse" first appeared in *Dick Tracy: The Secret Files*, edited by Max Allan Collins, Copyright 1990 by Ed Gorman

"Long Time Till Morning Comes" first appeared in *Narrow Houses*, edited by Peter Crowther, Copyright 1992 by Ed Gorman

"My Friend Bobby" first appeared (in different form) in *The Coe Review*, Copyright 1981, 1992 by Ed Gorman

"Stalker" first appeared in *Stalkers*, Copyright 1990 by Ed Gorman

"The Monster" first appeared in *Cemetery Dance Magazine*, Copyright 1990 by Ed Gorman

"The Ugly File" appears here for the first time, Copyright 1992 by Ed Gorman

"Bless us, Oh Lord" first appeared in *Shivers*, edited by Richard T. Chizmar, Copyright 1992 by Ed Gorman

"Turn Away" first appeared in *The First Black Lizard Anthology*, Copyright 1987 by Ed Gorman

"The Coming of Night" first appeared in *Masques 4*, edited by J.N. Williamson, Copyright 1992 by Ed Gorman

"The Long Silence After" first appeared in *Dark at Heart*, edited by Karen and Joe R. Lansdale, Copyright 1992 by Ed Gorman

"The Wind From Midnight" first appeared in *Bradbury's Friends*, edited by William F. Nolan and Martin H. Greenberg, Copyright 1992 by Ed Gorman

"Prisoners" first appears in *New Crimes 1*, edited by Maxim Jakubowski, Copyright 1990 by Ed Gorman

"Afterword" appears here for the first time, Copyright 1992 by Dean R. Koontz

*For my mother and father
who bought me the books
and listened to the dreams.*

Trade Hardcover Edition ISBN 1-881475-00-X
Signed & Slipcased Hardcover Edition ISBN 1-881475-01-8

The publishers would like to extend sincere thanks to the following people: William and Olga Chizmar and family, John and Ruth Tipton and family, Bill Caughron, Kim Bouder, Adam Fusco, Mark Ziesing, and Thomas F. Monteleone.

And very special thanks go to Ed and Carol Gorman, Bob Korn, and Dean R. Koontz.

FIRST EDITION

CD Publications / P.O. Box 18433 / Baltimore, MD / 21237

CONTENTS

INTRODUCTION

My seventh grade nun, Sister Mary Rosalinda, must have liked the first short story I ever wrote and showed to her because she soon encouraged me to write one a week, which she kept in a special three-ring notebook on her desk.

She was my first editor, and a more charitable and loving editor would be hard to find.

I hope she would approve of this book, and keep it proudly on her desk alongside that other one, because I have included here only those stories that are true in some way, by which I mean personal. The writers I like always write this way. A short story is a letter from a good friend. He wants to tell you about something that has touched or frightened or pleased him, and he wants to tell you honestly so you can share his experience with him.

I hope these stories touch or frighten or please you in some way, and I hope that Sister Mary Rosalinda, wherever she may be, understands how often and how fondly I think of her.

–Ed Gorman

A few years before I met my wife Carol, I ran into the most beautiful girl in my high school class. She was still beautiful. We saw each other for a few weeks and she told me a great deal about herself, mostly how she'd never forgotten the abortion she'd had in the back seat of a car when we were in but the eighth grade, and how terrified she was—four husbands down and God only knew how many to go—of losing her looks. A year later, she got married again, this time to a very wealthy man indeed, and so I decided it was time to write all this down somehow.

THE REASON WHY

"I'm scared."

"This was your idea, Karen."

"You scared?"

"No."

"You bastard."

"Because I'm not scared I'm a bastard?"

"You not being scared means you don't believe me."

"Well."

"See. I knew it."

"What?"

"Just the way you said 'Well.' You bastard."

I sighed and looked out at the big red brick building that sprawled over a quarter mile of spring grass turned silver by a fat June moon. Twenty-five years ago a 1950 Ford fastback had sat in the adjacent parking lot. Mine for two summers of grocery store work.

We were sitting in her car, a Volvo she'd cadged from her last marriage settlement, number four if you're interested, and sharing a pint of bourbon the way we used to in high school when we'd been more than friends but never quite lovers.

The occasion tonight was our twenty-fifth class reunion. But there was another occasion, too. In our senior year a boy named Michael Brandon had jumped off a steep clay cliff called Pierce Point to his death on the winding river road below. Suicide. That, anyway, had been the official version.

A month ago Karen Lane (she had gone back to her maiden

13

name these days, the Karen Lane-Cummings-Todd-Brown-LeMay getting a tad too long) had called to see if I wanted to go to dinner and I said yes, if I could bring Donna along, but then Donna surprised me by saying she didn't care to go along, that by now we should be at a point in our relationship where we trusted each other ("God, Dwyer, I don't even look at other men, not for very long anyway, you know?"), and Karen and I had had dinner and she'd had many drinks, enough that I saw she had a problem, and then she'd told me about something that had troubled her for a long time . . .

In senior year she'd gone to a party and gotten sick on wine and stumbled out to somebody's backyard to throw up and it was there she'd overheard the three boys talking. They were earnestly discussing what happened to Michael Brandon the previous week and they were even more earnestly discussing what would happen to them if "anybody ever really found out the truth."

"It's bothered me all these years," she'd said over dinner a month earlier. "They murdered him and they got away with it."

"Why didn't you tell the police?"

"I didn't think they'd believe me."

"Why not?"

She shrugged and put her lovely little face down, dark hair covering her features. Whenever she put her face down that way it meant that she didn't want to tell you a lie so she'd just as soon talk about something else.

"Why not, Karen?"

"Because of where we came from. The highlands."

The Highlands is an area that used to ring the iron foundries and factories of this city. Way before pollution became a fashionable concern, you could stand on your front porch and see a peculiarly beautiful orange haze on the sky every dusk. The Highlands had bars where men lost ears, eyes, and fingers in just garden-variety fights, and streets where nobody sane ever walked after dark, not even cops unless they were in pairs. But it wasn't the physical violence you remembered so much as the emotional violence of poverty. You get tired of hearing your mother scream because there isn't enough money for food and hearing your father scream back because there's nothing he can do about it. Nothing.

Karen Lane and I had come from the Highlands, but we were smarter and, in her case, better looking than most of the people from the area, so when we went to Wilson High School— one of those nightmare conglomerates that shoves the poorest kids in a city in with the richest—we didn't do badly for ourselves. By senior year we found ourselves hanging out with the sons and daughters of bankers and doctors and city officials and lawyers and riding around in new Impala convertibles and attending an occasional party where you saw an actual maid. But wherever we went, we'd manage for at least a few minutes to get away from our dates and talk to each other. What we were doing, of course, was trying to comfort ourselves. We shared terrible and confusing feelings—pride that we were acceptable to those we saw as glamorous, shame that we felt disgrace for being from the Highlands and having fathers who worked in factories and mothers who went to Mass as often as nuns and brothers and sisters who were doomed to punching the clock and yelling at ragged kids in the cold factory dusk. (You never realize what a toll such shame takes till you see your father's waxen face there in the years-later casket.)

That was the big secret we shared, of course. Karen and I, that we were going to get out, leave the place once and for all. And her brown eyes never sparkled more Christmas-morning bright than at those moments when it all was ahead of us, money, sex, endless thrills, immortality. She had the kind of clean good looks brought out best by a blue cardigan with a line of white button-down shirt at the top and a brown suede car coat over her slender shoulders and moderately tight jeans displaying her quietly artful ass. Nothing splashy about her. She had the sort of face that snuck up on you. You had the impression you were talking to a pretty but in no way spectac-ular girl, and then all of a sudden you saw how the eyes burned with sad humor and how wry the mouth got at certain times and how the freckles enhanced rather than detracted from her beauty and by then of course you were hopelessly entangled. Hopelessly.

This wasn't just my opinion, either. I mentioned four divorce settlements. True facts. Karen was one of those prizes that powerful and rich men like to collect with the understanding that it's only something you hold in trust, like a yachting cup. So, in her time, she'd been an ornament for a professional football player (her college beau), an orthodontist ("I think he used to have sexual fantasies about Barry Goldwater"), the owner of a large commuter airline ("I slept with half his pilots; it was kind of a company benefit"), and a sixty-nine-year-old millionaire who was dying of heart disease ("He used to have me sit next to his bedside and just hold his hand—the weird thing was that of all of them, I loved him, I really did—and his eyes would be closed and then every once in a while tears would start streaming down his cheeks as if he was remembering something that really filled him with remorse; he was really a sweetie, but then cancer got him before the heart disease and I never did find out what he regretted so much, I mean if it was about his son or his wife or what"), and now she was comfortably fixed for the rest of her life and if the crow's feet were a little more pronounced around eyes and mouth and if the slenderness was just a trifle too slender (she weighed, at five-three, maybe ninety pounds and kept a variety of diet books in her big sunny kitchen), she was a damn good-looking woman nonetheless, the world's absurdity catalogued and evaluated in a gaze that managed to be both weary and impish, with a laugh that was knowing without being cynical.

So now she wanted to play detective.

I had some more bourbon from the pint—it burned beautifully—and said, "If I had your money, you know what I'd do?"

"Buy yourself a new shirt?"

"You don't like my shirt?"

"I didn't know you had this thing about Hawaii?"

"If I had your money I'd just forget about all of this."

"I thought cops were sworn to uphold the right and the

true."

"I'm an ex-cop."

"You wear a uniform."

"That's for the American Security Agency."

She sighed. "So I shouldn't have sent the letters?"

"No."

"Well, if they're guilty, they'll show up at Pierce Point tonight."

"Not necessarily."

"Why?"

"Maybe they'll know it's a trap. And not do anything."

She nodded to the school. "You hear that?"

"What?"

"The song?"

It was Bobby Vinton's "Roses are Red."

"I remember one party when we both hated our dates and we ended up dancing to that over and over again. Somebody's basement. You remember?"

"Sort of, I guess," I said.

"Good. Let's go in the gym and then we can dance to it again."

Donna, my lady friend, was out of town attending an advertising convention. I hoped she wasn't going to dance with anybody else because it would sure make me mad.

I started to open the door and she said, "I want to ask you a question."

"What?" I sensed what it was going to be so I kept my eyes on the parking lot.

"Turn around and look at me."

I turned around and looked at her. "Okay."

"Since the time we had dinner a month or so ago I've started receiving brochures from Alcoholics Anonymous in the mail. If you were having them sent to me, would you be honest enough to tell me?"

"Yes, I would."

"Are you having them sent to me?"

"Yes, I am."

"You think I'm a lush?"

"Don't you?"

"I asked you first."

So we went into the gym and danced.

Crepe of red and white, the school colors, draped the ceiling; the stage was a cave of white light on which stood four balding fat guys with spit curls and shimmery gold lamé dinner jackets (could these be the illegitimate sons of Bill Haley?) playing guitars, drum, and saxophone; on the dance floor couples who'd lost hair, teeth, jaw lines, courage, and energy (everything, it seemed, but weight) danced to lame cover versions of "Breaking Up Is Hard To Do" and "Sheila," "Runaround Sue" and "Running Scared" (tonight's lead singer sensibly not even trying Roy Orbison's beautiful falsetto) and then, they broke into a medley of dance tunes— everything from "Locomotion" to "The Peppermint Twist" —and the place went a little crazy, and I went right along with it.

"Come on," I said.

"Great."

We went out there and we burned ass. We'd both agreed not to dress up for the occasion so we were ready for this. I wore the Hawaiian shirt she found so despicable plus a blue blazer, white socks and cordovan penny-loafers. She wore a salmon-colored Merikani shirt belted at the waist and tan cotton fatigue pants and, sweet Christ, she was so adorable half the guys in the place did the kind of double-takes usually reserved for somebody outrageous or famous.

Over the blasting music, I shouted, "Everybody's watching you!"

She shouted right back, "I know! Isn't it wonderful?"

The medley went twenty minutes and could easily have been confused with an aerobics session. By the end I was sopping and wishing I was carrying ten or fifteen pounds less and sometimes feeling guilty because I was having too much fun (I just hoped Donna, probably having too much fun, too, was feeling guilty), and then finally it ended and mate fell into the arms of mate, hanging on to stave off sheer collapse.

Then the head Bill Haley clone said, "Okay, now we're going to do a ballad medley," so then we got everybody from Johnny Mathis to Connie Francis and we couldn't resist that, so I moved her around the floor with clumsy pleasure and she moved me right back with equally clumsy pleasure. "You know something?" I said.

"We're both shitty dancers?"

"Right."

But we kept on, of course, laughing and whirling a few times, and then coming tighter together and just holding each other silently for a time, two human beings getting older and scared about getting older, remembering some things and trying to forget others and trying to make sense of an existence that ultimately made sense to nobody, and then she said, "There's one of them."

I didn't have to ask her what "them" referred to. Until now she'd refused to identify any of the three people she'd sent the letters to.

At first I didn't recognize him. He had almost white hair and a tan so dark it looked fake. He wore a black dinner jacket with a lacy shirt and a black bow tie. He didn't seem to have put on a pound in the quarter century since I'd last seen him.

"Ted Forester?"

"Forester," she said. "He's president of the same savings and loan his father was president of."

"Who are the other two?"

"Why don't we get some punch?"

"The kiddie kind?"

"You could really make me mad with all this lecturing about alcoholism."

"If you're really not a lush then you won't mind getting the kiddie kind."

"My friend, Sigmund Fraud."

We had a couple of pink punches and caught our respective breaths and squinted in the gloom at name tags to see who we were saying hello to and realized all the terrible things you realize at high school reunions, namely that people who thought they were better than you still think that way, and that all the sad people you feared for—the ones with blackheads and low IQs and lame left legs and walleyes and lisps and every other sort of unfair infirmity people get stuck with—generally turned out to be deserving of your fear, for there was melancholy in their eyes tonight that spoke of failures of every sort, and you wanted to go up and say something to them (I wanted to go up to nervous Karl Carberry, who used to twitch—his whole body twitched—and throw my arm around him and tell him what a neat guy he was, tell him there was no reason whatsoever for his twitching, grant him peace and self-esteem and at least a modicum of hope; if he needed a woman, get him a woman, too), but of course you didn't do that, you didn't go up, you just made edgy jokes and nodded a lot and drifted on to the next piece of human carnage.

"There's number two," Karen whispered.

This one I remembered. And despised. The six-three blond movie-star looks had grown only slightly older. His blue dinner jacket just seemed to enhance his air of malicious superiority. Larry Price. His wife Sally was still perfect, too, though you could see in the lacquered blond hair and maybe a hint of face lift that she'd had to work at it a little harder. A year out of high school, at a bar that took teenage IDs checked by a guy who must have been legally blind, I'd gotten drunk and told Larry that he was essentially an asshole for beating up a friend of mine who hadn't had a chance against him. I had the street boy's secret belief that I could take anybody whose father was a surgeon and whose house included a swimming pool. I had hatred, bitterness, and rage going, right? Well, Larry and I went out into the parking lot, ringed by a lot of drunken spectators, and before I got off a single punch, Larry hit me with a shot that stood me straight up, giving him a great opportunity to hit me again. He hit me three times before I found his face and sent him a shot hard enough to push him back for a time. Before we could go at it again, the guy who checked IDs got himself between us. He was madder than either Larry or me. He ended the fight by taking us both by the ears (he must have trained with nuns) and dragging us out to the curb and telling neither of us to come back.

"You remember the night you fought him?"

"Yeah."

"You could have taken him, Dwyer. Those three punches he got in were just lucky."

"Yeah, that was my impression, too. Lucky."

She laughed. "I was afraid he was going to kill you."

I was going to say something smart, but then a new group of people came up and we gushed through a little social dance of nostalgia and lies and self-justifications. We talked success (at high school reunions, everybody sounds like Amway representatives at a pep rally) and the old days (nobody seems to remember all of the kids who got treated like shit for reasons they had no control over) and didn't so-and-so look great (usually this meant they'd managed to keep their toupees on straight) and introducing new spouses (we all had to explain what happened to our original mates; I said mine had been eaten by alligators in the Amazon, but nobody seemed to find that especially believable) and in the midst of all this, Karen tugged my sleeve and said, "There's the third one."

Him I recognized, too. David Haskins. He didn't look any happier than he ever had. Parent trouble was always the explanation you got for his grief back in high school. His parents had been rich, truly so, his father an importer of some kind, and their arguments so violent that they were as eagerly discussed as who was or was not pregnant. Apparently David's parents weren't getting along any better today because although the features of his face were open and friendly enough, there was still the sense of some terrible secret stooping his shoulders and keeping his smiles to furtive wretched imitations. He was a paunchy balding little man who might have been a church usher with a sour stomach.

"The Duke of Earl" started up then and there was no way we were going to let that pass so we got out on the floor; but by now, of course, we both watched the three people she'd sent

letters to. Her instructions had been to meet the anonymous
letter writer at nine-thirty at Pierce Point. If they were going
to be there on time, they'd be leaving soon.

"You think they're going to go?"

"I doubt it, Karen."

"You still don't believe that's what I heard them say that
night?"

"It was a long time ago and you were drunk."

"It's a good thing I like you because otherwise you'd be a
distinct pain in the ass."

Which is when I saw all three of them go stand under one
of the glowing red EXIT signs and open a fire door that led to
the parking lot.

"They're going!" she said.

"Maybe they're just having a cigarette."

"You know better, Dwyer. You know better."

Her car was in the lot on the opposite side of the gym.

"Well, it's worth the drive even if they don't show up.
Pierce Point should be nice tonight."

She squeezed against me and said, "Thanks, Dwyer. Really."

So we went and got her Volvo and went out to Pierce Point
where twenty-five years ago a shy kid named Michael Brandon
had fallen or been pushed to his death.

Apparently we were about to find out which.

The river road wound along a high wall of clay cliffs on the
left and a wide expanse of water on the right. The spring night
was impossibly beautiful, one of those moments so rich with
sweet odor and even sweeter sight you wanted to take your
clothes off and run around in some kind of crazed animal
circles out of sheer joy.

"You still like jazz," she said, nodding to the radio.

"I hope you didn't mind my turning the station."

"I'm kind of into country."

"I didn't get the impression you were listening."

She looked over at me. "Actually, I wasn't. I was thinking about you sending me all of those AA pamphlets."

"It was arrogant and presumptuous and I apologize."

"No, it wasn't. It was sweet and I appreciate it."

The rest of the ride, I leaned my head back and smelled flowers and grass and river water and watched moonglow through the elms and oaks and birches of this new spring. There was a Dakota Staton song, "Street of Dreams," and I wondered as always where she was and what she was doing, she'd been so fine, maybe the most unappreciated jazz singer of the entire fifties.

Then we were going up a long, twisting gravel road. We pulled up next to a big park pavilion and got out and stood in the wet grass, and she came over and slid her arm around my waist and sort of hugged me in a half-serious way. "This is probably crazy, isn't it?"

I sort of hugged her back in a half-serious way. "Yeah, but it's a nice night for a walk so what the hell."

"You ready?"

"Yep."

"Let's go then."

So we went up the hill to the Point itself, and first we looked out at the far side of the river where white birches glowed in the gloom and where beyond you could see the horseshoe shape of the city lights. Then we looked down, straight down the drop of two hundred feet, to the road where Michael Brandon had died.

When I heard the car starting up the road to the east, I said, "Let's get in those bushes over there."

A thick line of shrubs and second-growth timber would give us a place to hide, to watch them.

By the time we were in place, ducked down behind a wide elm and a mulberry bush, a new yellow Mercedes sedan swung into sight and stopped several yards from the edge of the Point.

A car radio played loud in the night. A Top 40 song. Three men got out. Dignified Forester, matinee-idol Price, anxiety-tight Haskins.

Forester leaned back into the car and snapped the radio

off. But he left the headlights on. Forester and Price each had cans of beer. Haskins bit his nails.

They looked around in the gloom. The headlights made the darkness beyond seem much darker and the grass in its illumination much greener. Price said harshly, "I told you this was just some kind of goddamn prank. Nobody knows squat."

"He's right. He's probably right," Haskins said to Forester. Obviously he was hoping that was the case.

Forester said, "If somebody didn't know something, we would never have gotten those letters."

She moved then and I hadn't expected her to move at all. I'd been under the impression we would just sit there and listen and let them ramble and maybe in so doing reveal something useful.

But she had other ideas.

She pushed through the undergrowth and stumbled a little and got to her feet again and then walked right up to them.

"Karen!" Haskins said.

"So you did kill Michael," she said.

Price moved toward her abruptly, his hand raised. He was drunk and apparently hitting women was something he did without much trouble.

Then I stepped out from our hiding place and said, "Put your hand down, Price."

Forester said, "Dwyer."

"So," Price said, lowering his hand, "I was right, wasn't I?" He was speaking to Forester.

Forester shook his silver head. He seemed genuinely saddened. "Yes, Price, for once your cynicism is justified."

Price said, "Well, you two aren't getting a goddamned penny, do you know that?"

He lunged toward me, still a bully. But I was ready for him, wanted it. I also had the advantage of being sober. When he was two steps away, I hit him just once and very hard in the solar plexus. He backed away, eyes startled, and then he turned abruptly away.

We all stood looking at one another, pretending not to hear

the sounds of violent vomiting on the other side of the splendid new Mercedes.

Forester said, "When I saw you there, Karen, I wondered if you could do it alone."

"Do what?"

"What?" Forester said. "What? Let's at least stop the games. You two want money."

"Christ," I said to Karen, who looked perplexed, "they think we're trying to shake them down."

"Shake them down?"

"Blackmail them."

"Exactly," Forester said.

Price had come back around. He was wiping his mouth with the back of his hand. In his other hand he carried a silver-plated .45, the sort of weapon professional gamblers favor.

Haskins said, "Larry, Jesus, what is that?"

"What does it look like?"

"Larry, that's how people get killed." Haskin's sounded like Price's mother.

Price's eyes were on me. "Yeah, it would be terrible if Dwyer here got killed, wouldn't it?" He waved the gun at me. I didn't really think he'd shoot, but I sure was afraid he'd trip and the damn thing would go off accidentally. "You've been waiting since senior year to do that to me, haven't you, Dwyer?"

I shrugged. "I guess so, yeah."

"Well, why don't I give Forester here the gun and then you and I can try it again."

"Fine with me."

He handed Forester the .45. Forester took it all right, but what he did was toss it somewhere into the gloom surrounding the car. "Larry, if you don't straighten up here, I'll fight you myself. Do you understand me?" Forester had a certain dignity and when he spoke, his voice carried an easy authority. "There will be no more fighting, do you both understand that?"

"I agree with Ted," Karen said.

Forester, like a teacher tired of naughty children, decided

to get on with the real business. "You wrote those letters, Dwyer?"

"No."

"No?"

"No. Karen wrote them."

A curious glance was exchanged by Forester and Karen.

"I guess I should have known that," Forester said.

"Jesus, Ted," Karen said, "I'm not trying to blackmail you, no matter what you think."

"Then just exactly what are you trying to do?"

She shook her lovely little head. I sensed she regretted ever writing the letters, stirring it all up again. "I just want the truth to come out about what really happened to Michael Brandon that night."

"The truth," Price said. "Isn't that goddamn touching?"

"Shut up, Larry," Haskins said.

Forester said, "You know what happened to Michael Brandon?"

"I've got a good idea," Karen said. "I overheard you three talking at a party one night."

"What did we say?"

"What?"

"What did you overhear us say?"

Karen said, "You said that you hoped nobody looked into what really happened to Michael that night."

A smile touched Forester's lips. "So on that basis you concluded that we murdered him?"

"There wasn't much else to conclude."

Price said, weaving still, leaning on the fender for support, "I don't goddamn believe this."

Forester nodded to me. "Dwyer, I'd like to have a talk with Price and Haskins here, if you don't mind. Just a few minutes." He pointed to the darkness beyond the car. "We'll walk over there. You know we won't try to get away because you'll have our car. All right?"

I looked at Karen.

She shrugged.

They left, back into the gloom, voices receding and fading into the sounds of crickets and a barn owl and a distant roaring train.

"You think they're up to something?"

"I don't know," I said.

We stood with our shoes getting soaked and looked at the green green grass in the headlights.

"What do you think they're doing?" Karen asked.

"Deciding what they want to tell us."

"You're used to this kind of thing, aren't you?"

"I guess."

"It's sort of sad, isn't it?"

"Yeah, it is."

"Except for you getting the chance to punch out Larry Price after all these years."

"Christ, you really think I'm that petty?"

"I know you are. I know you are."

Then we both turned to look back to where they were. There'd been a cry and Forester shouted, "You hit him again, Larry, and I'll break your goddamn jaw." They were arguing about something and it had turned vicious.

I leaned back against the car. She leaned back against me. "You think we'll ever go to bed?"

"I'd sure like to, Karen, but I can't."

"Donna?"

"Yeah. I'm really trying to learn how to be faithful."

"That been a problem?"

"It cost me a marriage."

"Maybe I'll learn how someday, too."

Then they were back. Somebody, presumably Forester, had torn Price's nice lacy shirt into shreds. Haskins looked miserable.

Forester said, "I'm going to tell you what happened that night."

I nodded.

"I've got some beer in the back seat. Would either of you like one?"

27

Karen said, "Yes, we would."

So he went and got a six pack of Michelob and we all had a beer and just before he started talking he and Karen shared another one of those peculiar glances and then he said, "The four of us— myself, Price, Haskins, and Michael Brandon— had done something we were very ashamed of."

"Afraid of," Haskins said.

"Afraid that if it came out, our lives would be ruined. Forever," Forester said.

Price said, "Just say it, Forester." He glared at me.

"We raped a girl, the four of us."

"Brandon spent two months afterward seeing the girl, bringing her flowers, apologizing to her over and over again, telling her how sorry we were, that we'd been drunk and it wasn't like us to do that and—" Forester sighed, put his eyes to the ground. "In fact we had been drunk; in fact it wasn't like us to do such a thing—"

Haskins said, "It really wasn't. It really wasn't."

For a time there was just the barn owl and the crickets again, no talk, and then gently I said, "What happened to Brandon that night?"

"We were out as we usually were, drinking beer, talking about it, afraid the girl would finally turn us into the police, still trying to figure out why we'd ever done such a thing—"

The hatred was gone from Price's eyes. For the first time the matinee idol looked as melancholy as his friends. "No matter what you think of me, Dwyer, I don't rape women. But that night—" He shrugged, looked away.

"Brandon," I said, "You were going to tell me about Brandon."

"We came up here, had a case of beer or something, and talked about it some more, and that night," Forester said, "that night Brandon just snapped. He couldn't handle how ashamed he was or how afraid he was of being turned in. Right in the middle of talking—"

Haskins took over. "Right in the middle, he just got up and ran out to the Point." He indicated the cliff behind us. "And before we could stop him, he jumped."

"Jesus," Price said, "I can't forget his screaming on the way down. I can't ever forget it."

I looked at Karen. "So what she heard you three talking about outside the party that night wasn't that you'd killed Brandon but that you were afraid a serious investigation into his suicide might turn up the rape?"

Forester said, "Exactly." He stared at Karen. "We didn't kill Michael, Karen. We loved him. He was our friend."

But by then, completely without warning, she had started to cry and then she began literally sobbing, her entire body shaking with some grief I could neither understand nor assuage.

I nodded to Forester to get back in his car and leave. They stood and watched us a moment and then they got into the Mercedes and went away, taking the burden of years and guilt with them.

This time I drove. I went far out the river road, miles out, where you pick up the piney hills and the deer standing by the side of the road.

From the glove compartment she took a pint of J&B, and I knew better than to try and stop her.

I said, "You were the girl they raped, weren't you?"

"Yes."

"Why didn't you tell the police?"

She smiled at me. "The police weren't exactly going to believe a girl from the Highlands about the sons of rich men."

I sighed. She was right.

"Then Michael started coming around to see me. I can't say I ever forgave him, but I started to feel sorry for him. His fear—" She shook her head, looked out the window. She said, almost to herself, "But I had to write those letters, get them there tonight, know for sure if they killed him." She paused. "You believe them?"

"That they didn't kill him?"

"Right."

"Yes, I believe them."

"So do I."

Then she went back to staring out the window, her small face childlike there in silhouette against the moonsilver river. "Can I ask you a question, Dwyer?"

"Sure."

"You think we're ever going to get out of the Highlands?"

"No," I said, and drove on faster in her fine new expensive car. "No, I don't."

One spring I lived with a forlorn woman who spoke frequently of suicide. When I was away one evening, she tried it. Fortunately, I got home early enough to get her to the hospital.

For weeks after, I visited her in the drab brick institution that her family doctor had recommended, the one with bars on the windows and the steady slap-slap-slap of slippers as the lobotomized man passed endlessly back and forth, and one night when drugs had made her lucid, she said, "You never believe me when I tell you how sad it is. You think you know but you don't." She made it sound as if I had betrayed her in some way, as perhaps I had.

Years later I saw her on the street, her beauty long gone, a gray and hunched woman who looked twenty years older than she was.

Maybe she'd been right; maybe in the ways of grief I'm a tourist after all.

MOTHER DARKNESS

The man surprised her. He was black.

Alison had been watching the small filthy house for six mornings now and this was the first time she'd seen him. She hadn't been able to catch him at seven-thirty or even six-thirty. She'd had to try six o'clock. She brought her camera up and began snapping.

She took four pictures of him just to be sure.

Then she put the car in gear and went to get breakfast.

An hour-and-a-half later, in the restaurant where social workers often met, Peter said, "Oh, he's balling her all right."

"God," Alison Cage said. "Can't we talk about something else? Please."

"I know it upsets you. It upsets me. That's why I'm telling you about it."

"Can't you tell somebody else?"

"I've tried and nobody'll listen. Here's a forty-three year old man and he's screwing his seven-year-old daughter and nobody'll listen. Jesus."

Peter Forbes loved dramatic moments and incest was about as dramatic as you could get. Peter was a hold-over hippie. He wore defiantly wrinkled khaki shirts and defiantly torn Lee jeans. He wore his brown hair in a ponytail. In his cubicle back at social services was a faded poster of Robert Kennedy. He still smoked a lot of dope. After six glasses of cheap wine at an office party, he'd once told Alison that he thought she was

33

beautiful. He was forty-one years old and something of a joke and Alison both liked and disliked him.

"Talk to Coughlin," Alison said.

"I've talked to Coughlin."

"Then talk to Friedman."

"I've talked to Friedman, too."

"And what did they say?"

Peter sneered. "He reminded me about the Skeritt case."

"Oh."

"Said I got everybody in the department all bent out of shape about Richard Skeritt and then I couldn't prove anything about him and his little adopted son."

"Maybe Skeritt wasn't molesting him."

"Yeah. Right."

Alison sighed and looked out the winter window. A veil of steam covered most of the glass. Beyond it she could see the parking lot filled with men and women scraping their windows and giving each other pushes. A minor ice storm was in progress. It was seven thirty-five and people were hurrying to work. Everybody looked bundled up, like children trundling to school.

Inside the restaurant the air smelled of cooking grease and cigarettes. Cold wind gusted through the front door when somebody opened it, and people stamped snow from their feet as soon as they reached the tile floor. Because this was several blocks north of the black area, the juke box ran to Hank Williams, Jr. and The Judds. Alison despised country western music.

"So how's it going with you?" Peter said, daubs of egg yolk on his graying bandito mustache.

"Oh. You know." Blonde Alison shrugged. "Still trying to find a better apartment for less money. Still trying to lose five pounds. Still trying to convince myself that there's really a God."

"Sounds like you need a Valium."

The remark was so—Peter. Alison smiled. "You think Valium would do it, huh?"

"It picks me up when I get down where you are."

"When you get to be thirty-six and you're alone the way I am, Peter, I think you need more than Valium."

"I'm alone."

"But you're alone in your way. I'm alone in my way."

"What's the difference?"

Suddenly she was tired of him and tired of herself, too. "Oh, I don't know. No difference, I suppose. I was being silly I guess."

"You look tired."

"Haven't been sleeping well."

"That doctor from the medical examiner's office been keeping you out late?"

"Doctor?"

"Oh, come on," Peter said. Sometimes he got possessive in a strange way. Testy. "I know you've been seeing him."

"Doctor Connery, you mean?"

Peter smiled, the egg yolk still on his mustache. "The one with the blue blue eyes, yes."

"It was strictly business. He just wanted to find out about those infants."

"The ones who smothered last year?"

"Yes."

"What's the big deal? Crib death happens all the time."

"Yes, but it still needs to be studied."

Peter smiled his superior smile. "I suppose but—"

"Crib death means that the pathologist couldn't find anything. No reason that the infant should have stopped breathing—no malfunction or anything, I mean. They just die mysteriously. Doctors want to know why."

"So what did your new boyfriend have to say about these deaths? I mean, what's his theory?"

"I'm not going to let you sneak that in there," she said, laughing despite herself. "He's not my boyfriend."

"All right. Then why would he be interested in two deaths that happened a year ago?"

She shrugged and sipped the last of her coffee. "He's

exchanging information with other medical data banks. Seeing if they can't find a trend in these deaths."

"Sounds like an excuse to me."

"An excuse for what?" Alison said.

"To take beautiful blondes out to dinner and have them fall under his sway." He bared yellow teeth a dentist could work on for hours. He made claws of his hands. "Dracula; Dracula. That's who Connery really is."

Alison got pregnant her junior year of college. She got an abortion of course but only after spending a month in the elegant home of her rich parents, "moping" as her father characterized that particular period of time. She did not go back to finish school. She went to California. This was in the late seventies just as discos were dying and AIDs was rising. She spent two celibate years working as a secretary in a record company. James Taylor, who'd stopped in to see a friend of his, asked Alison to go have coffee. She was quite silly during their half hour together, juvenile and giggly, and even years later her face would burn when she thought of how foolish she'd been that day. When she returned home, she lived with her parents, a fact that seemed to embarrass all her high school friends. They were busy and noisy with growing families of their own and here was beautiful quiet Alison inexplicably alone and, worse, celebrating her thirty-first birthday while still living at home.

There was so much sorrow in the world and she could tell no one about it. That's why so many handsome and eligible men floated in and out of her life. Because they didn't *under-stand*. They weren't worth knowing, let alone giving herself to in any respect.

She worked for a year-and-a-half in an art gallery. It was what passed for sophisticated in a midwestern city of this size. Very rich but dull people crowded it constantly, and men both with and without wedding rings pressed her for an hour or two alone.

She would never have known about the income maintenance job if she hadn't been watching a local talk show one day. Here sat two earnest women about her own age, one white, one black, talking about how they acted as liaisons between poor people and the Social Services agency. Alison knew immediately that she would like a job like this. She'd spent her whole life so spoiled and pampered and useless. And the art gallery—minor traveling art shows and local ad agency artists puffing themselves up as artistes—was simply an extension of this life.

These women, Alison could tell, knew well the sorrow of the world and the sorrow in her heart.

She went down the next morning to the Social Services agency and applied. The black woman who took her application weighed at least three-hundred-and-fifty pounds which she'd packed into lime green stretch pants and a flowered polyester blouse with white sweat rings under the arms. She smoked Kool filters at a rate Alison hated to see. Hadn't this woman heard of lung cancer?

Four people interviewed Alison that day. The last was a prim but handsome white man in a shabby three-piece suit who had on the wall behind him a photo of himself and his wife and a small child who was in some obvious but undefined way retarded. Alison recognized two things about this man immediately: that here was a man who knew the same sorrow as she; and that here was a man painfully smitten with her already. It took him five-and-a-half months but the man eventually found her a job at the agency.

Not until her third week did she realize that maintenance workers were the lowest of the low in social work, looked down upon by bosses and clients alike. What you did was this: you went out to people—usually women—who received various kinds of assistance from various government agencies and you attempted to prove that they were liars and cheats and scoundrels. The more benefits you could deny the people who made up your case load, the more your bosses liked you. The people in the state house and the people in Washington, D.C. wanted you to allow your people as little as possible. That was the one and only way to keep tax-payers happy. Of course, your clients had a different version of all this. They needed help. And if you wouldn't give them help, or you tried to take away help you were already giving them, they became vocal. Income maintenance workers were frequently threatened and sometimes punched, stabbed, and shot, men and women alike. The curious thing was that not many of them quit. The pay was slightly better than you got in a factory and the job didn't require a college degree and you could pretty much set your own hours if you wanted to. So, even given the occasional violence, it was still a pretty good job.

Alison had been an income maintenance worker for nearly three years now.

She sincerely wanted to help.

An hour after leaving Peter in the restaurant, Alison pulled her gray Honda Civic up to the small house where earlier this morning she'd snapped photos of the black man. Her father kept trying to buy her a nicer car but she argued that her clients would just resent her nicer car and that she wouldn't blame them.

The name of this particular client was Doreen Hayden. Alison had been trying to do a profile of her but Doreen hadn't exactly cooperated. This was Alison's second appointment with the woman. She hoped it went better than the first.

After getting out of her car, Alison stood for a time in the middle of the cold, slushy street. Snow sometimes had a way of making even rundown things look beautiful. But somehow it only made this block of tiny, aged houses look worse. Brown frozen dog feces covered the sidewalk. Smashed front windows bore masking tape. Rusted-out cars squatted on small front lawns like obscene animals. And factory soot touched everything, everything. It was nineteen days before Christmas—Alison had just heard this on the radio this morning—but this was a neighborhood where Christmas never came.

Doreen answered the door. Through the screen drifted the oppressive odors of breakfast and cigarettes and dirty diapers. In her stained white sweater and tight red skirt, Doreen still showed signs of the attractive woman she'd been a few years ago until bad food and lack of exercise had added thirty pounds to her fine-boned frame.

The infant in her arms was perhaps four months old. She had a sweet little pink face. Her pink blanket was filthy.

"I got all the kids here," Doreen said. "You all comin' in? Gettin' cold with this door open."

All the kids, Alison thought. My God, Doreen was actually going to try that scam.

Inside, the hot odors of food and feces were even more oppressive. Alison sat on the edge of a discount-store couch and looked around the room. Not much had changed since her last visit. The old Zenith color TV set—now blaring Bugs Bunny cartoons—still needed some kind of tube. The floor was still an obstacle course of newspapers and empty Pepsi bottles and dirty baby clothes. There was a crucifix on one wall with a piece of faded, drooping palm stuck behind it. Next to it a photo of Bruce Springsteen had been taped to the soiled wallpaper.

"These kids was off visitin' last time you was here," Doreen said.

She referred to the two small boys standing to the right of the armchair where she sat holding her infant.

"Off visiting where?" Alison said, keeping her voice calm.

"Grandmother's."

"I see."

"They was stayin' there for awhile but now they're back with me so I'm goin' to need more money from the agency. You know."

"Maybe the man you have staying here could help you out." There. She'd said it quickly. With no malice. A plain simple fact.

"Ain't no man livin' here."

"I took a picture of him this morning."

"No way."

Alison sighed. "You know you can't get full payments if

you have an adult male staying with you, Doreen."

"He musta been the garbage man or somethin'. No adult male stayin' here. None at all."

Alison had her clipboard out. She noted on the proper lines of the form that a man was staying here. She said, "You borrowed those two boys."

"What?"

"These two boys here, Doreen. You borrowed them. They're not yours."

"No way."

Alison looked at one of the ragged little boys and said, "Is Doreen your mother?"

The little boy, nervous, glanced over at Doreen and then put his head down.

Alison didn't want to embarrass or frighten him anymore.

"If I put these two boys down on the claim form and they send out an investigator, it'll be a lot worse for you, Doreen. They'll try and get you for fraud."

"God damn you."

"I'll write them down here if you want me to. But if they get you for fraud—"

"Shit," Doreen said. She shook her head and then she looked at the boys. "You two run on home now, all right?"

"Can we take some cookies, Aunt Doreen?"

She grinned at Alison. "They don't let their Aunt Doreen forget no promises, I'll tell you that." She nodded to the kitchen. "You boys go get your cookies and then go out the back door, all right? Oh, but first say goodbye to Alison here."

Both boys, cute and dear to Alison, smiled at her and then grinned at each other and then ran with heavy feet across the faded linoleum to the kitchen.

"I need more money," Doreen said. "This little one's breakin' me."

"I'm afraid I got you all I could, Doreen."

"You gonna tell them about Ernie?"

"Ernie's the man staying here?"

"Yeah."

"No. Not since you told me the truth."

"He's the father."

"Of your little girl?"

"Yeah."

"You think he'll actually marry you?"

She laughed her cigarette laugh. "Yeah, in about fifty or sixty years."

The house began to become even smaller to Alison then. This sometimes happened when she was interviewing people. She felt entombed in the anger and despair of the place.

She stared at Doreen and Doreen's beautiful little girl.

"Could I hold her?" Alison said.

"You serious?"

"Yes."

"She maybe needs a change. She poops a lot."

"I don't mind."

Doreen shrugged. "Be my guest."

She got up and brought the infant across to Alison.

Alison perched carefully on the very edge of the couch and received the infant like some sort of divine gift. After a moment the smells of the little girl drifted away and Alison was left holding a very beautiful little child.

Doreen went back and sat in the chair and looked at Alison. "You got any kids?"

"No."

"Wish you did though, huh?"

"Yes."

"You married?"

"Not so far."

"Hell, bet you got guys fallin' all over themselves for you. You're beautiful."

But Alison rarely listened to flattery. Instead she was watching the infant's sweet white face. "Have you ever looked at her eyes, Doreen?"

" 'course I looked at her eyes. She's my daughter, ain't she?"

"No. I mean looked really deeply."

41

" 'course I have."

"She's so sad."

Doreen sighed. "She's got a reason to be sad. Wouldn't you be sad growin' up in a place like this?"

Alison leaned down to the little girl's face and kissed her tenderly on the forehead. They were like sisters, the little girl and Alison. They knew how sad the world was. They knew how sad their hearts were.

When the time came, when the opportunity appeared, Alison would do the same favor for this little girl she'd done for the two other little girls.

Not even the handsome Doctor Connery had suspected anything. He'd just assumed that the other two girls had died from crib death.

On another visit, someday soon, Alison would make sure that she was alone with the little girl for a few minutes. Then it would be done and the little girl would not have to grow up and know the even greater sadness that awaited her.

"You really ain't gonna tell them about Ernie livin' here?"

"I've got a picture of him that I can turn in any time as evidence. But I'll tell you what, Doreen; you start taking better care of your daughter—changing her diapers more often and feeding her the menu I gave you—and I'll keep Ernie our secret."

"Can't afford to have no more money taken from me," Doreen said.

"Then you take better care of your daughter," Alison said, holding the infant out for Doreen to take now. "Because she's very sad, Doreen. Very very sad."

Alison kissed the little girl on the forehead once more and then gave her up to her mother.

Soon, little one, Alison thought; soon you won't be so sad. I promise.

Following my divorce, I embarked on a long, boozy journey that led me to several dead-end jobs and the sort of rooming house front porches described in this story. Each porch was a different cross section of people, mostly rough or used-up people. Their stories were better than many of the novels I was then reading. But there was one porch that was as hushed and tense as a bar just before a fight. Two or three times a week the man in the downstairs apartment beat his wife. And we all knew it. And no matter what we did to stop it—threaten him, call the police, try and convince her to leave before it was too late—she seemed paralyzed in some terrible and frightening way.

Many years laters, when I saw on TV a story of a man who had beaten his wife to death with his fists, I thought of that fragile, pretty young woman on that long ago front porch . . . and wrote this story . . . tying it into a portrait of the cat-crazy old man who'd also sat on that porch.

RENDER UNTO CAESAR

I never paid much attention to their arguments until the night he hit her.

The summer I was twenty-one I worked construction upstate. This was 1963. The money was good enough to float my final year-and-a-half at college. If I didn't blow it the way some of the other kids working construction did, that is, on too many nights at the tavern, and too many weekends trying to impress city girls.

The crew was three weeks in Cedar Rapids and so I looked for an inexpensive sleeping room. The one I found was in a neighborhood my middle-class parents wouldn't have approved of but I wasn't going to be here long enough for them to know exactly where I was living.

The house was a faded frail Victorian. Upstairs lived an old man named Murchison. He'd worked forty years on the Crandic as a brakeman and was retired now to sunny days out at Ellis park watching the softball games, and nights on the front porch with his quarts of cheap Canadian Ace beer and the high sweet smell of his Prince Albert pipe tobacco and his memories of WW II. Oh, yes, and his cat Caesar. You never saw Murch without that hefty gray cat of his, usually sleeping in his lap when Murch sat in his front porch rocking chair.

And Murch's fondness for cats didn't stop there. But I'll tell you about that later.

Downstairs lived the Brineys. Pete Briney was in his early twenties, handsome in a roughneck kind of way. He sold new

Mercurys for a living. He came home in a different car nearly every night, just at dusk, just at the time you could smell the dinner his wife Kelly had set out for him.

According to Murch, who seemed to know everything about them, Kelly had just turned nineteen and had already suffered two miscarriages. She was pretty in a sweet, already tired way. She seemed to spend most of her time cleaning the apartment and taking out the garbage and walking up to Dlask's grocery, two blocks away. One day a plump young woman came over to visit but this led to an argument later that night. Pete Briney did not want his wife to have friends. He seemed to feel that if Kelly had concentrated on her pregnancy, she would not have miscarried.

Briney did not look happy about me staying in the back room on the second floor. The usual tenants were retired men like Murch. I had a tan and was in good shape and while I wasn't handsome girls didn't find me repulsive, either. Murch laughed one day and said that Briney had come up and said, "How long is that guy going to be staying here, anyway?" Murch, who felt sorry for Kelly and liked Briney not at all, lied and said I'd probably be here a couple of years.

A few nights later Murch and I were on the front porch. All we had upstairs were two window fans that churned the ninety-three degree air without cooling it at all. So, after walking up to Dlask's for a couple of quarts of Canadian Ace and two packs of Pall Malls, I sat down on the front porch and prepared myself to be dazzled by Murch's tales of WW II in the Pacific Theater. (And Murch knew lots of good ones, at least a few of which I strongly suspected were true.)

Between stories we watched the street. Around nine, dusk dying, mothers called their children in. There's something about the sound of working class mothers gathering their children — their voices weary, almost melancholy, at the end of another grinding day, the girls they used to be still alive somewhere in their voices, all that early hope and vitality vanishing like the faint echoes of tender music.

And there were the punks in their hot rods picking up the

meaty young teenage girls who lived on the block. And the sad factory drunks weaving their way home late from the taverns to cold meals and broken-hearted children. And the furtive lonely single men getting off the huge glowing insect of the city bus, and going upstairs to sleeping rooms and hot plates and lonesome letters from girlfriends in far and distant cities.

And in the midst of all this came a brand new red Mercury convertible, one far too resplendent for the neighborhood. And it was pulling up to the curb and—

The radio was booming "Surf City" with Jan and Dean— And—

Before the car even stopped, Kelly jerked open her door and jumped out, nearly stumbling in the process.

Briney slammed on the brakes, killed the headlights and then bolted from the car.

Before he reached the curb, he was running.

"You whore!" he screamed.

He was too fast for her. He tackled her even before she reached the sidewalk.

Tackled her and turned her over. And started smashing his fists into her face, holding her down on the ground with his knees on her slender arms, and smashing and smashing and smashing her face—

By then I was off the porch. I was next to him in moments. Given that his victim was a woman, I wasted no time on fair play. I kicked him hard twice in the ribs and then I slammed two punches into the side of his head. She screamed and cried and tried rolling left to escape his punches, and then tried rolling right. I didn't seem to have phased him. I slammed two more punches into the side of his head. I could feel these punches working. He pitched sideways, momentarily unconscious, off his wife.

He slumped over on the sidewalk next to Kelly. I got her up right away and held her and let her sob and twist and moan and jerk in my arms. All I could think of were those times when I'd seen my otherwise respectable accountant father beat up my mother, and how I'd cry and run between them terrified

47

and try to stop him with my own small and useless fists . . .

Murch saw to Briney. "Sonofabitch's alive, anyway," he said looking up at me from the sidewalk. "More than he deserves."

By that time, a small crowd stood on the sidewalk, gawkers in equal parts thrilled and sickened by what they'd just seen Briney do to Kelly . . .

I got her upstairs to Murch's apartment and started taking care of her cuts and bruises . . .

I mentioned that Murch's affection for cats wasn't limited to Caesar. I also mentioned that Murch was retired, which meant that he had plenty of time for his chosen calling.

The first Saturday I had off, a week before the incident with Pete and Kelly Briney, I sat on the front porch reading a John D. MacDonald paperback and drinking a Pepsi and smoking Pall Malls. I was glad for a respite from the baking, bone-cracking work of summer road construction.

Around three that afternoon, I saw Murch coming down the sidewalk carrying a shoebox. He walked toward the porch, nodded hello, then walked to the backyard. I wondered if something was wrong. He was a talker, Murch was, and to see him so quiet bothered me.

I put down my Pepsi and put down my book and followed him, a seventy-one year old man with a stooped back and liver-spotted hands and white hair that almost glowed in the sunlight and that ineluctable dignity that comes to people who've spent a life at hard honorable work others consider menial.

He went into the age-worn garage and came out with a garden spade. The wide backyard was burned stubby grass and a line of rusted silver garbage cans. The picket fence sagged with age and the walk was all busted and jagged. To the right of white flapping sheets drying on the clothesline was a small plot of earth that looked like a garden.

He set the shoebox down on the ground and went to work with the shovel. He was finished in three or four minutes. A nice fresh hole had been dug in the dark rich earth.

He bent down and took the lid from the shoebox. From inside he lifted something with great and reverent care. At first I couldn't see what it was. I moved closer. Lying across his palms was the dead body of a small calico cat. The blood on the scruffy white fur indicated that death had been violent, probably by car.

He knelt down and lowered the cat into the freshly dug earth. He remained kneeling and then closed his eyes and made the sign of the cross.

And then he scooped the earth in his hands and filled in the grave.

I walked over to him just as he was standing up.

"You're some guy, Murch," I said.

He looked startled. "Where the hell did you come from?"

"I was watching." I nodded to the ground. "The cat, I mean."

"They've been damn good friends to me—cats have—figure it's the least I can do for them."

I felt I'd intruded; embarrassed him. He picked up the spade and started over to the garage.

"Nobody gives a damn about cats," he said. "A lot of people even hate 'em. That's why I walk around every few days with my shoebox and if I see a dead one, I pick it up and bring it back here and bury it. They're nice little animals." He grinned. "Especially Caesar. He's the only good friend I've made since my wife died ten years ago."

Murch put the shovel in the garage. When he came back out, he said, "You in any kind of mood for a game of checkers?"

I grinned. "I hate to pick on old farts like you."

He grinned back. "We'll see who's the old fart here."

When I got home the night following the incident with Kelly and Briney, several people along the block stopped to ask me about the beating. They'd heard this and they'd heard that but since I lived in the house, they figured I could set them right. I couldn't, or at least I said I couldn't, because I didn't like the quiet glee in their eyes, and the subtle thrill in their voices.

Murch was on the porch. I went up and sat down and he put Caesar in my lap the way he usually did. I petted the big fellow till he purred so hard he sounded like a plane about to take off. Too bad most humans weren't as appreciative of kindness as good old Caesar.

When I spoke, I sort of whispered. I didn't want the Brineys to hear.

"You don't have to whisper, Todd," Murch said, sucking on his pipe. "They're both gone. Don't know where he is, and don't care. She left about three this afternoon. Carrying a suitcase."

"You really think she's leaving him?"

"Way he treats her, I hope so. Nobody should be treated like that, especially a nice young woman like her." He reached over and petted Caesar who was sleeping in my lap. Then he sat back and drew on his pipe again and said, "I told her to go. Told her what happens to women who let their men beat them. It keeps on getting worse and worse until— " He shook his head. "The missus and I knew a woman whose husband beat her to death one night. Right in front of her two little girls."

"Briney isn't going to like it, you telling her to leave him."

"To hell with Briney. I'm not afraid of him." He smiled. "I've got Caesar here to protect me."

Briney didn't get home till late. By that time we were up off the porch and in our respective beds. Around nine a cool rain had started falling. I was getting some good sleep when I heard him down there.

The way he yelled and the way he smashed things, I knew he was drunk. He'd obviously discovered that his compliant little wife had left him. Then there was an abrupt and anxious silence. And then there was his crying. He wasn't any better at it than I was, didn't really know how, and so his tears came out in violent bursts that resembled throwing up. But even though I was tempted to feel sorry for him, he soon enough made me hate him again. Between bursts of tears he'd start

50

calling his wife names, terrible names that should never have been put to a woman like Kelly.

I wasn't sure of the time when he finally gave it all up and went to bed. Late, with just the sounds of the trains rushing through the night in the hills, and the hoot of a barn owl lost somewhere in leafy midnight trees.

The next couple days I worked overtime. The road project had fallen behind. In the early weeks of the job there'd been an easy camaraderie on the work site. But that was gone for good now. The supervisors no longer took the time to joke, and looked you over skeptically every time you walked back to the wagon for a drink of water.

Kelly came back at dusk on Friday night. She stepped out of a brand new blue Mercury sedan, Pete Briney at the wheel. She carried a lone suitcase. When she reached the porch steps and saw Murch and me, she looked away and walked quickly toward the door. Briney was right behind her. Obviously he'd told her not to speak to us.

That night, Murch and I spoke in whispers, both of us naturally wondering what had happened. Briney had gone over to her mother's, where Murch had suggested she go, and somehow convinced Kelly to come back.

They kept the curtains closed, the TV low and if they spoke, it was so quietly we couldn't hear them.

I spent an hour with Caesar on my lap and Murch in my ear about politicians. He was a John Kennedy supporter and tried to convince me I should be, too.

For the next two days and nights, I didn't see or hear either of the Brineys. On Saturday afternoon, Murch returned from one of his patrols with his shoebox. He went in the back and buried a cat he'd found and then came out on the porch to smoke a pipe. "Poor little thing," he said. "Wasn't any bigger than this." With his hands, he indicated how tiny the kitten had been.

Kelly came out on the porch a few minutes later. She wore a white blouse and jeans and had her auburn hair swept back into a loose ponytail. She looked neat and clean. And nervous. She muttered a hello and started down the stairs.

"Ain't you ever going to talk to us again, Kelly?" Murch said. There was no sarcasm in his voice, just an obvious sadness.

She stopped halfway toward the sidewalk. Her back was to us. For long moments she just stood there.

When she turned around and looked at us, she said, "Pete don't want me to talk to either of you." Then, gently, "I miss sitting out on the porch."

"He's your husband, honey. You shouldn't let him be your jailer," Murch said.

"He said he was sorry about the other night. About hitting me." She paused. "He came over to my mother's house and he told my whole family he was sorry. He even started crying."

Murch didn't say anything.

"I know you don't like him, Murch, but I'm his wife and like the priest said, I owe him another chance."

"You be careful of him, especially when he's drinking."

"He promised he wouldn't hit me no more, Murch. He gave his solemn word."

She looked first at him and then at me, and then was gone down the block to the grocery store. From a distance she looked fifteen years old.

He went two more nights, Briney did, before coming home drunk and loud.

I knew just how drunk he was because I was sitting on the porch around ten o'clock when a new pink Mercury came up and scraped the edge of its right bumper long and hard against the curbing.

The headlights died. Briney sat in the dark car smoking a cigarette. I could tell he was staring at us.

Murch just sat there with Caesar on his lap. I just sat there waiting for trouble. I could sense it coming and I wanted it over with.

Briney got out of the car and tried hard to walk straight up the walk to the porch. He wasn't a comic drunk, doing an alcoholic rhumba, but he certainly could not have passed a sobriety test.

He came up on the porch and stopped. His chest was heaving from anger. He smelled of whiskey and sweat and Old Spice.

"You think I don't fucking know the shit you're putting in my old lady's mind," he said to Murch. "Huh?"

Murch didn't say anything.

"I asked you a fucking question, old man."

Murch said, softly, "Why don't you go in and sleep it off, kid?"

"You're the god damned reason she went to her mother's last week. You told her to!"

And then he lunged at Murch and I was up out of my chair. He was too drunk to swing with any grace or precision but he caught me on the side of the head with the punch he'd intended for Murch, and for a dizzy moment I felt my knees go. He could hit. No doubt about that.

And then he was on me, having given up on Murch, and I had to take four or five more punches while I tried to gather myself and bring some focus to my fear and rage.

I finally got him in the ribs with a good hooking right, and I felt real exhilaration when I heard the air *whoof* out of him, and then I banged another one just to the right off his jaw and backed him up several inches and then—

Then Kelly was on the porch crying and screaming and putting herself between us, a child trying to separate two mindless mastodons from killing each other and—

"You promised you wouldn't drink no more!" she kept screaming over and over at Briney.

All he could do was stand head hung and shamed like some whipped giant there in the dirty porchlight she'd turned on. "But honey . . . " he'd mumble. Or "But sweetheart . . . " Or "But Kelly, jeeze I . . . "

"Now you get inside there, and right now!" she said, no longer his wife but his mother. And she sternly pointed to the door. And he shambled toward it, not looking back at any of us, just shuffling and shambling, drunk and dazed and sweaty, depleted of rage and pride, and no longer fierce at all.

When he was inside, the apartment door closed, she said, "I'm real sorry, Todd. I heard everything from inside."

"It's all right."

"You hurt?"

"I'm fine."

"I'm real sorry."

"I know."

She went over to Murch and touched him tenderly on the shoulder. He was standing up, this tired and suddenly very old looking man, and he had good gray Caesar in his arms. Kelly leaned over and petted Caesar and said, "I wish I had a husband like you Caesar."

She went back inside. The rest of our time on the porch, the Brineys spoke again in whispers.

Just before he went up to bed, Murch said, "He's going to kill her someday. You know that, don't you, Todd?"

This time I was ready for it. Six hours had gone by. I'd watched the late movie and then lay on the bed smoking a cigarette in the darkness and just staring at the play of street-light and tree shadow on the ceiling.

The first sound from below was very, very low and I wasn't even sure what it was. But I threw my legs off the bed and sat up, grabbing for my cigarettes as I did so.

When the sound came again, I recognized it immediately for what it was. A soft sobbing. Kelly.

Voices. Muffled. Bedsprings squeaking. A curse—Briney.

And then, sharp and unmistakable, a slap.

And then two, three slaps.

Kelly screaming. Furniture being shoved around.

I was up from the sweaty bed and into my jeans, not bothering with a shirt, and down the stairs two-at-a-time.

By now, Kelly's screams filled the entire house. Behind me, at the top of the stairs, I could hear Murch shouting down, "You gotta stop him, son! You gotta stop him!"

More slaps; the muffled thud of closed fists pounding into human flesh and bone.

I stood back from the door and raised my foot and kicked with the flat of my heel four times before shattering the wood into jagged splinters.

Briney had Kelly pinned on the floor as he had last week, and he was putting punches into her at will. Even at a glance, I could see that her nose was broken. Ominously, blood leaked from her ear.

I got him by the hair and yanked him to his feet. He still wasn't completely sober so he couldn't put up the resistance he might have at another time.

I meant to make him unconscious and that was exactly what I did. I dragged him over to the door. He kept swinging at me and occasionally landing hard punches to my ribs and kidney but at the moment I didn't care. He smelled of sweat and pure animal rage and Kelly's fresh blood. I got him to the door frame and held him high by his hair and then slammed his temple against the edge of the frame.

It only took once. He went straight down to the floor in an unmoving heap.

Murch came running through the door. "I called the cops!"

He went immediately to Kelly, knelt by her. She was over on her side, crying crazily and throwing up in gasps that shook her entire body. Her face was a mask of blood. He had ripped her nightgown and dug fierce raking fingers over her breasts. She just kept crying.

Even this late at night, the neighbors were up for a good show, maybe two dozen of them standing in the middle of the street as the whipping red lights of police cars and ambulance gave the crumbling neighborhood a nervous new life.

Kelly had slipped into unconsciousness and was brought out strapped to a stretcher.

Two uniformed cops questioned Briney on the porch. He kept pointing to me and Murch, who stood holding Caesar and stroking him gently.

There was an abrupt scuffle as Briney bolted and took a punch at one of the cops. He was a big man, this cop, and he brought Briney down with two punches. Then he cuffed him and took him to the car.

From inside the police vehicle, Briney glared at me and kept glaring until the car disappeared into the shadows at the end of the block.

Kelly was a week in the hospital. Murch and I visited her twice. In addition to a broken nose, she'd also suffered a broken rib and two broken teeth. She had a hard time talking. She just kept crying softly and shaking her head and patting the hands we both held out to her.

Her brother, a burly man in his twenties, came over to the house two days later with a big U-Haul and three friends and cleaned out the Briney apartment. Murch and I gave him a hand loading.

The newspaper said that Peter James Briney had posted a $2500 bond and had been released on bail. He obviously wasn't going to live downstairs. Kelly's brother hadn't left so much as a fork behind, and the landlord had already nailed a dayglo FOR RENT sign on one of the front porch pillars.

As for me, the crew was getting ready to move on. In two more days, we'd pack up and head up the highway toward Des Moines.

I tried to make my last two nights with Murch especially good. There was a pizza and beer restaurant over on Ellis Boulevard and on the second to last night, I took him there for dinner. I even coerced him into telling me some of those good old WW II stories of his.

The next night, the last night in Cedar Rapids, we had to work overtime again.

I got home after nine, when it was full and starry dark.

I was walking up the street when one of the neighbors came down from his porch and said, "They took him away."

I stopped. My body temperature dropped several degrees. I knew what was coming. "Took who off?"

"Murch. You know, that guy where you live."

"The cops?"

The man shook his head. "Ambulance. Murch had a heart attack."

I ran home. Up the stairs. Murch's place was locked. I had a key for his apartment in my room. I got it and opened the place up.

I got the lights on and went through each of the four small rooms. Murch was an orderly man. Though all the furnishings were old, from the ancient horsehair couch to the scarred chest of drawers, there was an obstinate if shabby dignity about them, much like Murch himself.

I found what I was looking for in the bathtub. Apparently the ambulance attendants hadn't had time to do anything more than rush Murch to the hospital.

Caesar, or what was left of him anyway, they'd left behind.

He lay in the center of the old claw-footed bathtub. He had been stabbed dozens of times. His gray fur was matted and stiff with his own blood. He'd died in the midst of human frenzy.

I didn't have to wonder who'd done this or what had given Murch his heart attack.

I went over to the phone and called both hospitals. Murch was at Mercy. The nurse I spoke with said that he had suffered a massive stroke and was unconscious. The prognosis was not good.

After I hung up, I went through the phone book looking for Brineys. It took me six calls to get the right one but finally I found Pete Briney's father. I convinced him that I was a good friend of Pete's and that I was just in town for the night and that I really wanted to see the old sonofagun. "Well," he said, "he hangs out at the Log Cabin a lot."

The Log Cabin was a tavern not far away. I was there within fifteen minutes.

The moment I stepped through the bar, into a working

class atmosphere of clacking pool balls and whiney country western music, I saw him.

He was in a booth near the back, laughing about something with a girl with a beehive hair-do and a quick beery smile.

When he saw me, he got scared. He left the booth and ran toward the back door. By now, several people were watching. I didn't care.

I went out the back door after him. I stood beneath a window unit air-conditioner that sounded like a B-52 starting up and bled water like a wound. The air was hot and pasty and I slapped at two mosquitos biting my neck.

Ahead of me was a gravel parking lot. The only light was spill from the back windows of the tavern. The lot was about half full. Briney hadn't had time to get into that nice golden Mercury convertible at the end of the lot. He was hiding somewhere behind one of the cars.

I walked down the lot, my heels adjusting to the loose and wobbly feel of the gravel beneath.

He came lunging out from behind a pick-up truck. Because I'd been expecting him, I was able to duck without much problem.

I turned and faced him. He was crouched down, ready to jump at me.

"I'd still have a wife if it wasn't for you two bastards," he said.

"You're a pretty brave guy, Briney. You wait till Murch goes somewhere and then you sneak in and kill his cat. And then Murch comes home and finds Caesar dead and— "

But I was through talking.

I kicked him clean and sharp. I broke his nose. He gagged and screamed and started puking—he must have had way too much to drink that night—and sank to his knees and then I went over and kicked him several times in the ribs.

I kicked him until I heard the sharp brittle sound of bones breaking, and until he pitched forward, still screaming and crying, to the gravel. Then I went up and kicked him in the back of the head.

A couple of his friends from the tavern came out and started toward me but I was big enough and angry enough that they were wary.

"Personal dispute," I said. "Nothing to do with you boys at all."

Then they went over and tried to help their friend to his feet. It wasn't easy. He was a mess.

Murch died an hour and ten minutes after I got to the hospital. I went into his room and looked at all the alien tentacles stretching from beeping cold metal boxes to his warm but failing body. I stood next to his bed until a doctor came in and asked very softly and politely if I'd mind waiting in the hall while they did some work.

It was while the doctor was in there that Murch died. He had never regained consciousness and so we'd never even said proper goodbyes.

At the house, I went into Murch's apartment and found the shoebox and took it into the bathroom and gathered up the remains of poor Caesar.

I took the box down the stairs and out to the garage where I got the garden spade. Then I went over and in the starry prairie night, buried Caesar properly. I even blessed myself, though I wasn't a Catholic, and then knelt down and took the rich damp earth and covered Caesar's grave.

I didn't sleep that night. I just sat up in my little room with my last quart of Canadian Ace and my last pack of Pall Malls and thought about Kelly and thought about Caesar and especially I thought about Murch.

Just at dawn, it started to rain, a hot dirty city rain that would neither cool nor cleanse, and I packed my bags and left.

This story is completely fictional yet I think it's a true tale about alcoholism. In retrospect, it seems sexist and for that I apologize, yet I think it's tender enough, in its weary way, to offset the selfishness of the protagonist. I think most alcoholics would recognize themselves as one—or both—of these people. It is also a story very much written about the singles scene of the 1970s.

DANCERS

Ass stomach (nice tummy) tits neck hair. Her hair feels blond. His fingers are very sensitive. But blond, she could be one of several. His fingers are not that sensitive.

He is checking her out blind because between his hangover and his exhaustion, he can't get his eyes open. And besides, he enjoys the game. Plays it often. Seeing if by touch alone he can remember whom he took home the previous night from this or that bar or party.

Then he withdraws his fingers, rolls over on his back again, and surrenders himself to his hangover. The worst of it is the dehydration. He once drank a six-pack of Pepsi in less than an hour. He paid for it later on the john, with bright hemorrhoidal blood.

In his head, his hangover is like a tumor. In his stomach, like a virus. Even his feet hurt, inexplicable.

The worst of his hangover wanes then, at least for the moment, and he starts to speculate again on the woman beside him.

He wonders if she is awake. He wonders if he knows her well enough (whoever she is) to fart. Really fart. He farts. Really farts.

He feels much better. As if some tense introduction has just been gotten through.

Next to him in the bed, she snores. Lightly. Peacefully.

Who could she be? There was the blonde who giggled and had buck teeth. There was the blonde who said that her main

61

interest was art but kept mispronouncing Cezanne. There was the blonde who told him every ten minutes (and for no discernable reason) that she was originally from Los Angeles.

Probably she is one of them, this woman next to him.

And then he remembers a fourth blonde. The one who predicted that his son would end up on a shrink's couch clutching his balls. The one who told him that he was a piss-poor father and no better human being. The one who slapped him.

Now he can't recall how the episode started or finished. It seems he was just standing there, weaving lightly, talking to the blonde with the buck teeth, when for no reason this woman, who was actually nice-looking, made her way through the party and came right up to him. He recalls that her voice was hysterical and that for a long moment her otherwise lovely blue eyes were terrifying.

Then she slapped him. And after she slapped him, he left. Or she left. He can't remember which, and now it isn't important.

Now what matters is to open his eyes, the hell with the guessing game, the hell with this hangover, and see for sure who is lying next to him.

"Jesus Christ," he says.

Then, more roughly than he needs to, he begins shaking her shoulder. "Wake up."

As she struggles up through the fathoms of her sleep, he finds himself wishing she were bad-looking. But she's pretty. Very, in fact.

She even has a more than perfunctory smile for him. She asks, "What time is it?"

"Let's get one thing straight, lady. I see my son every chance I get."

Again she smiles. Her face is sensual with sleep. "I just asked the time."

"And I call him twice a week."

"I thought we settled this last night," she says.

"We didn't settle anything."

"We must've settled something," she says, "or what would I be doing here?"

He tries to glare at her. With the trouble he's having focusing, he probably just looks silly.

"Do you have a hangover?" she asks.

He says nothing and rolls to the other side of the bed, facing away from her.

His hangover is bad enough. And the day (whatever day it is) is ruined—in this condition, he'd have trouble jerking off, let alone doing anything constructive. And now her.

"Are you hungry?" she asks.

"No."

"Do you mind if I use your toothbrush?"

"Yes, I mind."

"Look," she says, moving closer to him. He can feel the heat of her all along the back of his body. "Look. We really did settle this. I apologized for saying what I did and for slapping you. Then we came over here and had a nice time. Don't you remember?"

He says nothing.

"Don't you remember?" she asks.

"Of course I remember."

"Well then?"

"Well then, nothing."

"I only said what I did because I was drunk. Because for some reason you reminded me of my ex-husband. But you're nothing alike. I told you that last night. When I apologized. You're nothing alike. He only sees our daughter once or twice a year. You see your son regularly."

"Not regularly."

"You said you did. Last night."

"Then I lied."

"Oh," she says, "Well, you see him sort of regularly."

"What the hell does that mean? 'Sort of' regularly?"

"More than once or twice a year."

"I don't see him as often as I could, and that's what matters. Not as often as I could."

"Well, you've talked to him then. On the phone."

"Not for three weeks."

"Oh," she says, "Then you've been busy and when you're not busy you'll start seeing him again. And phoning him again. Things come up from time to time. Women don't expect miracles."

He feels trapped now, hunched into a half-fetal, naked, cold, lonely-as-a-monk position, unable to remember her name, let alone the crazy evening she's been describing in bits and pieces, guilty about his son and suffocatingly sorry for himself.

So she slapped him, he thinks. Well, maybe he had it coming. Maybe it was somehow his son slapping him.

"Women don't expect miracles," she repeats.

Now he rolls on his side the other way. Facing her. "Oh, really? Then what do women expect?"

She seems unimpressed by his hostility. "Women expect help."

He says, "He doesn't call her?"

"Sometimes when he's drunk. And then he cries and that just upsets her."

"Maybe he's got a reason to cry."

"Of course he does. We all do. But he should think of our daughter before he thinks of himself."

He doesn't know how to deal with her. If she'd remained the woman who shrieked at him, who slapped him, maybe now they could have some mean sex and then he could kick her out. But she's not that simple.

"You want some breakfast?" he asks.

"If you let me use the bathroom."

"There's a new toothbrush in the medicine cabinet. I'll start breakfast."

He lets her get up first. With his hangover, he will dodder like an old man and he looks old enough these days.

But she doesn't go into the bathroom immediately. She stands naked at the foot of the bed looking down at him, combing through her blonde hair with her fingers. He guesses her age at thirty. She has small breasts and tender-looking thighs. And light freckles across her nose. About freckles he can get sentimental. He doesn't like women he can't get sentimental about.

"I really am sorry about last night," she says.

"I've done things like that myself. I'm a bad drunk."

He expects her to deny this. To say that she's the bad drunk, not he.

She says nothing.

"As a matter of fact, I can be a very nasty drunk."

"I'll be right back," she says and gives him a tricky, nervous smile and starts off for the john.

He decides against dressing, not even underwear, though his stomach after thirty-six years is not exactly flat and his body is not exactly tanned. His first steps are painful. The tumor in his head expands. This morning he could drink a case of Pepsi, not just a six-pack.

As she moves toward the little kitchenette concealed behind the latticework doors, he wonders again why she was silent when he said he was a nasty drunk. Then his stomach tightens. It occurs to him that he has no real recollection of the previous night. For a moment he is terrified, thinking of all the things he might have said or done. But if he'd gone off, really fucked it up, why would she be here?

He opens the latticework doors.

The stove top is gummy with the grease of three thousand eggs and ten thousand strips of bacon, but not half as gummy as the fry pan into which he puts the fresh eggs and bacon. His coffeepot burned out long ago, so he now boils water for instant coffee in a battered little sauce pan. He can hear her pissing and then flushing the toilet. He puts two plates and some reasonably clean silver on the table. He hears her running water in the sink and then gargling. He sets two slices of bread in the toaster. He hears her closing the medicine cabinet and opening the bathroom door.

He turns to watch her walk toward him. He is still wondering why she wouldn't deny that he's a terrible drunk. He looks at her face carefully. She looks happy enough.

"You need any help?" she asks.

"It's all ready," he says, coming away from the kitchenette with a sticky jug of orange juice in his hand.

"Not bad," she says after taking the first bite of her omelet.

"Not good, though."

She laughs, "Not bad."

"So how did we finally get together?" he asks after he finishes his first cup of coffee.

She looks disappointed. "You don't remember any of it, do you?"

"Some of it. Not all of it."

"None of it. It's not worth talking about anyway," she says.

"I'm just curious."

"There's nothing to be curious about."

"Well, why did you slap me?"

"Because I was drunk."

"How did we get from there to here?"

"You don't remember any of it, do you?"

He sighs. "Not much."

"Not any."

Now she sighs. "All right. All right, but then we drop the subject, okay?"

"Okay."

"After I slapped you, I left the party and went downstairs. I was so upset I couldn't even start my car. I just sat there crying. The more sober I got, the more embarrassed I got. Then I noticed you sort of weaving your way to your car. I decided to apologize. Which is what I tried to do. But you wouldn't let me."

The tumor is working on the front part of his brain now. He wants to tell her to stop. Why upset her more by making her go through it all again? Why risk upsetting himself by hearing about something he did or said while drunk? "You mean I wouldn't accept your apology?"

She smiles. "You didn't think I owed you an apology. You said that you didn't know who I was. At first I thought you were just being belligerent. How could you forget somebody who'd just slapped you ten minutes ago? But then I realized how drunk you were. You honestly didn't know who I was."

He tries for a smile. "Sometimes I drink too much."

"So I told you all about it. About what I'd said to you, how you were a terrible father and a selfish person. And about how I slapped you."

"Did I get hostile?" he asks.

"You tried to seduce me."

"Right there in the parking lot?"

"Right on the car hood."

"That isn't funny. I apologize."

"At least I persuaded you to get inside the car."

"We did it inside the car?"

"In the front seat. Just like high school. It was sad. But I thought it would settle our debt."

"So how did we get to my place?" he asks.

"I drove us. Your car is still in the parking lot."

"Christ," he says. He remembers none of what she's describing. None of it. He is terrified. "Could we get back into bed?"

"Into bed?" She looks surprised. "Why?"

"Why do you think?"

As a boy he played a certain game. He imagined that his bed was a life raft and that as long as he stayed in bed nothing could harm him. Not the sharks. Not the ocean. Now, as he makes love to her, he feels this same peace and security again. He watches her face. She looks at peace, too. And now he no longer worries about last night, or even about his hangover.

"Thank you," he says afterward.

For a while then he is silent, here on his life raft, surrounded by sharks and the cold eternal ocean.

But he knows his contentment is not permanent. He still has questions. What else he said. What else he did. He has to know. His raft is a bed again.

He says, "I'd like to apologize for last night."

"We're not going to talk about last night anymore, remember?"

"But I do owe you an apology."

"For what?" she asks. "I was the one who slapped you."

"But after that," he says. "For the parking lot. For that I owe you an apology. For that I apologize."

"Well," she says. "For the parking lot I guess I would accept an apology. A small one."

"A big one. I know what I'm like when I'm that drunk."

"A small one will be fine," she says.

"Is there anything else I should apologize for? About last night?"

"Please. Forget about last night," she says.

"Did I talk about my son?"

"Please."

"Well, did I?"

"You said he was very bright and very kind and that you loved him very much."

"Did I talk about visiting him?"

"You said you visited him regularly."

"Well, I don't. That was an exaggeration. I don't visit him regularly."

She says nothing.

He says, "I don't want you to think I'm like your ex-husband."

"He's not so bad," she says. "Not really. It's just when he hurts Jennifer. But after being with you, I understand him a little better."

"Me? What did I have to do with it?"

"Why the hell do you keep pushing?"

"I want you to tell me. You're holding something back and I want you to tell me what it is."

"Please. I have to leave in an hour. I don't want to waste it talking about last night."

"You can always leave now."

"Maybe I will," she says, angry.

"But before you go, I want you to tell me about last night."

"What you did is nothing to be ashamed of."

"I'll be the judge of that."

"Can't we just lie here?"

"What did I do?"

She says, "You tried to call your son."

"What?"

"You tried to call your son. It was three-thirty in the morning. I wouldn't let you. We wrestled by the phone over there."

"Jesus," he says.

She says nothing.

He says, "Why the hell did I try to call my son at three-thirty in the morning?"

"Because you felt sorry for yourself."

"For him."

"For yourself."

"Jesus Christ," he says.

"It's nothing to be ashamed of. All of us have reasons to feel sorry for ourselves."

"Jesus," he says.

She tries to put her arms around him. He leans back to make this impossible. Now he is sick of her, of himself. His hangover threatens to push his eyes out of his head.

"I suppose you feel really smug about all this," he says after a while.

"Hardly."

"You know I could make a point right here."

"If it will make you feel better," she says, "make it."

"I could ask you where your daughter is at this very moment. And where she's been all night."

"At home. With my mother."

"With your mother. You don't think your daughter misses you when you're gone?"

"Of course she does."

"But even knowing that she misses you, you go out anyway? And stay out all night?"

"Yes."

"Well what kind of mother does that make you? Your

daughter's at home missing you and here you are in some man's bed. What kind of mother does that make you?"

"I only go out one night a month," she says.

"Very noble."

"One night a month," she says. "One night a month I have my mother watch Jennifer so I can stay out all night. So I can get laid, screwed, fucked, whatever you want to say. I don't have a steady boyfriend. This is the only thing I can do and I make no apologies for it. No fucking apologies whatsoever. Do you understand?"

He says nothing. What can he say? Then he says, "I'm sorry."

She says nothing.

He says, "I'm sorry."

"Of course you're sorry," she says. "Of course you're sorry. And I'm sorry. And Jennifer's sorry. And my ex-husband's sorry. We're all sorry."

"Your one night a month," he says. "You could've found somebody better to spend it with than me."

"Or somebody worse," she says. "There are lots worse."

"Not 'lots' worse," he says.

"All right," she sighs. "Not 'lots' worse."

I wrote this for a Horror Writers of America anthology. I got up one morning and there it was in the word processor, just waiting for me to type out the words. I wish they all came this easily.

DUTY

Earlier this morning, just as the sun had begun to burn the dew off the farm fields, Keller got out his old Schwinn and set off from the box-like tarpaper shack where he lived with a goat, three chickens he'd never had the heart to eat, four cats and a hamster. The hamster had been Timmy's.

Today he traveled the old two-lane highway. The sun hot on his back, he thought of how it used to be on this stretch of asphalt, the bright red convertibles with the bright pink blondes in them and the sound of rock and roll waving like a banner in the wind. Or the green John Deere tractors moving snail-slow, trailing infuriated city drivers behind.

The old days. Before the change. He used to sit in a chair in front of his shack and talk to his wife Martha and his son Timmy till Timmy went to sleep in Martha's lap. Then Keller would take the boy inside and lay him gently in bed and kiss his boy-moist brow goodnight. The Kellers had always been referred to locally, and not unkindly, as "that hippie family." Keller had worn the tag as a badge of honor. In a world obsessed with money and power, he'd wanted to spend his days discovering again and again the simple pleasures of starry nights, of clear quick country streams, of mountain music strummed on an old six-string and accompanied by owls and kitties and crocuses. Somehow back in time he'd managed to get himself an advanced degree in business and finance. But after meeting Marsha, the happiest and most contented person he'd ever known, he'd followed her out here and he never once

73

yearned for the treacherous world he'd deserted.

He thought of these things as he angled the Schwinn down the center of the highway, his golden collie Andy running alongside, appreciative of the exercise. Across Keller's shoulder was strapped his ancient backpack, the one he'd carried twenty years ago in college. You could see faintly where the word "Adidas" had been.

He rode on. The Schwinn's chain was loose and banged noisily sometimes, and on a particularly hard bump the front fender sometimes rubbed the tire. He fixed the bike methodically, patiently, at least once a week, but the Schwinn was like a wild boy and would never quite be tamed. Timmy had been that way.

The trip took two hours. By that time, Andy was tired of running, his pink tongue lolling rightward out of his mouth, exhausted, and Keller was tired of pedaling.

The farmhouse was up a high sloping hill, east of the highway.

From his backpack Keller took his binoculars. He spent ten minutes scanning the place. He had no idea what he was looking for. He just wanted to reassure himself that the couple who'd sent the message with Conroy—a pig farmer ten miles to the west of Keller's—were who and what they claimed to be.

He saw a stout woman in a faded housedress hanging laundry on a backyard clothesline. He saw a sun-reddened man in blue overalls moving among a waving carpet of white hungry chickens, throwing them golden kernels of corn. He saw a windmill turning with rusty dignity in the southern wind.

After returning his binoculars to his backpack, he mounted the Schwinn again, patted Andy on the head, and set off up the steep gravel hill.

The woman saw Keller first. He had come around the edge of the big two-story frame house when she was just finishing her laundry.

She looked almost angry when she saw who he was.

She didn't speak to him; instead, she called out in a weary

voice for her husband. Somehow, the man managed to hear her above the squawking chickens. He set down the tin pan that held the kernels of corn then walked over and stood by his wife.

"You're a little early," the farmer said. His name was Dodds, Alcie Dodds, and his wife was Myrna. Keller used to see them at the pot luck dinners the community held back before the change.

"I wasn't sure how long it would take. Guess I left a little before I needed to."

"You enjoy what you do, Mr. Keller? Does it give you pleasure?" Myrna Dodds said.

"Now Myrna, don't be—"

"I just want him to answer me that question. I just want him to answer me honest."

By now, Keller was used to being treated this way. It was, he knew, a natural reaction.

Alcie Dodds said, "She hasn't had much sleep the last couple of nights, Keller. You know what I'm saying?"

Keller nodded.

"You want a cup of coffee?" Alcie Dodds said.

"I'd appreciate it."

Suddenly the woman started crying. She put her hands to her face and simply began wailing, her fleshy body shaking beneath the loose fitting housedress.

Keller saw such grief everywhere he went. He wished there was something he could do about it.

Dodds went over and slid his arm around his wife. "Why don't you go in and see Beth, honey?"

Mention of the name only caused the woman to begin sobbing even more uncontrollably.

She took her hands from her face and glared at Keller. "I hope you rot in hell, Mr. Keller. I hope you rot in hell."

Shadows cooled the kitchen. The air smelled of stew bubbling on the stove, of beef and tomatoes and onions and paprika.

The two men sat at a small kitchen table beneath a funeral home calendar that depicted a picture of Jesus as a young and very handsome bearded man. By now, they were on their second cup of coffee.

"Sorry about the missus."

"I understand. I'd feel the same way."

"We always assume it won't happen to us."

"Ordinarily, they don't get out this far. It isn't worth it for them. They stick to cities, or at least areas where the population is heavy."

"But they do get out here," Dodds said. "Oftener than people like to admit."

Keller sighed. He stared down into his coffee cup. "I guess that's true."

"I hear it happened to you."

"Yes."

"Your boy."

"Right."

"The fucking bastards. The fucking bastards." Dodds made a large fist and brought it down thunderously on the table that smelled of the red and white checkered oilcloth. In the window above the sink the sky was very blue and the blooming trees very green.

After a time, Dodds said, "You ever seen one? In person, I mean?"

"No."

"We did once. We were in Chicago. We were supposed to get back to our hotel room before dusk, before they came out into the streets but we got lost. Anybody ever tell you about their smell?"

"Yes."

"It's like rotting meat. You can't believe it. Especially when a lot of them are in one place at the same time. And they've got these sores all over them. Like leprosy. We made it back to the hotel all right but before we did we saw these two young children—they'd turned already—they found this old lady and they started chasing her, having a good time with her, really

76

prolonging it, and then she tripped in the street and one of them knelt beside her and went to work. You heard about how they puke afterwards?"

"Yes. The shock to their digestive systems. All the blood."

"Never saw anybody puke like this. And the noise she made when she was puking. Sickening. Then the old lady got up and let out this cry. I've never heard anything even close to it. Just this loud animal noise. She was already starting to turn."

Keller finished his coffee.

"You want more?"

"No, thanks, Mr. Dodds."

"You want a Pepsi? Got a six pack we save for special occasions." He shrugged. "I'm not much of a liquor drinker."

"No, thanks, Mr. Dodds."

Dodds drained his own coffee. "Can I ask you something?"

"Sure."

It was time to get it over with. Dodds was stalling. Keller didn't blame him.

"You ever find that you're wrong?"

"How so, Mr. Dodds?"

"You know, that you think they've turned but they really haven't?"

Keller knew what Dodds was trying to say, of course. He was trying to say—to whatever God existed—please let it be a mistake. Please let it not be what it seems to be."

"Not so far, I haven't, Mr. Dodds. I'm sorry."

"You know how it's going to be on her, don't you, on my wife?"

"Yes, I'm afraid I do, Mr. Dodds."

"She won't ever be the same."

"No, I don't suppose she will."

Dodds stared down at his hands and turned them to fists again. Under his breath, he said, "Fucking bastards."

"Maybe we'd better go have a look, Mr. Dodds."

"You sure you don't want another cup of coffee?"

"No, thanks, Mr. Dodds. I appreciate the offer though."

* * *

Dodds led them through the cool, shadowy house. The place was old. You could tell that by all the mahogany trim and the height of the ceilings and the curve of the time-swollen floor. But even given its age it was a pleasant and comfortable place, a nook of sweet shade on a hot day.

Down the hall Keller could hear Mrs. Dodds singing, humming really, soft noises rather than words.

"Forgive her if she acts up again, Mr. Keller."

Keller nodded.

And it was then the rock came sailing through the window in the front room. The smashing glass had an almost musical quality to it on the hot silent afternoon.

"What the hell was that?" Dodds wondered.

He turned around and ran back down the pink wallpapered hall and right out the front door, almost slamming the screen door in Keller's face.

There were ten of them on the lawn, in the shade of the elm, six men, four women. Two of the men held carbines.

"There he is," one of the men said.

"That sonofabitch Keller," another man said.

"You people get out of here, and now," Dodds said, coming down off the porch steps. "This is my land."

"You really gonna let him do it, Alcie?" a man said.

"That's my business," Dodds said, pawing at the front of his coveralls.

A pretty woman leaned forward. "I'm sorry we came, Alcie. The men just wouldn't have it any other way. Us women just came along to make sure there wasn't no violence."

"Speak for yourself, honey," a plump woman in a man's checkered shirt and jeans said. "Personally, I'd like to cut Keller's balls off and feed 'em to my pigs."

Two of the men laughed at her. She'd said it to impress them and she'd achieved her end.

"Go on, now, before somethin' is said or done that can't be unsaid or undone," Dodds said.

"Your wife want this done?" the man with the second

carbine said. He answered his own question: "Bet she don't.
Bet she fought you on it all the way."

A soft breeze came. It was an afternoon for drinking
lemonade and watching monarch butterflies and seeing the
foals in the pasture running up and down the summer green
hills. It was not an afternoon for angry men with carbines.

"You heard me now," Dodds said.

"How 'bout you, chickenshit? You got anything to say for
yourself, Keller?"

"God dammit, Davey—" Dodds started to say.

"Won't use my gun, Alcie. Don't need it."

And with that the man named Davey tossed his carbine to
one of the other men and then stepped up near the steps where
Dodds and Keller stood.

Keller recognized Davey. He ran the feed and grain in
town and was a legendary tavern bully. God forbid you should
ever beat him at snooker. He had freckles like a pox and fists
like anvils.

"You hear what I asked you, chickenshit?"

"Davey—" Dodds started saying again.

Keller stepped down off the steps. He was close enough
to smell the afternoon beer on Davey's breath.

"This wasn't easy for Mr. Dodds, Davey," Keller said. He
spoke so softly Davey's friends had to lean forward to hear.
"But it's his decision to make. His and his wife's."

"You enjoy it, don't you, chickenshit?" Davey said. "You're
some kind of pervert who gets his kicks that way, aren't you?"

Behind him, his friends started cursing Keller, and that
only emboldened Davey all the more.

He threw a big roundhouse right and got Keller right in
the mouth.

Keller started to drop to the ground, black spots alternat-
ing with yellow spots before his eyes, and then Davey raised his
right foot and kicked Keller square in the chest.

"Kill that fucker, Davey! Kill that fucker!" one of the men
with the carbines shouted.

And then, on the sinking afternoon, the shotgun was fired.

The birdshot got so close to Davey that it tore tiny holes in his right sleeve, like something that had been gnawed on by a puppy.

"You heard my husband," Mrs. Dodds said, standing on the porch with a sawed-off double barrel that looked to be one mean and serious weapon. "You get off our land."

Davey said, "We was only tryin' to help you, missus. We knew you didn't want—"

But she silenced him. "I was wrong about Keller here. If he didn't care about them, he couldn't do it. He had to do it to his own wife and son, or are you forgetting that?"

Davey said, "But—"

And Mrs. Dodds leveled the shotgun right at his chest. "You think I won't kill you, Davey, you're wrong."

Davey's wife took him by the sleeve. "C'mon, honey; you can see she's serious."

But Davey had one last thing to say. "It ain't right what he does. Don't you know that, Mrs. Dodds? It ain't right!"

But Mrs. Dodds could only sadly shake her head. "You know what'd become of 'em if he didn't do it, don't you? Go into the city sometime and watch 'em. Then tell me you'd want one of your own to be that way."

Davey's wife tugged on his sleeve again. Then she looked up at Mrs. Dodds and said, "I'm sorry for this, Mrs. Dodds. I really am. The boys here just had too much to drink and—" She shook her head. "I'm sorry."

And in ones and twos they started drifting back to the pickup trucks they'd parked on the downslope side of the gravel drive.

"It's a nice room," Keller said twenty minutes later. And it was. The wallpaper was blue. Teddy bears and unicorns cavorted across it. There was a tiny table and chairs and a globe and a set of junior encyclopedias, things she would grow up to use someday. Or would have, anyway.

In the corner was the baby's bed. Mrs. Dodds stood in front of it, protecting it. "I'm sorry how I treated you when you first came."

"I know."

"And I'm sorry Davey hit you."

"Not your fault."

By now he realized that she was not only stalling. She was also doing something else—pleading. "You look at little Jenny and you be sure."

"I will."

"I've heard tales of how sometimes you think they've turned but it's just some other illness with the same symptoms."

"I'll be very careful."

Mr. Dodds said, "You want us to leave the room?"

"It'd be better for your wife."

And then she spun around and looked down into the baby's bed where her seven-month-old daughter lay discolored and breathing as if she could not catch her breath, both primary symptoms of the turning.

She picked the infant up and clutched it to her chest. And began sobbing so loudly, all Keller could do was put his head down.

It fell to Mr. Dodds to pry the baby from his wife's grip and to lead Mrs. Dodds from the baby's room.

On his way out, starting to cry a man's hard embarrassed tears, Mr. Dodds looked straight at Keller and said, "Just be sure, Mr. Keller. Just be sure."

Keller nodded that he'd be sure.

The room smelled of sunlight and shade and baby powder.

The bed had the sort of slatted sides you could pull up or down. He put it down and leaned over to the baby. She was very pretty, chunky, blonde, with a cute little mouth. She wore diapers. They looked very white compared to the blue, asphyxiated color of her skin.

His examination was simple. The Dodds could easily have done it themselves but of course they didn't want to. It would only have confirmed their worst fears.

He opened her mouth. She started to cry. He first examined her gums and then her teeth. The tissue on the former had started to harden and scab; the latter had started to elongate.

The seven-month-old child was in the process of turning.

Sometimes they roamed out here from the cities and took what they could find. One of them had broken into the Dodds' two weeks ago and had stumbled on the baby's room.

He worked quickly, as he always did, as he'd done with his wife and son when they'd been ambushed in the woods one day and had then started to turn.

All that was left of civilization was in the outlands such as these. Even though you loved them, you could not let them turn because the life ahead for them was so unimaginably terrible. The endless hunt for new bodies; the feeding frenzies; the constant illness that was a part of the condition and the condition was forever—

No, if you loved them, you had only one choice.

In this farming community, no one but Keller could bring himself to do what was necessary. They always deluded themselves that their loved ones hadn't really been infected, hadn't really begun turning—

And so it fell to Keller.

He rummaged quickly through his Adidas backpack now, finding hammer and wooden stake.

He returned to the bed and leaned over and kissed the little girl on the forehead. "You'll be with God, honey," he said. "You'll be with God."

He stood up straight, took the stake in his left hand and set it against her heart, and then raised with great sad weariness the hammer.

He killed her as he killed them all, clean and quick, hot infected blood splattering his face and shirt, her final cry one more wound in his soul.

On the porch, Mrs. Dodds inside in her bedroom, Mr. Dodds put his hand on Keller's shoulder and said, "I'll pray for you, Mr. Keller."

"I'll be needing your prayers, Mr. Dodds," Keller said, and

then he nodded goodbye and left.

In half an hour, he was well down the highway again, Andy getting another good run for the day, pink tongue lolling.

In his backpack he could feel the sticky hammer and stake, the same tools he used over and over again as the sickness of the cities spread constantly outward.

In a while it began to rain. He was still thinking of the little Dodds girl, of her innocent eyes there at the very last.

He did not seem to notice the rain, or the soft quick darkness.

He rode on, the bicycle chattering, the front wheel wobbling from the twisted fender, and Andy stopping every quarter mile or so to shake the rain off.

The fucking sonofabitches, he thought.

The fucking sonofabitches.

Much like the narrator of this story, I drank my way through my divorce, ending up one bright spring morning with a gun in my hand, determined to kill myself or give up the bottle. My life was completely out of control. Somehow, I had strength enough to quit (I don't agree with Alcoholics Anonymous that God grants everybody the same strength to quit.)

"Failed Prayers" captures the drab brutal sorrow of the years following my divorce. I knew many men like the narrator, and even more alas like his friend. I even recall, with the perfect memory of remorse, smashing up a car much as the narrator does early on in the tale. It was not my car. Rather it belonged to a well-dressed middle-aged man who kept saying through rage and tears, "The bitch dumped me; the bitch dumped me," referring only occasionally to his wife by name. I had no idea who he was but when he invited me outside the bar to help kick in his new Audi, I found myself thinking that the man must be some kind of Shaman, for clearly his idea was possessed of thunderous cosmic truth.

FAILED PRAYERS

In my days as a police officer I mostly laughed at the few private investigators I knew. For some reason, they were usually small men with fierce little eyes and sour little mouths and enough comic-opera swagger to do an entire rodeo of cowboys proud. And they carried weapons of unimaginable size, which was especially curious when you considered that their prime job was installing electronic bugs.

But that wasn't why I disliked them so much. I mean, we're all foolish in our way, and each of us whores to survive.

No, what I disliked about them was the fact that they traded on human misery for their money. Here, sir, are the pictures of your wife you wanted; I even got her smiling mid-orgasm. (Here, ma'am, is your husband. A pitiful figure, isn't he, his fat ass bucking up and down?)

Living is a matter of choices, and private investigators have made the worst choice of all.

I say this with no little hypocrisy. There is the matter of my present employer, the American Security Agency. There is the matter of my own private investigator's license. There is the matter two weeks ago, of my following a married woman to an assignation so that I could snap several 35 mm. shots of her. (I did not go up to the motel room; I did not slide a bug beneath the mattress. Even hypocrites have some scruples.)

So how did I get from reasonably honest cop to reasonably dishonest private investigator?

It was winter, a very bitter winter . . .

When she slapped him, everybody turned around and

looked, including me. I'm just as addicted to the spectacle of human misery as anybody else.

This was six years ago, back when I was still married. Ostensibly, anyway. I had just discovered acting and my wife had just discovered her husband-to-be. It was a trade, of sorts.

Anyway, that's how I came to be in Belmondo's that snowy Friday night. Belmondo's is a singles bar where cops hang out. I had already passed on the all available cop groupies and was hoping that the door was going to open up and somebody female was going to come in with sunshine in her smile.

Which is when the woman, seated at a small cuddling table near the middle of the place, leaned over and slapped the man she was with very hard.

My partner Ryan said, "Jesus." Ryan had a mournful way of cursing that was more a failed prayer than blasphemy. As if he wanted to appeal to God but had learned through bitter experience that the Big Guy didn't always come through for you.

Everybody tried to look away after it was all over, but you couldn't help but let your eyes drift back to them, to see what they were doing.

And what they were doing, of course, was suffering.

They were my age, early thirties, a spawn of good colleges and good taste. He was probably an investment banker or something very much like it—preppy blonde hair, pin-striped shirt with collar pin, slightly condescending smile for waitresses and anybody else who wasn't a member of whatever Club these guys are always members of—and she was the prize upper middle-class men always fight for, one of those gentle dark women with the glistening impenetrable gaze of a Spanish Madonna and a presence that was both dignified and erotic. In their college days they'd probably made love in the back seat of any number of Volvos. But they were long past their college days now, so long past that she'd done the unthinkable. Created a scene in a public place.

Ryan said "Jesus" again and I looked up from my drink.

"Yeah," I said.

Ryan so happened to be going through the same kind of divorce I was. He'd done what I'd proposed doing but couldn't get my wife to agree to—gone to a counselor. Whom he told all the things he'd told me and presumably other things, too. Ryan, or so Ryan told me anyway one drunken blistering night in a parking lot when we'd both beat the hell out of our cars in useless and adolescent rage, Ryan hadn't had a decent hard-on in a year and every time he thought about his wife leaving him, he started crying. You don't expect this from a guy who looks like a middleweight fighter, including the tattoos, gone slightly to flesh.

"Wonder who's dumping who," Ryan said, nodding in their direction. "I mean, between them?"

"Does it matter? The result is the same."

"Yeah."

So we spent more time watching the door. Frank Ryan was waiting for a sweetheart bearing sunshine, too. You meet the right woman suddenly it's no longer gray November. It's spring. But even above the juke box I could hear the winter wind whip and feel the night abandon me.

Some other cops came and we talked cop stuff, or I did anyway. Ryan, who's never had a reliable bladder, went several times to the john and when he wasn't peeing, he stared openly at the couple in the center of the place. They still looked miserable.

Nothing else of note happened that night. I did find a woman finally and we went to her place and she asked me a lot of questions about herpes with the lights still on and then in the darkness she told me about a kid she'd lost in a custody battle and a second husband who'd turned out to be gay. I managed a forlorn little erection and got out of there as soon as I could. I was really looking forward to being single again. You meet such a lot of happy people.

Six months went by, during which time my wife told me about her lover and our two kids went through the pain of deciding which parent to hate most, me for being Dad *in*

absentia, Mom for being at least a bit of a tart. Both of us
deserved to be put in the same bag and tossed in the same river.
You never forget how your kids sound just then, sobbing over
how you've betrayed them. Their sobbing goes down the
timelines. Forever.

I saw Ryan from time to time of course, usually in a singles
bar. By then his wife had been through a few more affairs and
he was spending all his money on a shrink. He had pretty much
given up looking for women. Instead he was spending most of
his time being both father and mother to his daughter. It's
amazing how the pain of betrayal turns normally intensive men
like Ryan into real people. For a couple of weeks we did what
most dumped lovers do—took up racquetball. We had big
hopes for racquetball. We were going to pound that frigging
ball so hard it was going to be a creative act in and of itself, and
our human sweat was going to cleanse us of our griefs. We
paid something like a $200 fee to join the club and I think we
went maybe seven times in all. I found an excuse not to go one
night and then he found an excuse, then the next time we both
found excuses and right then we decided, without words of
course, to blow off our $200 per initiation fee. What the hell,
I was rich.

Then it was spring again and the Cubs were sending hope-
ful messages from training camp (sort of like the message
General Custer sent from Little Big Horn) and along the river
you saw women strolling whom God put on the planet just so
you'd have somebody to dream about.

Then one night I saw the man's picture on the six o'clock
news. At first I didn't recognize him. Instead of the investment
banker suit, they had him here in a mug shot. He looked out
of sleep and out of luck. Amazing how a single bad night can
transform you into a derelict.

The reason he was on TV was simple enough. The fellows
at one of the downtown precincts were accusing him of murder.
The next shot was of his Madonna-like wife. Her you didn't
forget. I remembered them then. The night in the singles bar.

The slap. The slow grinding misery in their eyes afterward. Now she was dead, murdered, and he was accused. Was it really a surprise? Doubtful.

I can't say I followed the trial, not at first anyway, with more than perfunctory interest. I had my own work at the precinct and my own life. Anyway there was a lot of murder trials on the tube and this one didn't have as much inherent interest as the one, say, that involved the guy who drove around chopping people in half, then trying to sell their carcasses to slaughter houses. He now resides downstate in a room with only one window but many bars.

But the singles bar guy came back to my attention when he tore up the courtroom. Just went berserk one day. All the while shouting his innocence.

The TV boys and girls got a shot of him leaving the courtroom. He had the look of somebody who is no longer quite human—rage and sorrow had turned him into a man without grace notes. All he could do was scream one thing, over and over again, till he died, "I AM INNOCENT." Not that this meant he was innocent. He might well have killed her and was now simply in the process of denying it to himself. Or he might be a great, or at least flamboyant, actor.

Then Ryan showed up at my apartment one night with a six-pack of Miller's Lite and said, "He didn't kill her."

"Who?"

"Dobbs."

"Hell, Frank, you were there that night. You saw the slap. You know what it's like when you're in a state like that." The press had detailed how this perfect Yuppie couple had gone gradually to hell. Neighbors testified to the violence of their arguments. Lovers, a blonde lady for him, a swarthy man for her, attested to how much Dobbs hated his wife falling in love with somebody else, and how much his wife hated Dobbs for not letting her go.

"He didn't kill her," Ryan said.

"How do you know?"

"I've just got a feeling."

"You know how far that'll take you in court?"

"He didn't kill her. It's that goddamn simple."

"Let's watch the Cubs."

"Who they playing?"

"Dodgers."

For the first time that night, he grinned. "Let's just go down and watch them make sausage instead. It's the same thing."

Three days later, over sub sandwiches, Ryan convinced me to help him check out the dead woman's boyfriend.

So that afternoon we went to the health club where Carlos Sanchez worked.

He had hot brown eyes, hotter still when we identified ourselves as detectives. We sat in a sunny room, his office, and watched him pat aftershave onto his cheeks. He had biceps that did little dances each time he asked them to.

"Damn," he said. Here he'd been looking perfect, a magazine doll, but the dirty word spoiled the effect.

"Meaning what?" I said.

"Meaning Dobbs' lawyer hired three different private investigators to check me out. To prove that I killed Melissa."

"And they didn't get anywhere?" Ryan said.

"They got right here," and he jammed his arm up in bitter salute.

"Maybe we're smarter than private cops," I said.

"If you were smart, you wouldn't be any kind of cops at all."

"Right," Ryan said, "We'd work in health clubs so we could be around big muscular guys and smell their sweat all day."

"I don't have to take this shit. I can call my lawyer."

"Call him," Ryan said.

"You have an alibi for that night?" I said.

He laughed. "You haven't been reading the papers, have you? I've got the best alibi of all."

"What's that?"

"I was out of town."

"And you can prove it?"

He rubbed brown hands on his clean white T-shirt. "I have a witness who says that I was with her all night. In Detroit."

"If you were so hot for Melissa, what were you doing with another woman?" I asked.

"Who said I was hot for Melissa?"

"The papers seem to give that impression."

"You know what the papers can do."

"So you weren't hot for Melissa?"

"She was so messed up, man. Totally messed up. Tranks. Booze. Crying jags. Jesus."

"So why did you have an affair with her?"

"She came out to the club here. Often. I have affairs with lots of the ladies."

I could see Ryan's blood anger working up. He wasn't the kind of guy who could sit in the presence of a gigolo for long. Especially not a gigolo as callous as this one.

"So if you wanted rid of her why didn't you send her back to her husband?" I said.

"Hey, man, what the hell you think I tried to do? But she wouldn't go. She blew this whole thing out of proportion."

"What's the name of your witness?" Ryan said.

"Angie Swanson."

"Where do we find her?" I asked.

"Towel room."

"She works here?"

He grinned again, as if he were about to impart some pleasingly shocking secret. "Sure, man. Sometimes I have affairs with the staff, too."

I got Ryan out of there while there was still time.

Over the next few days we interviewed Angie Swanson twice, but it didn't work at all (Carlos seemed to inspire the sort of desperate loyalty brought out frequently by lust and only rarely by love) and then we interviewed Dobbs' girlfriend who turned out to be a beautiful but somewhat hysterical interior designer with expensive clothes and nails bitten into blood.

91

She was like a prom queen with stigmata. She was no help at all.

In the car, I said, "You know what?"

"What?"

"I think he did it."

"Dobbs?"

"Yeah."

"Why?"

"Because it's starting to be obvious."

"He's like us, Dwyer." His voice was somber.

"What?"

"He's like us. Went through the number. Bad wife."

"Hey, Frank, Christ. I'm past the stage now."

"What stage?"

"Blaming my wife for everything. Hell, I was a bad father and an even worse husband. It was at least a fifty-fifty failure."

"That's what the shrinks all try to convince you of, anyway. You think it was my fault that my wife liked to go out with every strange jerk that came her way?"

He said it with such heat and hatred that I knew it was a good time to be still. To just look at the traffic.

A couple of blocks later, he said, "Sorry."

"It's all right."

"We're buddies, Dwyer, you and me."

"I know."

"We went through the same stuff together."

"Right."

"Just like Dobbs."

"So you want to keep on?"

"I'll keep on alone if I have to—soon as I get back, I mean."

"Where you going?"

"This friend of mine's got a cabin downstate. Fishing for a few days."

"It'll be good for you."

"Yeah, I started calling her again. My ex-wife I mean."

He said it sadly, the way he said "Jesus" sometimes. "She's still a bitch."

* * *

Next day was my day off. I went to an audition for a stage play and watched all the parts go to other actors and then I went out and had a few beers and then I decided to go home and study for another commercial part my agent felt I had a shot at. Thus far I'd done three spots—public safety things about being a good driver. They had led to promises of work that, for now, remained only that. Promises.

There was a call on my machine and I imagined it was the director back at the dinner theater saying he'd made a big mistake and why didn't I come back and take the lead in the play they were doing.

It turned out to be Dobbs' girlfriend, the one with the bitten nails. She said she wanted to see me as soon as she could.

I started watching a Cubs game, but there were two wild pitches in the first inning so I thought I might as well spare myself some grief and go over and talk to Rita Tavers.

She was showing carpet samples and handling them with the care one would a newborn infant. A young couple returned her reverence by gazing on the samples as if they were precious stones.

I listened to Rita work—she had a certain nervous verve and I liked her sad edge despite myself—and when the couple was gone and she came over, I said, "You've really got it down."

She bit her nails. "I wish I had my own life down as well."

I smiled. "I know the feeling."

She surprised me by smiling back. "Yes, for some reason I think you do."

"You want a drink? There's a nice bar around the corner."

She bit her nails again. I wanted to buy her a pair of insulated gloves. "Yes, why not?"

"I don't think he's ever realized how much I love him," Rita Tavers said.

She was about to cry. We were sitting in a restaurant built of redwood and ferns.

"Don't you tell him that?"

93

"Yes, but—well, he's almost in a trance these days. Since the verdict I mean."

"He'll be out in six years."

"He didn't do it."

I sighed. "I've spent some time on this. I've got a friend who doesn't think he did it, either. But I think you're both wrong. His wife betrayed him and he couldn't take it and he killed her. It's not a new story."

"She was seeing someone else."

"Carlos."

"Other than him."

"What?"

From her purse she took a small bound book. "This is her diary."

"Melissa Dobbs'?"

"Yes."

"Where did you get it?"

She flushed. She had green eyes and very white skin and a wry little mouth. I liked the hell out of her. "I broke in. To their home I mean."

"When?"

"This was just before she died."

"Why?"

"Why did I break in you mean?"

"Right."

"I was—insane sort of. He didn't want me around him anymore. He said that he was going to figure out a way that she'd take him back. He was insane, too. So I broke in—I didn't know what I was looking for, but I wanted some evidence of just how much he needed me instead of her. I found—this. I wasn't sure it was important till now." She nodded to the book. Then she glanced at her watch. "I've really got to get back. But take the diary. Read it carefully. Then you'll see what I mean."

I walked her back to her office in the bright summer day and then I went home and read the diary and then I made my plans.

* * *

Frank Ryan said, "How did you figure it out?"

"This." I handed him the diary.

We were riding down the street. I'd called as soon as he'd gotten back from fishing, told him I needed to see him. For the first time—obviously sensing something—he seemed nervous.

"What does it say?"

"Just about how this guy stopped her one day—this guy she'd never seen before—and seemed to know all about her life. And told her to go back to her husband."

We sat at a stoplight.

"All I really wanted to do was help them," he said.

"The weird thing is, Frank, I believe you."

"I mean, that night in the bar, when she slapped him, I got their names. I wasn't even sure why, then. But then I started following them around, trying to find out everything I could about them. I found out a lot. I followed them for months. I didn't make any contact with either of them. I just followed them. It was like I was—monitoring them, or something. They were both decent people—they really were—but they were a little spoiled, especially her. She needed more excitement than Dobbs so she took up with that fucking Carlos asshole. She really thought it was love. All I wanted her to do was stop seeing him for a couple of weeks. Give Dobbs another chance."

"So you strangled her?"

"I just—got carried away. Jesus."

"You thought you could throw any suspicion off yourself— if it ever came up—by investigating the murder yourself."

He sighed. "You're not giving me anything, Dwyer."

"I want to give you something, Frank. Help me."

"It wasn't that I wanted to throw suspicion off *me*. I didn't want him to do time. I figured if we investigated we could nail Carlos for it in some way."

I laughed. "I almost wish it would have worked, Frank. Because you're a friend of mine, and this is all crazy."

"You know what my wife's gonna say?" he said.

I didn't say anything for a time. Then, "What's she gonna say?"

"She's gonna say—I always knew he was a killer. Then she'll completely absolve herself of all the crap she did to me and everybody will feel real sorry for her."

Now it was my turn. "Jesus," I said.

I said it just the way Frank always did.

As a prayer.

A failed prayer.

I went to see him a couple of times upstate in prison. Both times he tried looking jaunty—a lot of grinning and diddly-bopping—but he couldn't do anything about his eyes.

He'd done three years when they got him that night just after dinner and put a spoon fashioned into a knife straight up deep into his chest. There were three of them and they must have got all caught up in the frenzy of it because they didn't stop stabbing him once—they stabbed him thirty-four times. "Savages," the warden said for the sake of the press.

So I left the force and started picking up bits as an actor and meanwhile I supported myself as a part-time security guard and private investigator.

Ryan wouldn't have been able to handle it, of course, my job. Listening to tapes of laughter and betrayal. Watching that particular type of smirk only adultery seems to produce.

No, Ryan wouldn't have been able to handle it at all.

Whenever I wanted to escape, I took a Greyhound. I'd pack some clothes and get some cash and just take off for a few days. I was on a Greyhound the night Martin Luther King was murdered, and a white woman sitting next to me said, "I knew somebody'd get that nigger someday," and the black teenager behind me said, "You better watch your mouth, bitch." All that sorrow; all that rage.

There is no ambience quite like that of a Greyhound hurtling through the midwestern darkness, and that's what I tried to capture here in a story written originally for a men's pulp magazine.

LAYOVER

In the darkness, the girl said, "Are you all right?"

"Huh?"

"I woke you up because you sounded so bad. You must have been having a nightmare."

"Oh. Yeah. Right." I tried to laugh but the sound just came out strangled and harsh.

Cold midnight. Deep midwest. A Greyhound bus filled with old folks and runaway kids and derelicts of every kind. Anybody can afford a Greyhound ticket these days, that's why you find so many geeks and freaks aboard. I was probably the only guy on the bus who had a real purpose in life. And if I needed a reminder of that purpose, all I had to do was shove my hand into the pocket of my P-coat and touch the chill blue metal of the .38. I had a purpose all right.

The girl had gotten on a day before, during a dinner stop. She wasn't what you'd call pretty but then neither was I. We talked of course, the way you do when you travel; dull grinding social chatter at first, but eventually you get more honest. She told me she'd just been dumped by a guy named Mike, a used car salesman at Belaski Motors in a little town named Burnside. She was headed to Chicago where she'd find a job and show Mike that she was capable of going on without him. Come to think of it, I guess Polly here had a goal, too, and in a certain way our goals were similar. We both wanted to pay people back for hurting us.

Sometime around ten, when the driver turned off the tiny

99

overhead lights and people started falling asleep, I heard her start crying. It wasn't loud and it wasn't hard but it was genuine. There was a lot of pain there.

I don't know why—I'm not the type of guy to get involved—but I put my hand on her lap. She took it in both of her hands and held it tightly. "Thanks," she said and leaned over and kissed me with wet cheeks and a trembling hot little mouth.

"You're welcome," I said, and that's when I drifted off to sleep, the wheels of the Greyhound thrumming down the highway, the dark coffin inside filled with people snoring, coughing and whispering.

According to the luminous hands on my wrist watch, it was forty-five minutes later when Polly woke me up to tell me I'd been having a nightmare.

The lights were still off overhead. The only lumination was the soft silver of moonlight through the tinted window. We were in the back seat on the left hand side of the back aisle. The only thing behind us was the john, which almost nobody seemed to use. The seats across from us were empty.

After telling me about how sorry she felt for me having nightmares like that, she leaned over and whispered, "Who's Kenny?"

"Kenny?"

"That's the name you kept saying in your nightmare."

"Oh."

"You're not going to tell me, huh?"

"Doesn't matter. Really."

I leaned back and closed my eyes. There was just darkness and the turning of the wheels and the winter air whistling through the windows. You could smell the faint exhaust.

"You know what I keep thinking?" she said.

"No. What?" I didn't open my eyes.

"I keep thinking we're the only two people in the world, you and I, and we're on this fabulous boat and we're journeying to someplace beautiful."

I had to laugh at that. She sounded so naive yet desperate too. "Someplace beautiful, huh?"

"Just the two of us."

And she gave my hand a little squeeze. "I'm sorry I'm so corny," she said.

And that's when it happened. I started to turn around in my seat and felt something fall out of my pocket and hit the floor, going *thunk*. I didn't have to wonder what it was.

Before I could reach it, she bent over, her long blonde hair silver in the moonlight, and got it for me.

She looked at it in her hand and said, "Why would you carry a gun?"

"Long story."

She looked as if she wanted to take the gun and throw it out the window. She shook her head. "You're going to do something with this, aren't you?"

I sighed and reached over and took the gun from her. "I'd like to try and catch a little nap if you don't mind."

"But—"

And I promptly turned over so that three-fourths of my body was pressed against the chill wall of the bus. I pretended to go to sleep, resting there and smelling diesel fuel and feeling the vibration of the motor.

The bus roared on into the night. It wouldn't be long before I'd be seeing Dawn and Kenny again. I touched the .38 in my pocket. No, not long at all.

If you've taken many Greyhounds, then you know about layovers. You spend an hour-and-a-half gulping down greasy food and going to the bathroom in a john that reeks like a city dump on a hot day and staring at people in the waiting area who seem to be deformed in some way. Or that's how they look at 2:26 A.M., anyway.

This layover was going to be different. At least for me. I had plans.

As the bus pulled into a small brick depot that looked as if it had been built back during the Depression, Polly said, "You're going to do it here, aren't you?"

"Do what?"

"Shoot somebody."

"Why would you say that?"

"I've just got a feeling is all. My mom always says I have ESP."

She started to say something else but then the driver lifted the microphone and gave us his spiel about how the layover would be a full hour and how there was good food to be had in the restaurant and how he'd enjoyed serving us. There'd be a new driver for the next six hours of our journey, he said.

There weren't many lights on in the depot. Passengers stood outside for a while stretching and letting the cold air wake them up.

I followed Polly off the bus and immediately started walking away. An hour wasn't a long time.

Before I got two steps, she snagged my arm. "I was hoping we could be friends. You know, I mean, we're a lot alike." In the shadowy light of the depot, she looked younger than ever. Young and well-scrubbed and sad. "I don't want you to get into trouble. Whatever it is, you've got your whole life ahead of you. It won't be worth it. Honest."

"Take care of yourself," I said, and leaned over and kissed her.

She grabbed me again and pulled me close and said, "I got in a little trouble once myself. It's no fun. Believe me."

I touched her cheek gently and then I set off walking quickly into the darkness.

Armstrong was a pretty typical midwestern town, four blocks of retail area, a fading brick grade school and junior high, a small public library with a white stone edifice, a court house, a Chevrolet dealership and many blocks of small white frame houses that all looked pretty much the same in the early morning gloom. You could see frost rimmed on the windows and lonely gray smoke twisting up from the chimneys. As I walked, my heels crunched ice. Faint streetlight threw everything into deep shadow. My breath was silver.

A dog joined me for a few blocks and then fell away. Then I spotted a police cruiser moving slowly down the block. I jumped behind a huge oak tree, flattening myself against the rough bark so the cops couldn't see me. They drove right on past, not even glancing in my direction.

The address I wanted was a ranch house that sprawled over the west end of a cul-de-sac. A sweet little red BMW was parked in front of the two-stall garage and a huge satellite dish antenna was discreetly hidden behind some fir trees. No lights shone anywhere.

I went around back and worked on the door. It didn't take me long to figure out that Kenny had gotten himself one of those infra-red security devices. I tugged on my gloves, cut a fist-size hole in the back door window, reached in and unlocked the deadbolt, and then pushed the door open. I could see one of the small round infra-red sensors pointing down from the ceiling. Most fool burglars wouldn't even think to look for it and they'd pass right through the beam and the alarm would go off instantly.

I got down on my haunches and half-crawled until I was well past the eye of the infra-red. No alarm had sounded. I went up three steps and into the house.

The dark kitchen smelled of spices, paprika and cinnamon and thyme. Dawn had always been a good and careful cook.

The rest of the house was about what I'd expect. Nice but not expensive furnishing, lots of records and videotapes, and even a small bumper pool table in a spare room that doubled as a den. Nice, sure, but nothing that would attract attention. Nothing that would appear to have been financed by six hundred thousand dollars in bank robbery money.

And then the lights came on.

At first I didn't recognize the woman. She stood at the head of a dark narrow hallway wearing a loose cotton robe designed to conceal her weight.

The flowing dark hair is what misled me. Dawn had always been a blonde. But dye and a gain of maybe fifteen pounds had changed her appearance considerably. And so had time. It hadn't been a friend to her.

She said, "I knew you'd show up someday, Chet."

"Where's Kenny?"

"You want some coffee?"

"You didn't answer my question."

She smiled her slow, sly smile. "You didn't answer mine, either."

She led us into the kitchen where a pot of black stuff stayed warm in a Mr. Coffee. She poured two cups and handed me one of them.

"You came here to kill us, didn't you?" she said.

"You were my wife. And we were supposed to split everything three ways. But Kenny got everything—you and all the dough. And I did six years in the slam."

"You could have turned us in."

I shook my head, "I have my own way of settling things."

She stared at me. "You look great, Chet. Prison must have agreed with you."

"I just kept thinking of this night. Waiting."

Her mouth tightened and for the first time her blue eyes showed traces of fear. Softly, she said, "Why don't we go in the living room and talk about it."

I glanced at my wristwatch. "I want to see Kenny."

"You will. Come on now."

So I followed her into the living room. I had a lot ahead of me. I wanted to kill them and then get back on the bus. While I'd be eating up the miles on a Greyhound, the local cops would be looking for a local killer. If only my gun hadn't dropped out and Polly seen it. But I'd have to worry about that later.

We sat on the couch. I started to say something but then she took my cup from me and set it on the glass table and came into my arms.

She opened her mouth and kissed me dramatically.

But good sense overtook me. I held her away and said, "So while we're making out, Kenny walks in and shoots me. Is that it?"

"Don't worry about Kenny. Believe me."

And then we were kissing again. I was embracing ghosts,

ancient words whispered in the back seats of cars when we were in high school, tender promises made just before I left for Nam. Loving this woman had always been punishment because you could never believe her, never trust her, but I'd loved her anyway.

I'd just started to pull away when I heard the floor creak behind me and I saw Kenny. Even given how much I hated this man—and how many long nights I'd laid on my prison bunk dreaming of vengeance—I had to feel embarrassed. If Kenny had been his old self, I would have relished the moment. But Kenny was different now. He was in a wheelchair and his entire body was twisted and crippled up like a cerebral palsy victim. A small plaid blanket was thrown across his legs.

He surprised me by smiling. "Don't worry, Chet. I've seen Dawn entertain a lot of men out here in the living room before."

"Spare him the details," she said. "And spare me, too, while you're at it."

"Bitch," he whispered loud enough for us to hear.

He wheeled himself into the living room. The chair's electric motor whirred faintly as he angled over to the fireplace. On his way, he said, "You didn't wait long, Chet. You've only been out two weeks. You never did have much patience."

You could see the pain in his face when he moved.

I tried to say something but I just kept staring at this man who was now a cripple. I didn't know what to say.

"Nice set-up, huh?" Kenny said as he struck a stick match on the stone of the fireplace. With his hands twisted and gimped the way they were, it wasn't easy. He got his smoke going and said, "She tell you what happened to me?"

I looked at Dawn. She dropped her gaze. "No," I said.

He snorted. The sound was bitter. "She was doin' it to me just the way she did it to you. Right, bitch?"

She sighed then lighted her own cigarette. "About six months after we ran out on you with all the money, I grabbed the strongbox and took off."

Kenny smirked. "She met a sailor. A fucking sailor, if you can believe it."

"His name was Fred," she said. "Anyway, me and Fred had all the bank robbery cash—there was still a couple hundred thousand left—when Kenny here came after us in that red Corvette he always wanted. He got right up behind us but it was pouring rain and he skidded out of control and slammed into a tree."

He finished the story for me. "There was just one problem, right, bitch? You had the strongbox but you didn't know what was inside. Her and the sailor were going to have somebody use tools on the lock I'd put on it. They saw me pile up my 'vette but they kept on going. But later that night when they blew open the strongbox and found out that I'd stuffed it with old newspapers, the sailor beat her up and threw her out. So she came back to me 'cause she just couldn't stand to be away from 'our' money. And this is where she's been all the time you were in the slam. Right here waitin' for poor pitiful me to finally tell her where I hid the loot. Or die. They don't give me much longer. That's what keeps her here."

"Pretty pathetic story, huh?" she said. She got up and went over to the small wet bar. She poured three drinks of pure Jim Beam and brought them over to us. She gunned hers in a single gulp and went right back for another.

"So she invites half the town in so she can have her fun while I vegetate in my wheelchair." Now it was his turn to down his whiskey. He hurled the glass into the fireplace. A long, uneasy silence followed.

I tried to remember the easy friendship the three of us had enjoyed back when we were in high school, before Kenny and I'd been in Nam, and before the three of us had taken up bank robbery for a living. Hard to believe we'd ever liked each other at all.

Kenny's head dropped down then. At first I thought he might have passed out but then the choking sound of dry tears filled the room and I realized he was crying.

"You're such a wimp," she said.

And then it was her turn to smash her glass into the fireplace.

I'd never heard two people go at each other this way. It was degrading.

He looked up at me. "You stick around here long enough, Chet, she'll make a deal with you. She'll give you half the money if you beat me up and make me tell you where it is."

I looked over at her. I knew what he said was true.

"She doesn't look as good as she used to—she's kind of a used car now instead of a brand-new Caddy—but she's still got some miles left on her. You should hear her and some of her boyfriends out here on the couch when they get goin'."

She started to say something but then she heard me start to laugh.

"What the hell's so funny?"

I stood up and looked at my watch. I had only ten minutes left to get back to the depot.

Kenny glanced up from his wheelchair. "Yeah, Chet, what's so funny?"

I looked at them both and just shook my head. "It'll come to you. One of these days. Believe me."

And with that, I left.

She made a play for my arm and Kenny sat there glowering at me but I just kept on walking. I had to hurry.

The cold, clean air not only revived me, it seemed to purify me in some way. I felt good again, whole and happy now that I was outdoors.

The bus was dark and warm. Polly had brought a bag of popcorn along. "You almost didn't make it," she said as the bus pulled away from the depot.

In five minutes we were rolling into countryside again. In farmhouses lights were coming on. In another hour, it would be dawn.

"You took it, didn't you?" I said.

"Huh?"

"You took it. My gun."

"Oh. Yes. I guess I did. I didn't want you to do anything foolish."

Back there at Kenny's I'd reached into my jacket pocket for the .38 and found it gone. "How'd you do it? You were pretty slick."

"Remember I told you I'd gotten into a little trouble? Well, an uncle of mine taught me how to be a pickpocket and so for a few months I followed in his footsteps. Till Sheriff Baines arrested me one day."

"I'm glad you took it."

She looked over at me in the darkness of the bus and grinned. She looked like a kid. "You really didn't want to do it, did you?"

"No," I said, staring out the window at the midwestern night. I thought of them back there in the house, in a prison cell they wouldn't escape till death. No, I hadn't wanted to shoot anybody at all. And, as things had turned out, I hadn't had to either. Their punishment was each other.

"We're really lucky we met each other, Chet."

"Yeah," I said, thinking of Dawn and Kenny again. "You don't know how lucky we are."

When you make your living writing, and are neither rich nor famous, you sometimes take on assignment work. An editor called me recently, for example, and said that he had an anthology ready to go —cover printed, type set—but that his boss didn't think any of the stories had enough "bite." Could I write "sort of a dark" piece for the book? In a hurry? That's what's called assignment work.

Some might call it, and perhaps fairly, hackwork. Certainly not all of it works out so well.

But in a few cases—and here I offer four examples— the writer comes up with tales that are at least readable and, in rare instances, maybe even a little better than that.

"Idol" was inspired by a most unpleasant experience I'd had in a comic book store. Four quite geeky middle-aged comic book fans were making fun of a poor stranger whose body was misshapen so badly I almost had to look away. Somehow all my rage and sorrow went into the "Batman" story I'd been asked to produce. It is also based on a PBS biography of John Lennon's killer I'd seen.

Martin H. Greenberg, the world's best anthologist and my partner in Mystery Scene magazine, asked me to do a story for our anthology Stalkers. "I'd like to see a different kind of crime story," he said. And I tried to oblige with "The Jungle."

"My Cousin Cal" is a lark, written to disprove the notion that I never have happy thoughts. It owes much in tone and spirit to one of my favorite mystery stylists, the estimable Rex Stout, and was written over the course of three long, rainy and quite pleasant April days.

Max Allan Collins, one of my favorite people and writers, asked me to do a "Dick Tracy" story for the tie-in anthology that was appearing at the same time as the movie. For inspiration, I reread several John D. MacDonald pulp stories from the late forties, trying to emulate that odd bleak melancholy that was so much a part of John D.'s early work. For two days I couldn't come up with an idea I really cared about. Then I went for a long highway drive in the midnight rain and when I got back home "The Curse" was waiting for me.

IDOL

1984

Knock.

"Hi, hon. Just wanted to tell you that—"

His mother peeks around the edge of his bedroom door and says, "Gosh, hon. You're kind of old for that, aren't you?"

Her voice and eyes say she wishes she had not seen her seventeen-year-old son doing what he's doing.

Pause, then: "Are you OK, hon?"

"Why wouldn't I be OK?"

"Well—"

"I'm fine. Now get the hell out of here."

"Hon, I've asked you not to talk to me that way. I'm your own mother. I'm—"

"You heard me."

She knows this tone. Is afraid of it. Has been afraid of it ever since he was seven or eight years old.

He is not like other boys. Never has been.

"Yes, hon," she says, already starting to cry useless tears. "Yes, hon."

they don't know my loneliness. they only see my strength. they don't know my loneliness.

1986

Open window. Autumn. Smell of leaves burning. In the distance a marching band practicing on the edge of campus. Smell of leaves rich as marijuana smoke.

He lies in his white undershorts on a bed in this tiny off-campus apartment. Next to him a girl sits stroking his chest. She is naked except for pink bikini panties.

"It's all right. Really."

"Sure," he says.

"It's happened to me a lot. You're probably just tired."

"Just shut up."

"Please," she says. "I really like you. Isn't that all that really matters?"

He slaps her, startling her as much as hurting her.

Startling her.

i am beginning to understand my problem. i don't cause the headaches. he does. the impostor.

the impostor.

1987

·"So how do you feel about this man?"

"You know how I feel, doctor."

"Angry? Resentful?"

"Of course. Wouldn't you?"

Pause. "Tell me about the headaches."

"What time is it?"

"Pardon me?"

"The time, doctor. The time. I forgot my watch."

Sigh. "Two-ten. Why?"

"I'm in sort of a hurry today."

"We're not through till three."

"You, maybe. I'm in a hurry."

"You know your mother wants you to stay here for the entire session."

"Screw my mother."

"Please. Tell me about the headaches."

"What about them?"

"Do you know what triggers them?"

"No."

"Think about it a moment. Please."

Sigh. "Him."

"Him?"

"The impostor."'

"Ah."

"Whenever I see him on tv or in the paper, the headaches start."

Writes quickly in his notebook. "What do you feel when you see him?"

"Nothing."

"Nothing?"

"Literally, nothing. People think he's me. It's as if I don't exist."

He thinks: how seriously can you take a shrink who has three big warts on his face and who wears falling-down socks with battered old Hush-Puppies?

Anyway, he is beginning to suspect that the shrink may well be a friend of the impostor's.

Yes. Of course.

My God, why didn't he think of that before?

He stands up.

"It's only two-fifteen. It's only—"

But he's already going out the door. "Goodbye, doctor."

1988

He sits in his room with the white kitten his mother bought him to cheer him up after he quit college a few months ago. He lazes warm and drifting in the soft May sunlight the same way the white kitten with the damp black nose and the quick pink tongue lazes.

"Kitty," he says, stroking her, "You're my only friend. My

only friend."

He starts crying then—sobbing really. He doesn't know why.

i saw him on TV last night. waving, accepting their applause. he's convinced them now. everybody. they really think he's me. they really believe it.

1989

"I'd like to talk to you."

"I'm in a hurry."

"I'm serious about this."

He's never seen his mother like this. No "hon." No backing down. Almost angry.

"All right."

"Upstairs."

"Why?"

"Your room, come on."

What is going on here? She seems almost . . . crazed.

So up the stairs.

So past where the white kitty with the damp black nose and quick pink tongue lies on the landing in the sunlight.

Into his room.

Throwing open the closet door.

Pointing.

Voice half-hysterical.

"I thought you told me you were getting rid of all this stuff."

Feeling himself flush. "This is none of your business. You have no right—"

"I have every right. I've put up with this since you were eight years old and I can't handle it anymore. You're a man now, or supposed to be. Get rid of this silly junk, and get rid of it now!"

Instead of becoming angry, he just stands there, allowing himself to understand the truth of this moment. The real truth.

So the impostor has gotten to her, too.

His own mother.

Sensing this shift in his mood, she seems less certain of herself. Backs away from the closet.

"What's wrong with you?" she says.

"Did you let him touch you?"

"Who? What are you *talking* about?"

"You know, mother. You know very well what I'm talking about." Pause. Stares at her. For a forty-two-year-old woman she is quite attractive. All those aerobic shows on daytime tv. All that eating of fruit and lean meat and almost never any bread. Certainly no desserts. "You did let him touch you, didn't you?"

"My God, are you—"

But then she stops herself, obviously realizing that would be the wrong thing to say. The very wrongest thing to say. (Are . . . you . . . crazy?)

He grabs her, then.

By the throat.

Choking her before she has time to scream and alert the neighbors.

It is so easy.

His thumbs press down on her trachea.

Her eyes roll white.

Spittle silver and useless runs down the sides of her mouth as she tries to form useless words.

He watches the way her breasts move so gracefully inside the cotton of her housedress.

Harder harder.

"Please," she manages to say.

Then drops to the floor.

He has no doubt she is dead.

the impostor has taken over every aspect of my life. i have no friends (sometimes i even suspect that it was really he who put the white kitty here) i have no prospects for a career because nobody believes me when i tell them who i am i have no—

he leaves me no choice

no choice whatsoever

Same Day (Afternoon)

He has never flown before. He is frightened at takeoff, having heard that the two most dangerous times aboard a plane are takeoff and landing.

Once in the air—except for those brief terrifying moments of turbulence, anyway—he starts to enjoy himself.

He had never realized before what a burden she'd been, his mother.

He thinks of her back there in his room, crumpled and dead in a corner. He wonders how many days it will be before they find her. Will she be black? Will maggots be crawling all over her? He hopes so. That will teach the impostor to mess with him.

He spends the rest of the flight watching a dark-haired stewardess open a very red and exciting mouth as she smiles at various passengers.

Very red.

Very exciting.

Same Day (Evening)

The city terrifies him. He has checked into a good hotel. Thirty-sixth floor. People below so many ants.

Stench and darkness of city.

All those people in the thrall of the impostor.

Terrifying.

He has come here without an exact plan, but as he lies on the firm hotel bed eating donuts and drinking milk the late news comes on and the very first story gives him a beautiful plan. A wonderful plan.

Tomorrow the impostor will receive an award from the mayor.

So easy to—

so easy

*tomorrow the world will know. my long struggle will be over and
i will be able to assume my rightful place. tomorrow.*

Next Day (Morning)

Warm spring day. The rear of the city jail where the
impostor often brings the criminals he apprehends.
Smell of city—gasoline and smoke and filth and loneliness—
sight of city: the helpless, the arrogant, the predatory.
His room, he wants to be back in his room . . . (the gun
sweatily in his hand as he hides behind a parked car) but
suddenly now the impostor is here—
—leading a prisoner into the rear metal door—
—the impostor; so confident-looking—
—in full costume—
—going into the door as—
—the gunfire starts
Two quick cracks on the soft still air
Two quick cracks
(you bastard—father-of-mine—you've been fooling people
too long; I exist now and you do not)
crack of pistol . . .
(and you do not . . .)

Same Day (Afternoon)

Around noon the story was on all the news media, bulletins
on the networks, even.
And the would-be assassin (shot to death by police) was
identified.
So a neighbor came over to see how his mother was doing
after hearing such horrible news
and knocked and knocked
and went and called police
and
They find the body with no problem. Good-looking fortyish woman strangled to death, stuffed into a corner of the

117

bedroom.

One cop, the mournful sort, shakes his head.

What a waste.

He sees the closet door partially open and, being a cop, curious and all, edges it open with a pencil (you've got to be extra careful at a crime scene; evidence can be destroyed so easily).

He looks inside.

"What the hell," he says.

His partner, who has been directing the lab man and the man from the coroner's office and the ambulance attendants, walks over next to him. "What?"

"Look inside."

So the second cop looks inside. And whistles. "All these costumes. They're just like—"

"Just like the guy he tried to kill."

"But if he had all these costumes you'd think he would have respected the guy, not wanted to kill him."

The first cop shakes his head. "It's a strange old world. A strange old world."

Same Afternoon (Later)

"Hey. Look at this," the first cop says.

"What?"

"Some kind of diary."

"Let's see."

They flip through pages. Open at a spot and read.

"it is no longer tolerable. the impostor must be killed because there can't be two of us. one is real, one is false. and after today, the real one will assume the throne of power. me."

"Now what the hell could he have meant by that?"

The second cop shrugs. "You got me, partner. You sure got me."

(For Max Allan Collins, who helped)

118

THE JUNGLE

In the darkness and the cold, silver rain, I climbed to the top of the empty gondola car I'd been riding in since the Wyoming border, and looked down the rails at the hobo jungle that was maybe a quarter mile ahead.

A couple of nights ago I'd heard President Roosevelt on the radio talk about 'bo jungles, how they were unsafe places and robbed men of their dignity and that Americans shouldn't have to live in such conditions and wouldn't have to much longer now that he'd become President a few months back. He didn't seem to understand that a lot of men and women didn't have much choice, not when bread lines stretched around the block and people rioted trying to get into soup kitchens.

You can always spot a jungle at night just by looking for the fires. 'bos got lots of uses for fire so they always keep them going. Even on rainy nights, they manage to keep the flames alive in the darkness.

Just thinking of the jungle, I was getting hungry. And I was starting to imagine what it would be like to be dry again. I'd been maybe two days without food and maybe one hundred miles in the rain.

But the biggest reason I wanted to hit the jungle was because of the newspaper headline I'd read three days ago: NEBRASKA GIRL FOUND MUTILATED; *Police Can't Explain Curious, Savage Death.*

I was getting closer to the man I'd been chasing the last five years.

I'd been looking for him all this time and now I knew I was getting closer. He was running out of jungles to hide in. Maybe tonight I was going to get real lucky.

I climbed over the top of the gondola—this was the good kind without the sloping bottom you could fall through—and grabbed the side ladder so I could jump. Some of the older 'bos like to talk big about throwing yourself off a freight car going twenty miles per hour but it's all just talk because no matter how long you do it, the shock to your legs and back still hurts. Plus you see a lot of men and women, even experienced ones, break legs and arms and even get concussions from time to time. Not to mention getting cut in half if you fall between the wheels.

The train swept around a wide curve, slowing slightly to do so. Now was the best chance I was going to get. I said a little Hail Mary for luck and closed my eyes and flung myself out into the wind and the night.

The rain had turned the roadbed to mud and that made my landing fairly soft.

I kept my feet and stood there till the train rocked past, a blur of freight cars and a cry of iron wheels needing oil. Half the cars would have men in them. What with the Depression and all, you found some trains that freighted maybe two hundred 'bos per trip.

Then it was just me and the night and the rain, the light of the caboose receding in the gloom, the wail of the train fainter and fainter.

It was spring, and everything was just turning, so the night smelled clean and fresh of pine and mint and mud, and down the gully and across the creek in the jungle, the aroma of hot 'bo stew.

I was ten yards from the bonfire when the guy stepped out of the shadows.

He was no-argument big and no-argument mean. He wore a derby and a ragged suit with no shirt beneath the jacket. He kept a cigar tucked in the corner of his mouth. He grasped my shoulder with one big hand and started grinding it into a fine powder.

Just for safety's sake, he snicked open a switchblade and put the point of it right against my Adam's apple.

"I'm Rollins," he said. "Who're you?"

"Thought jungles welcomed 'bos?"

"We got law problems here, friend, and we figger the coppers are prob'ly gonna plant one of their own undercover." While he looked me up and down, I returned the favor. In his grimy, sour way, he was an impressive piece of work, with a forehead an ape would envy and hands Jack Dempsey himself wouldn't want to run into. Most jungles have their enforcers and obviously Rollins here was doing the honors in this one.

He patted me down. Then he lifted the paper bag I always carried and went through the contents. Apparently he didn't find anything very interesting because he shoved everything back inside and slammed the bag into my stomach. Then he surprised me by grinning and clapping me on the same shoulder he'd just been grating into bone meal.

"Come on in and meet the boys," he said, still keeping that wide, dumb grin on his wide, dumb face.

He was some piece of work, all right; the friendly executioner.

There were maybe fifty men in this jungle, some living in little tarpaper shacks, some living in lean-tos, some living right outdoors in blankets. Now that the rain had let up, a fellow could probably sleep on the ground all right, if he was tired enough, anyway.

The bonfire was in the center of the camp. Men stood around it drinking coffee from battered tin cups, men of every age and every type. What they had in common were the rags on their backs and the look of desperation in their eyes. The yellow fire playing across their beard-stubbled faces gave them the look of soldiers who'd been fighting a war for long, weary years.

Behind the fire stretched clotheslines. The rain over, men had hung their tattered shirts and trousers out to dry again. At a smaller fire, in a big five gallon can, I found the stew simmering.

"Grab yerself a plate," Rollins said, nodding to the tree trunks with dozens of pie tins nailed to them. 'bos believed in communal living. When you were done with your pie tin, you took it down to the creek to wash it out with sand and water, and then you brought it back to nail to a tree so that somebody else could use it. 'bos took pride in how clean they kept their eating utensils.

The stew smelled mostly of vegetables and that was plenty good for me.

I grabbed a tin, took a spoon Rollins handed me, and dug into the can.

I loaded up the tin with meaty chunks of carrots and onions and potatoes, and then Rollins dropped a big chunk of wheat bread on top of my tin, and I went over and crouched down next to a tree and ate my dinner and started watching every-body around the camp.

A Mex played a harmonica. A couple of other guys started talking about their favorite radio shows, especially "The Shadow" and then some of the other 'bos joined in wondering out loud if maybe there was a real Shadow, in real life that is, that the show was based on.

I finished off the meal with one of the three Luckies I'd been able to save from the last time I had a little change.

Then I sat down flat on the ground with my back against the tree. I slept. I didn't plan to sleep, I didn't even want to sleep—I wanted to look around camp and see if I could find the guy I was looking for—but suddenly my eyes started closing, and then I couldn't help myself.

When I woke up, it was real cold. The fire had burned out. I started to move my arms but found them covered with a woolen blanket that somebody had draped over me. It was so quiet you could hear fat raindrops plopping off the budding spring tree limbs to the muddy earth. My bones ached from years of sleeping on damp, hard ground. But I told myself it was soon all going to be worth it. I had a real sense that I'd found the camp where my man was staying.

I got up and went down to the fast-running creek. They'd dug latrines there and I used one to piss in. The steam off the urine rose like ghosts to the full moon riding the dark sky.

I was halfway back to the jungle when I heard the cry of the wolf.

I stopped and stood so still all I could hear was my heartbeat.

The wolf cried again.

I turned and saw him then on the hill, silhouetted perfectly against the silver disc of moon. Even his cold breath was dark against the silver circle.

Now he turned and looked down the hill at me.

A low rumbling sound seemed to work its way through his entire body and then come out of his mouth as a growl.

He knew who I was and I knew who he was. He was giving me fair warning. His eyes were red in the darkness, and then they vanished as he turned eastward and disappeared over the grassy crest of the hill.

I went back to my tree and got under the blanket and pulled my hat low so nobody could see my eyes. I pretended to be asleep.

If I was right, he'd be along in the next few hours.

If I was wrong, I'd be on the first freight out in the morning, starting my search all over again.

Somebody in one of the lean-tos was having a pretty bad nightmare. He was crying for his mama. He sounded like a kid, and maybe he was. He sounded sad in a way that was almost scary. It was the kind of sadness that can crush the hell out of a human being, and make death seem welcome.

I was wondering what was bothering him when I heard the sound of heavy shoes tramping through the wet grass to my right.

Somebody was coming into the jungle.

I angled my head so that I could see out of one eye, just

below the brim of my hat.

He was an old man, white hair, with one of those sweet aged faces you sometimes see on country priests.

I couldn't believe this was the man I'd been searching for.

He came over to the guttering fire, crouched down and poured himself a cup of coffee. His hand trembled when he tipped the tin cup to his mouth. He drank it down in one long, single gulp.

Finished, he suddenly looked around the camp. He must have been aware of my watching him.

In his panic, he looked younger and more capable than I'd first thought.

He stood up and went back to the creek momentarily. He washed the cup out and brought it back to the fire for somebody else to use.

He stood near the fire, the first pearly streak of dawn lighting the sky now, and looked around some more. He still wanted to know who had been watching him.

He stayed there for the next few minutes, until somebody down the line got into a phlegmy coughing jag. Then he apparently decided it was time to leave. He walked six lean-tos down to an empty berth and disappeared. I took note of which one it was.

When I was pretty sure he was all snuggled in, I closed my eyes and got a little sleep before the day in the jungle started.

Most people have the impression that the hoboes sit around all day. That's the impression ministers like to give from the pulpit when they're thundering about the immoral men who ride the rails.

But they're wrong. For one thing, if you're a 'bo who's inclined to seasonal work such as picking apples in Washington state or detassling corn in the Midwest, then you spend your days on a flatcar traveling, which is no easy life believe me, not with railroad dicks—the meanest god damned guys who ever wore a badge—waiting to open your head like a melon at every stop, and the threat of getting pitched off the flatcar at least fifty percent. You don't want to see a corpse that's been pitched off a flatcar, believe me.

And if you stay in the jungle, as I did that day, you realize that every man has a task, and that the tasks more than keep you occupied. Mine was taking a hammer and nail and some leftover lumber somebody'd mooched at a lumberyard and building three new lean-tos. One of the men had asked me if I was good at carpentry and I'd made the mistake of allowing how I wasn't real bad anyway.

A couple times that sunny but cool morning I saw the old man. Once I caught him staring at me suspiciously—as if he knew that I'd been watching him last night—but then later I saw him staring at somebody else suspiciously, too. Apparently, he knew there was a spy in the jungle but he couldn't figure out who.

After lunch, which was pinto beans and bread and good hot strong coffee, some of the 'bos organized a begging expedition into town. Every once in a while, you've got to do that. You canvass some rural burg by going up and down the alleys and asking nice young plump housewives if there isn't maybe some yard work or something you could do for them, and most of them are so impressed with your initiative that they say no, sorry, there really isn't any work but here, why don't you take this piece of beef or take this dollar in change, or here's a couple packs of my husband's cigarettes. Spend an afternoon canvassing like that and you can get yourself a lot of goodies to take back to the jungle. Of course, sometimes the law hassles you, and occasionally a particularly mean bull will put you behind bars for a few days for pestering the townsfolk, but usually the housewives take pity on you and speak up on your behalf to the sheriff or the copper.

So just after noon, about seventy percent of the 'bos headed for town. There was a nice April breeze to warm their walk, and the smell of apple blossoms sweet on the Midwestern air.

I finished the second of two lean-tos and then decided to

ED GORMAN

make my move.

The old man had gone into town with the rest of the 'bos. Now was my chance to look through his belongings.

I was ten feet from his lean-to when a voice said, "You're doin' a fine job, brother."

I turned and saw Rollins the enforcer standing just behind me, his derby slanted wise-guy on his head, and his cigar tucked unmoving into the corner of his mouth.

"Thanks," I said.

He came over and stood next to me. He looked even bigger and scruffier in the daylight. You could see catsup and mustard stains on the lapels of his double-breasted suitcoat. One problem with fancy duds is that they're a bitch to wash in the creek.

"We been needin' a man who was good with a hammer and nails to come around," he said.

"Well, I'm grateful for the grub and the hospitality and I'm glad to oblige."

On the surface we were having a nice friendly chat but Rollins seemed to sense something funny here. He kept looking at the old man's lean-to and then back at me.

"Just wonderin' if you was lost or somethin'," he said, taking the cigar butt from his mouth. I tried not to notice all the saliva he had on the end of it.

"Lost?"

"Yeah, bein' back here with the lean-tos and all. Most of the men stay away from other men's sleepin' quarters—you know, in case somethin' should turn up missin', then they wouldn't get blamed or nothin'."

"Oh, yeah, right," I said. "That's a good idea."

And I started edging away from the old man's lean-to. I gave Rollins my best Sunday-school smile and said, "I just wanted to check out these other lean-tos. Make sure I'm doing my own right."

He stared at me. "Yer doin' fine. No reason to come back here."

"That's right," I said. "No reason at all."

He put the cigar butt back in his mouth and touched the rim of his derby as if for luck and then folded his massive arms across his chest. He was daring me to try and go past him. But I knew better.

I nodded goodbye to him and went back to my work.

The second time I tried to get to the old man's lean-to, I had better luck.

Around two that afternoon, there was a small derailment about a quarter mile down the track. One or two freight cars had gotten pitched off the roadbed.

Like most men who travel the rails, the men in camp couldn't resist seeing what had happened. Including Rollins. They ran up the hill to the roadbed for a better look.

I pitched my hammer and nails and started working my way through the jungle to the back where the lean-tos lay. I still had to be careful. There could be a 'bo dozing in one of the small shanties or lean-tos. Or Rollins could surprise me and come right back.

On the way back, I got choked up with the smells you encounter anytime a lot of men stay in a confined space in less than sanitary conditions—sweat and vomit and piss mostly but also some inexplicable stench that has to do with men without women and men without hope.

Two cotton blankets covered the floor of the old man's lean-to. A crude knapsack sat in one corner, a rolled-up ball of clean clothes in the other. Presumably the clothes would at some point be stuffed in the knapsack.

After checking again for any sign of Rollins, I opened the knapsack up like a piece of huge ripe fruit and found inside all the things you'd expect—a safety razor, a bar of shaving soap, a couple of pairs of spotted but washed underwear, two pairs of holey socks and a small hardback book entitled *Werewolves: Myth and Reality* by one Don Guido Amambenetti.

No doubt about it; I had found my man.

Then I saw the picture, faded yellow and cracked with age, a young girl, pretty, standing in front of a small farm house on a sunny day. I wondered who she was.

A few minutes later, a hammer in my right hand, two penny nails in my teeth, I was back building my lean-to.

At the bonfire that night I heard all about the day's events in town. While the begging part had gone all right, the local sheriff had hassled everybody about the mutilation death of the teenage girl a few weeks ago. The sheriff and his men had been out to the jungle many times trying to pin the murder on one of the 'bos. And the 'bos were concerned that he just might manage to do it.

All the time the men talked about this, I watched Carlyle there on the edge of the firelight. That had been the name written in pen on the front page of the book: *Horace Carlyle.*

He didn't seem interested in any of it. Just sipped coffee from his tin cup and stared up at the sky.

Once, he caught me looking at him but instead of acting suspicious, he gave me a sad little old man smile, as if we shared a pretty special secret which, I guess, we did after all.

The day's work had left me tired. I put my back to the tree and went to sleep early. Never getting much more than three or four hours sleep, I figured I'd wake up early, too. That way I'd be ready to follow Carlyle when he left.

When I woke up, the campfire was guttering and men were sprawled around the fire for the last flickering warmth it had to offer. In the distance, you could hear freight cars linking up, and further away still there was the sweet night music of the town itself, the songs of the flesh all those lucky white men got to sing with all those fine young silky white women of theirs. It had been a long time since I'd sipped that particular brand of wine, and sometimes when I thought about it I got so lonesome I almost cried on the spot.

Carlyle left camp just after a midnight freight had rattled its way around the westward curve.

I was only three minutes behind him.

* * *

The moon tonight was just a quarter's worth, hanging there like a silver scimitar used in some ancient battle.

Carlyle headed for town, taking the edge of the railroad bed for his trail.

The whole left side was deep forest so I didn't have any trouble staying part of the shadows. The fog didn't hurt either.

The town was mostly shut down. Near the end of the main street you could see the lights of a lone tavern, and hear the high beery noise men make around closing time. The dirt street held maybe ten Model-Ts. Just ten years ago horses would still have filled the parking spots in this part of the country.

There was a two-story red brick bank building and a nice white church with a needle-shaped spire and four blocks of businesses that ran to a Ford dealership and a grocery store and a general store and tiny city park with a Civil War memorial and a bandstand looking lonely in the rolling fog.

Between the bank and the only hotel I could see was a narrow alley and that's where he made the transformation.

He went in maybe sixty, seventy feet ahead of me, just this shambling old 'bo that nobody except maybe a mean copper would pay any mind to, and he came out of that alley a minute later a sleek, silver timber wolf, the same timber that had murdered my brother five years ago; the same timber wolf I carried the silver bullet for.

I ducked behind one of the Model-Ts and watched him pad out into the street.

What he did next surprised me.

He walked up and down the row of parked cars until he found one with the window open. Then he jumped inside and jumped once more behind the seat.

He'd picked out his prey for the evening. All he was doing now was waiting.

Over the next half hour, most of the cars disappeared. Their owners came wobbling out of the tavern, got in their cars and drove away. The law probably figured that these men wouldn't end up hurting anybody but themselves so what the hell.

Finally, we were down to two cars. I was crouched behind one of them. The wolf waited in the back seat of the other.

He was short and fat and walked with a waddle. He wore a white Panama more than slightly out of season and a double-breasted dark suit that only emphasized the vast slope of his belly. He was whistling and trying to flip a coin at the same time but he missed with the coin. It bounced off the sidewalk and rolled into the darkness and he waved it off with a derisive gesture.

I knew I'd have to move fast but I'd also have to wait until the fat man got into the car before I made my move.

He was the right man, all right. He went up to the car the wolf had selected, opened the door and then with very broad, almost comic movements, managed to stuff himself inside the box-shaped Model-T.

Now I made my move, coming out from behind the adjacent Ford and jumping up on the back bumper of the fat man's car. I held on tight to the spare tire as he flicked on his headlights and started the process of getting the car rolling.

Ten minutes later, me clinging to the spare, we made our way out of town.

The dirt roads were pretty bad. The rains had helped rut them so badly that the Ford was jerked right and left as it passed in and out of ruts.

The fat man got up to thirty miles-an-hour by the time we hit the country, distant farmhouses looking dark and snug in the moonlight, cows mooing in the shadows.

The engine was so loud, I couldn't hear anything from inside the car.

We were just coming up on a copse of pine trees and a small whitewashed schoolhouse, when I felt the fat man lose control of the car.

Before I could do anything—the car wrenching violently to

the right—I was thrown off the rear bumper, landing on my back in the rutted road.

The car shot ahead, smashing into the edge of the school-house.

There was a clatter of glass and the deep thunder of the car plowing several feet into the schoolhouse, ripping out the wall as it went.

Then there was the odd silence that always follows any act of violence; a silence not unlike that following lovemaking; not long, just seconds, but profound seconds of quiet and then—

—the wolf growled.

And the fat man screamed.

I was on my feet now, running toward the schoolhouse, when I saw a flash of silver as the wolf jumped over the back seat and attacked the fat man.

And then began to rip the fat man apart.

All I could do as I stood next to the smashed Ford was watch and listen. Several times I pounded on the side window with my useless fists but the wolf was in a frenzy now, the car rocking back and forth as he ate and supped of the fat man, the night obscene with the sounds of his feasting. I had once seen a sow eat her own pig, rend her own child, and that was all I could think of now.

And then there was the silence again as the wolf, finished, lay on the seat next to the fat man's bloody remains and stared up at me.

In the moonlight through the shattered windshield, I could see the round pupils of its red eyes, and see the streaks of the fat man's blood and innards on its silver-gray fur.

From behind my back, I took the gun I'd just loaded with the single silver bullet, and I raised the weapon and pointed it directly at the wolf and started to pull the trigger and—

—the wolf leapt on me.

Through the window it came, its powerful teeth bare, its backside shattering what was left of the glass in the windshield.

I crouched so the wolf would not be able to seize my throat but the animal surprised me by hurling himself at my hand and

133

the gun I held. This close, I could smell the hot sour stench of the fat man's meat and blood on the wolf's breath.

Then the wolf grabbed my hand and forced me to drop the gun to the ground. In moments, well before I realized what it was doing, the wolf picked up the gun in its terrible jaws and took off running.

It did not look back, not even once, but instead bounded down the road, back in the direction of town, its bushy tail flicking violently as it moved like a silver phantom in the moonlight.

After a time, I walked closer to the car and peered in. The fat man's throat was an empty bloody hole. One of his eyes had been ripped and now stared up at me from the seat next to him. I did not look any more closely; I particularly avoided looking down at what was left of his stomach.

In half an hour or so, still moving as if in a dream, I started walking at right angles across farm fields, corn stalks dead and brittle beneath my feet. Frost covered everything, as if it were autumn and not spring at all, and I kept trying to get the smell of the fat man out of my nostrils.

It took me three hours to find the 'bo jungle again.

When I reached the camp, Carlyle was crouched by the guttering fire, sipping coffee from his cup. Even given what I knew about him, his white hair and mild blue eyes and soft, sad smile gave him the look of a village priest.

He watched me emerge from the shadows and walk toward the faint, flickering light of the fire. Dawn would streak the sky in a few more hours, and a new day's fire would burn.

"You like some coffee, Mr. Davis?"

I don't know what I expected him to do or say but whatever it was, it wasn't offering me a cup of coffee.

All I could do was nod.

He filled a spare tin cup with the dregs of the day's coffee and handed it over to me as I sat down next to the fire.

In the surrounding darkness, I could hear men snore and turn violently in their sleep and make the little mewling sounds of bad dreams. In the distance, the clothes hanging to dry on the lines were like ghosts surrounding us.

I drank my coffee. I didn't say anything.

After a time, he said, "You've been after me for more than five years now, Mr. Davis." He smiled. "Surprised you, huh? That I knew you were trailing me?"

I nodded.

"There's just one trouble, Mr. Davis."

"And what would that be?"

He stared at me. "I know why you're really following me."

I looked straight into the fire. "You killed my brother."

He shook his venerable head. "That part's true enough as it goes, Mr. Davis. I did kill your brother. I worked for him in his department store on the loading dock and one night he came back unexpected and he saw me transform myself and kill a hobo. For the next year, he blackmailed me."

"Blackmailed you? For what? My brother was a rich man."

"Ah, Mr. Davis, but I possessed something more important than money to your brother. I possessed the secret of lycanthropy. That's what he wanted—he wanted to be just like me." He paused then and met my gaze. "And that's why you've been following me, Mr. Davis. Not to avenge your brother but because you want the same thing he did—my secret."

I said nothing. There was nothing to say.

He reached inside his ragged cloth coat and took out my gun.

Again, he did the unexpected. He handed it over to me. "I can save you the trouble of checking. The silver bullet's still in the chamber."

"Why would you give it to me?"

I hadn't noticed before now but his old eyes had grown watery. He was starting to cry. "I want to die, Mr. Davis, and I want you to kill me tonight."

I thought back to the car and the fat man. "Then why didn't you let me do it earlier when I had the chance?"

He shrugged and shook his head. "I'm sentimental. The other day when you went through my things, you probably saw

135

a photograph of a young girl? Well, she's my daughter. I haven't seen her in years, of course, given my condition and all. But before I died I—" He shrugged again and looked at me. "Well, I wanted to see the photograph—hold it in my hand and remember her. And now that I have—"

He nodded to the gun. "I'm ready, Mr. Davis, any time you are."

I put the gun in my hand, gripped the handle, let my finger lightly brush the trigger.

"But I've got to warn you of something, Mr. Davis. It's not what you think it is, the ability to transform yourself. The gypsies called it a curse and that's just what it is. Because once you drink the tainted blood, Mr. Davis, you are no longer human. You're an exile on your own planet. You'll look at women and children and lovely summer days and you'll want to appreciate them all but you won't be able to because the only thing that will matter is the transformation and the killing. You'll pray and you'll cry that you can be your old self again but it will never happen, Mr. Davis. Never." He raised his eyes and I could see the tears clearly now. "I'd give anything to be a human being again, Mr. Davis. Anything."

"I'm willing to take my chances, Carlyle. I haven't spent five years chasing you for nothing."

"All I can do is warn you, Mr. Davis."

But I was tired of talk and tired of dreaming. I wanted the reality of it now, the animal freedom of it.

"How about up by the tracks?" I said.

"Where you'll kill me, you mean?"

"Yes."

"It doesn't make much difference to me, Mr. Davis."

"Then let's go."

He watched me closely once again. "You didn't really hear anything I've just told you, did you, Mr. Davis? All you know is that you want the secret for yourself. I was just like you, Mr. Davis. All I cared about was the secret. And I sacrificed everything for it. But the killing makes you weary, Mr. Davis. That's what you don't understand. The killing makes you weary. I didn't want to kill that man tonight but I had no choice."

I stood up. "Come on, Carlyle. You've given me your little speech once. I don't want to hear it all over again."

By the creek, just down from where the tracks curve westward, Carlyle stood calmly with his hands straight down at his side.

"You want a cigarette or something?"

He smiled. "Sort of like in the movies, eh, Mr. Davis?"

"I'm trying to be nice."

"But you're making a mistake. You think I'm afraid to die. But I'm eager for it."

"Really?"

"Really, Mr. Davis."

So I killed him. One shot straight in the heart. The sound of the gun was like a dog barking under the dawning sky.

I moved quickly, then, putting my mouth to his chest and drinking the cursed blood hot and tart in my mouth.

I vomited, then, but I wasn't worried. I'd taken plenty of his blood into my system.

By mid-afternoon, I was far down the tracks at a water stop where I had no trouble hopping a freight car headed west.

There were a couple of 'bos already in the car, sharing giggles and a look of contempt for me.

I just sat in the corner and stared at them as the train jerked away from the water tower.

Later that night one of them was going to be my first meal.

* * *

"The Jungle" evolved from reading *McGoorty: The Story of A Billiard Bum*, one of the liveliest and most provocative autobiographies I've ever read. The author is Robert Byrne, the book was published by Lyle Stuart in 1972. You'd do well to make its acquaintance. I'd like to thank Dow Mossman for introducing me to McGoorty and his curious yet splendid life.

—EG

MY COUSIN CAL

1

By morning I had everything I needed to expose the killer. Now it was just a matter of convincing Cal to let me go through with my plan.

The train bearing President Harding's body was in the depot at the San Francisco station. Harding, who had fallen ill with ptomaine a week earlier and who had died suddenly of what appeared to be apoplexy, had been pronounced dead three days earlier.

My cousin Calvin Coolidge, formerly the vice president, had been spending the summer on the Vermont farm where we'd been raised. He'd been given the oath of presidential office right in his own living room by his own father, who was not only a champion woodcutter but also a justice of the peace.

Cal—or Mr. President as I was now going to be calling him—had then taken the Twentieth Century Limited out here so he could ride with the mourners back to Washington.

Hundreds of citizens—rich and poor, white and black and yellow—crowded the depot. I kept my White House Security badge in my hand, flashing it as a means of getting through the throng. Every twenty feet you saw army men in green khaki uniforms patrolling with the type of Enfield rifles that had been used a few years ago in WWI (Cal always saying that WW stood not for World War but Woodrow Wilson's War). There had been strong hints in the press that President Harding had not died of natural causes at all but had in fact been murdered by a piece of poisoned crab meat he'd eaten in Alaska (which explained the emphasis on security). Some claimed that it was his wife, a strange woman given to belief in astrology, who'd done it. Others claimed it was Harry S. Sinclair himself, the owner of the giant Mammoth Oil Company, who'd been his killer.

On board with me I took two things, the silver-plated Colt 1911 that Cal had given me when he'd brought me to work for him as a vice-presidential assistant, and a plain brown leather valise containing all the evidence I'd been gathering.

Finally, I boarded the train, had the black porter called George (all porters were called George for some reason) find me a Pullman, and then proceeded, at least for a time, to relax and hone my plan.

2

By now you've no doubt read about it. The spectacular response of Americans to the death of their beloved President Harding. We'd only been on the rails a day when a reporter for the *New York Times* said, "It is believed to be the most remarkable demonstration in American history of affection, respect, and reverence for the dead."

And he wasn't exaggerating.

Thousands of people packed the route. It seemed you could not look out your window even in stretches of desolate country without seeing mourners standing by the rails, waving small American flags or clutching their hats to their chests.

On the slopes of western hills we saw cowboys saluting us; in villages we saw freckle-faced children with silver tears the color of mercury sliding down their cheeks waving to us; and in cities the crowds became so overwhelming that the engineer had to slow the train to a crawl lest he kill them.

The mood on board was just as vexed. As twenty-ninth president of the United States, Warren G. Harding had been among the most beloved leaders of our time. Americans liked him particularly because he was not an imperious snob on the order of Woodrow Wilson nor a careless adventurer, however colorful, on the order of Theodore Roosevelt. The press liked to call him "This country's favorite uncle," and I guess that pretty much said it.

Of course, lately his air of industry and fairness had been tarnished by some of the men around him. Various charges of graft and bribery had driven several cabinet members from office.

But at that moment none of the administration's shortcomings were on the country's mind. We meant, by God, to mourn the passing of a decent man, and so we did.

3

I had a copy of *The American Mercury* spread out in front of me and was tracing over a photograph of Lillian Gish, who was that issue's major feature. That's always been one of my frustrations, wanting to be an illustrator but not having the talent. That's how I spent my winter nights in the Coolidge farm home back in Vermont (they'd taken me in after my parents died of influenza), tracing over every magazine illustration I could find.

A knock interrupted me this morning.

"Come in," I said.

"Morning," Cal said, sticking his head through the door. Then he smiled to see how I was spending my time in my compartment. "Tracing. You're never going to outgrow that are you, Bobby?"

"Afraid not, Cal." I laughed.

He closed the door and came into my compartment—a pretty fancy suite, actually, complete with a shiny nickel-plated washbowl and a small dining table on which sat the remnants of my breakfast: hot corn muffins, bacon, and jam.

Cal came in and sat down, a slender man with the sort of

robust looks that come from spending as much time as possible with one's family and with God's work in the outdoors. As always, he wore a three-piece dark suit, with a white shirt, gold tie bar, and dark blue tie. He helped himself to his only cup of coffee a day ("caffeine breaks your concentration," he usually told people) and said, "Sorry we haven't had more time to talk the last day and a half." His smile faded. "I thought the ceremonial duties were bad when I was vice-president—"

I said, "Somebody murdered President Harding."

He set down his coffee. "You know what I think about the newspaper stories." Though cousin Cal respected the press at their best, he thought that too many of them trafficked in gossip and innuendo. The reaction was typical of Cal. Here I'd just told him that a murder had taken place and he'd responded by mildly telling me that the press was not always to be believed.

"Do you remember how I spent my first years after college?" I asked.

"Of course. Woodrow Wilson's War."

"Right after that."

"The Pinkertons," he said.

"Exactly."

"Afraid I'm not following you, cousin." This he said with something of a New England accent, which was part of his color and charm when he was giving stump speeches. He sounded as down to earth as a New England farmer telling you about hickory or syrup. People loved it.

"I'm a trained investigator."

"No disputing that," he said, "And a good one."

"And I've been doing some investigating."

"I see." For the first time, apprehension sounded in his voice. Beyond him, out the window, rushed vast stretches of plains turned brown by summer sun stretched to the horizon. He chewed a bit on his lower lip. I'd only seen him do this on the most pressing of occasions, at the death of his beloved mother (whose photograph he kept in his pocket) and when his wife almost miscarried their first child.

"I need to tell you something," he said.

142

"All right."

He sat up a little straighter and folded his hands in his lap and looked hard at me with blue eyes lit with their own quiet wisdom. "I'm not sure this country can get through a murder plot—even if it eventually proves to be inaccurate."

I said, "We need to know the truth."

He continued to stare at me. Finally, sighing, he said, "You're right, Bobby. We need to know the truth. What are you proposing?"

"There's a drawing-room car second from the end of this train. A perfect place for a meeting. In one hour I'd like you to bring both Phoebe Harding and Harry Sinclair there."

"They're not on speaking terms." Phoebe and Harry had always had to vie for the president's attention and as a result disliked each other.

"You're the president, Cal. You can order them to be there."

He scratched his head. "I guess I could." Then he raised his eyes to me again and said, "You've got some proof, I take it?"

"Oh, yes."

"That one of them is implicated in his death?"

I nodded to the brown valise on the bed. "Cal, when I open that valise and present the material that's in it, you and Phoebe Harding and Harry S. Sinclair are going to be shocked."

"I've always trusted you, cousin. I certainly hope my trust won't be misplaced this time." And, happily, he was right. I'd worked for him for two years, handling some extremely delicate matters, and I'd completed each successfully.

He stood up, took his pocket watch from his vest, looked at it and said, again with the Yankee twang, "One hour then, Bobby."

"One hour, Cal," I said.

4

The drawing-room car was fancy beyond necessity, everything red-flecked wallpaper and gilt, with leather furnishings and even padded sills along the windows. Porters in starchy white jackets set out several kinds of refreshments as Cal and I waited for the guests to arrive.

Phoebe Harding came first, a once sumptuous woman given to brocaded dresses and pendants of splendiferous size and ornate design. The pendants each contained some astrological sign. Today she wore a great deal of makeup to cover the dark circles beneath her eyes and the way her cheeks had begun to sag.

She daintily put out a hand for cousin Cal to take but it was too beefy a hand to effect the feminine delicacy she wished. He took it anyway. To me she only nodded.

We had just passed through a town where the throngs had pressed right up to the Pullman windows. "He would have been so appreciative," Phoebe Harding said, pouring herself a healthy dose of bourbon.

Harry S. Sinclair came a few minutes later. As always, he looked angry about something and, as always, he looked like a cartoon tycoon: too much belly, too much ire, too much self-importance. He wore a dark suit and a stiff collar twenty years out of vogue. His face showed whiskey and his eyes showed malice.

He was solicitous as he could be—which was not very often—to cousin Cal. To Phoebe Harding and me, he scarcely offered any sort of recognition at all.

A young man in a khaki uniform came in and said, "Now, sir?"

"Now."

"Just what the blazes is this all about?" said Harry S. Sinclair, owner of Mammoth Oil and richest man in the country second only to John D. himself.

"A little discussion," I said mildly.

The soldier went down to one end of the car and secured the lock and then went to the other end of the car and said, "Will you lock this behind me, sir?"

"Yes," I said. "You've got armed guards posted at each

door?"

"Yessir."

"Thank you."

A few minutes later, fixing myself a straight seltzer water, I said to the three people who sat in front of me, "Each of us here knows something that the press is only speculating about."

"What would that be?" Phoebe Harding said, sounding as innocent as possible.

"That President Harding was murdered."

I let them react, her in her shocked way, Sinclair in his blustery one.

Then I produced the brown valise, setting it like a magician's prop on the table with the refreshments.

The first thing I produced were two sheets of lined paper. In fountain pen innumerable foodstuffs were listed. I handed the paper to Phoebe Harding and said, "Please look at this and pass it around."

Which she did.

Cousin Cal was the last to see it. He handed it back. "It looks like a very long list of groceries."

I took the paper and set it back in the valise. "As you three know, I went to Alaska with President Harding's party. As soon as he was struck by ptomaine, my Pinkerton training took over and I decided to do a little checking with the steward. President Harding ate crab meat—but this list of supplies that I had the steward draw up for me listed no crab meat."

"What are you saying?" demanded Harry S. Sinclair.

"That somebody served the president a very special meal. Very special. One that contained poison."

"But why would anybody want to kill him?" said Phoebe Harding. Again her voice was sweet and pure as a jay's on a spring morning. Only the eyes were old and hard.

I reached into my bag and produced a second document. This one was a letter written on presidential stationery.

I cleared my throat. "'I am setting this down now in case my sudden passing should be confused by anybody as accidental, which it will most definitely not be.

145

" 'I write this on a Tuesday evening when the apple blossoms in the White House garden waft on the soft breeze. I am of sound mind even if I am given to despondence.

" 'But who would not be despondent in my position? My wife is having a relationship with my physician Doctor Sawyer, and my secretary of the interior has disgraced both himself and this administration by nefarious and illegal dealings with Harry S. Sinclair, public knowledge of which would bring me down.

" 'So what would these people profit by my death? If I were done away with now, my wife could spend the rest of her years trading on the name of a martyred president, while enjoying the company of Doctor Sawyer. And Harry S. Sinclair would be spared the collapse of his entire financial empire once I've taken this to the press.

" 'Again, I am of sound mind as I write this and I entrust it to Robert "Bobby" Williams, the ex-Pinkerton man who now serves my vice-president, Mr. Coolidge. I have asked Bobby to accompany me to Alaska so as to keep me from peril.

" 'Sincerely, President Warren G. Harding.' "

I gave them the letter to scrutinize carefully, which of course they did. Then I asked for it back.

"Preposterous!" said Harry S. Sinclair.

"A libel!" cried Phoebe Harding.

I put the letter down and faced them both. "The fault here is mine, I suppose. I thought of several ways one of you might have tried to kill him—accidentally falling overboard being the most likely—but I didn't think of poisoning. I failed in my duty."

"And just what do you propose to do with your accusations?" said Harry S. Sinclair.

I said, "Nothing."

"What?" said my cousin Cal.

"Nothing."

I took the two documents—the steward's list and the letter from President Harding—and put them back in the valise.

My cousin Cal stood up and said, "But if you truly believe that one of these people killed the president—"

I held up my hand. "Please, Mr. President, let me finish, if

146

you will." It seemed an appropriate time to start calling him Mr. President.

He sighed then sat back down.

"There are major scandals brewing in this administration," I said. "You, Phoebe, and you, Harry, will only hinder my cousin the president from setting things right. Therefore, I am going to make you a proposal. I will not take this evidence to the press—and let the press decide which of you is guilty of murder—if you agree to withdraw all your interests from my cousin's administration and to leave him entirely alone so he can get rid of all the scoundrels and put the country back on the proper course."

They started to balk.

"Do you want the press to know about you and Doctor Sawyer?" I said to Phoebe. "And live the rest of your life in the public eye as an adultress?"

"And do you, Harry, want me to feed the press the kind of information about how you bribe public officials—information they've been looking for for so long?"

Their ardor for battle simmered.

Phoebe muttered something that former first ladies are not supposed to mutter and Harry stabbed out his cigar in my glass of seltzer.

I said, "I want you and all your cronies and friends—both of you—to be gone from Washington within three weeks. If that has not happened, then these documents will be turned over to the press. Is that understood?"

"You bastard," said Harry S. Sinclair.

"You dirty bastard," said Phoebe Harding.

I looked at my cousin Cal and smiled.

5

Three hours later I was sitting in my room, enjoying the clack of train wheels and the sight of piney hills in the distance, when somebody knocked. I was doing some more tracing.

"Come in," I said.

"Thought I'd bring these back," my cousin Cal said, coming into the room.

He'd borrowed the steward's list and the letter for examination.

I pointed to a chair and he sat down.

"Beautiful part of the country," I said.

"I read the letter several times, Bobby, and then it finally dawned on me what happened. All these years of tracing. You've become a forger. The letter's a fake."

I put down the book I was reading, one of the Zane Grey westerns I'm partial to, and said, "But the steward's list isn't."

"Then you admit forging the letter?"

"Of course."

"You're so blase about it."

"I want you to have a successful administration, Cal. I look out for your interests. There are so many scandals about to hit the newspaper that the entire Harding administration would have been brought down. This is a chance for you to clean house and become a national hero."

The blue eyes stared at me. "A few nights before he left for Alaska, the president called me to his office. You know what he said?"

"What?"

"He told me that he wanted to die."

The blue eyes continued to stare at me. "He told you the same thing, didn't he?"

I thought about telling him what President Harding had asked me to do. To shoot him in such a way that it would look like suicide. The friends he'd trusted who'd betrayed him—including not only his wife and Harry S. Sinclair but his secretary of the interior Albert B. Fall and many others—had driven him to the brink of suicide.

"Yes," I said.

"But you couldn't shoot him, could you?"

"No cousin, I couldn't."

"So you found a gentler way."'

"Yes."

"Poison."

"Correct."

"My Lord," he said, "My Lord."

"It was the best way to do it. This way you get rid of Phoebe and Harry and all the others—sending most of them to prison, I'm afraid—and history will officially record President Harding's death as accidental. He won't be thought of as a suicide. I liked him enough that saving his reputation was important to me."

"Then neither Phoebe or Harry killed him?"

"No. But now they both think the other did it and now they'll just want to get as far away from Washington as possible. Neither one of them can stand having the press look into their background and they know it."

"My Lord," he said again. "My Lord."

He followed my gaze out the window to the green hills and the blue sky and the rolling beauty of the prairie.

Then he turned back to me.

"In your own strange way, Bobby," he said, "you're a patriot."

"Oh, I hope so, cousin," I said, "I certainly hope so."

THE CURSE

He was not sure when the blue sedan had started following him. Sometime around Colliersville, probably, where Tracy had pulled into a trucker's diner for an egg sandwich and a cup of coffee.

Now he was back on the narrow two-lane blacktop that wound through the rolling hills and deep valleys you found only upstate. Ordinarily, Tracy would have entertained himself by watching the countryside roll by, the fat harvest moon tinting the September cornfields with gold, lights in distant farmhouse windows looking snug and comfortable, lazing cows mooing on the soft Indian summer breeze.

Tonight, however, Tracy had to keep both hands planted firmly on the wheel and his gaze set rapt ahead. The rain was coming in silver sheets that struck the windshield with the force and sound of hail. It was one of those vicious summer rainstorms that unnerve you just because of their unexpected—and unseasonal—ferocity.

The interior of the car was unpleasant. It was raining too hard to roll the window down, so the air was hot and moist. Even the air-conditioning didn't cut into the clamminess. The windows were steamed up and Tracy had to keep wiping a patch of the windshield clear. Before the rainstorm struck, Tracy had been listening to a tape that was a salute to the big bands. That was still Tracy's favorite era of music. Hearing Bob Crosby and the Bobcats' "Big Noise From Winnetka" was just as thrilling tonight as it had been back in 1939.

For the third time, the car behind him came shooting over a hill, pulling up too close given the slickness of the asphalt, and then falling abruptly back. The person following him was an amateur, overcompensating when Tracy vanished from sight by flying over the hill, then applying the brakes when he realized Tracy could easily see him.

Reaching inside his black suitcoat, Tracy jerked the .357 Magnum from his shoulder rig and set it on the seat. He was ready.

In all, the pursuit went on twenty-eight miles through the relentless rain. Several more times the driver behind lost Tracy, then shot forward as if through a time warp.

Tracy, who was driving up to see an old police friend of his who was gravely ill in a hospital, had been on this stretch of highway often enough to recall the two-pump gas station that lay on the right side of the road approximately five miles ahead. His idea was to lure his stalker there and find out just what was going on.

No lights shone in the rain. The station, a relic of the thirties, was shaped like a cottage except for its deep slanting roof. Fishscale-pattern shingles managed to look dirty even in the downpour. In the wash of his headlights, he could see the large red padlock on the front door. The owner had gone home long ago.

Tracy pulled up to one of the two gas pumps, killing his lights as he did so. Taking the .357 mag from the seat, he shrugged into his trenchcoat, pulled the brim of his fedora lower, and walked out from under the protection of the island overhang.

The rain hit him like rubber bullets, echoing off his hat, soaking into the fabric of his trenchcoat. The rain smelled fresh; the ground smelled muddy.

A quarter mile west, he could see the headlights of the car that had been following him. They shone through the gloom like tracer rounds in an endless nocturnal war.

He walked over to the far side of the gas station and crouched behind a dumpster that smelled of car oil and transmission fluid.

He had his weapon pointed at the spot where he estimated the stalker would pull up. Given the nature of his job, Tracy had a hundred enemies. He was curious about which one this would be.

The blue sedan obliged him by pulling off the asphalt, rolling along the gravel drive and stopping at almost the exact spot Tracy had in his gunsight.

The car sat there, lights still on, rain silver and slanting in the beams, the sound of the radio muffled behind the sound of the engine loudly idling. Tracy couldn't see who was inside. The steamy windows prevented that.

First the radio went off. Then the headlights. Then the engine.

All Tracy could hear for long minutes was the noise of the rain banging metallically on the roof of his car and the stalker's car. He was getting hot inside his trenchcoat. His mouth tasted dead and warm. He wanted a drink of water or a piece of gum.

The door of the stalker's car opened. A tall figure emerged, wearing a trenchcoat and fedora much like his own. From there, Tracy could see that in the figure's right gloved hand was a large silver handgun.

By the time the figure came around the front of the car, Tracy knew it was a woman. The steps were tentative, almost mincing, in the downpour, and the sway of the hips beneath the bulky material of the coat was unmistakably feminine. This didn't surprise him. He was sure he had as many female enemies as he did male ones.

Tracy got off one shot. Even in the rain, the muzzle flashed yellow-red and the acrid odor of gunsmoke filled his nostrils.

The shot tore a piece from the overhang. It was sufficient warning for the woman. She started to dive for the protection of her car.

Tracy raised himself upright and said, "If you throw your gun down, I won't fire anymore." He paused. "But I want to see you toss it out here on the gravel."

He couldn't see her. She was somewhere behind the

driver's side of her car. She was better than Tracy had assumed. Her first shot missed his left shoulder by a quarter of an inch.

He put two quick ones into her fender. He heard her scream and scramble toward the back end of the car.

Over the next two minutes, she returned fire three times. None of the shots came close to hitting him. He came out from behind the dumpster and started walking to her car. Every few steps, he'd fire a round just to keep her at bay.

He was five feet from the rear of the blue sedan when he saw her jump up and aim her .38 right at his face.

All he had time to do was pitch himself to the ground and start rolling. If he lay still, she'd have an easy target. When he was even with her bumper, he rolled himself to one knee, ducked under her frantic gunfire, and put two shots in the middle of her chest. She slumped against the trunk immediately, her gun falling to the gravel. She began moaning, saying words that were not audible through the hissing downpour, and crying in a way Tracy recognized at once. It was the sound people made when they knew for sure they were about to cross over to the other realm.

From his pocket, he took a flashlight. He walked over to the woman and put a beam in her face.

Her hat had fallen off and now he could see her shoulder-length blonde hair and her classically beautiful features. Even in dying, her face was almost painfully lovely to behold. He had no idea who she was.

"I'm going to call an ambulance," he said.

"No," she said. "It's too late for that." She started to slide from the trunk to the gravel. Tracy helped her so that she could lie on the ground beneath the overhang, out of the pounding rain. Like a huge flower, dark red blood had bloomed over the front of her yellow trenchcoat. A glistening stream of blood was also beginning to escape from the corner of her soft lips.

The strength of her grasp surprised him. She took his wrist and pulled him close to her. "I want to thank you, Tracy," she said.

"Thank me? For what?"

She smiled and in that moment he saw the madness in her blue eyes. "For killing me. Just the way I planned it." Blood was becoming so thick in her mouth, she could scarcely form words. "Purse," she managed to spit out. "Tape."

She died, then, Tracy cradling her blonde head in his arms.

"Who the hell are you?" he said, even though he knew there'd be no answer. "Why did you want me to kill you?"

The ambulance came from a small county hospital. Both the driver and the attendant were women bulky in their white jumpsuits. Like Sheriff Olsen, the man whose jurisdiction included this lonely stretch of county road, the women looked very angry and suspicious when Tracy admitted he'd killed the woman.

Unlike Olsen, the women obviously did not believe Tracy's tale of being drawn into a shootout and learning only afterwards that he'd been trapped into killing her. The women glared at him even while the white, boxy ambulance was wheeling out of the drive. Tracy didn't blame them. He knew how suspicious this looked.

Olsen told him to stay in touch, that there'd be an inquest and further questions, then bid Tracy goodnight.

Tracy hadn't told Olsen about the cassette tape he'd found in the woman's purse. He figured that was between himself and the dead woman.

In the car two hours later, continuing his drive to see his old friend, the rain little more than a mist now, Tracy put the tape into the deck and listened.

The woman's voice was as lovely as her face had been.

"I am Kendra Long, the daughter of Charles Long, a man you shot to death three years ago while trying to arrest him for holding up a bank in which a guard had been killed. I'm not making any claim that my father was innocent. He spent his whole life being a criminal.

"But when you killed him, Tracy, you doomed me to a life of wanting vengeance. All I could think of was killing you. I alienated my husband and two little girls because my obsession

155

with vengeance took the place of everything else. I could no longer love; I could only hate.

"Most people don't understand that hatred binds even more strongly than love. I could not let go.

"I spent six months following you. Learning your habits. Waiting for the one right moment.

"My plan at this time was to kill you and then return to my family.

"But gradually I began to realize that in a very real sense, my life was over. I had given it all up to kill you. So twice, I tried. Once I was about to send you a letter bomb and the other time I was about to shoot you when you were on vacation in Mexico.

"But both times, something stopped me. And after the second time, I realized what it was. It was not you I wanted dead; it was myself. Hatred had already killed my mind and soul so the killing of my body was little more than a formality.

"And how fitting that you'd be my executioner, Tracy. Just as you'd been my father's executioner.

"You will never forget me, Tracy, no matter how hard you try. You'll remember what it was like seeing me die; my face, the sounds I made. You'll know what it's like killing an innocent woman.

"Just as you cursed me, Tracy, now I've cursed you."

And that was it.

Blank tape passed through the heads silently.

She'd said what she wanted to say. Nothing more.

A pearl-colored dawn stretched across the black line of horizon as Tracy pulled into the small town where his friend lay in the hospital.

He kept thinking of the one word that Kendra Long had used to describe him—"executioner."

Tracy was not a man given to much doubt about the morality of his calling. Sometimes to catch killers, you had to become a killer yourself, and you could not allow yourself the luxury of doubt.

But as he climbed from his car in the hospital parking lot,

sunlight beginning to stream through the rainclouds, he realized that Kendra Long had had her vengeance indeed.

In a very real way, in a way that would trouble him and occasionally sap him with doubt if he was not careful, Dick Tracy had been cursed.

I love newspapers. Sure I like TV news with all its dazzle and drama. But for all its histrionics, TV news is short on content. A few years ago, The Cedar Rapids Gazette ran a long story about a murder in an adjacent county. The piece, which was quite well done, had the qualities of a William Faulkner story. I couldn't get the events or the people out of my head. Finally, I sat down and wrote my own version of it all.

LONG TIME TILL MORNING COMES

KJ grew up on an Iowa farm where funerals were as good as social events for seeing cousins and eating rich desserts and playing tag till you dropped in a human puddle from the sheer weight of sweat and pleasure.

This was true till he was nine when he went to the Karney funeral. Evelyn Karney, one of the valley's true young beauties, dead of a heart attack at twenty-six. Jake, Evelyn's husband, was KJ's first cousin and so KJ sat in the first row of folding chairs in the funeral parlor, the shining silver casket open, and lovely young Evelyn seeming to look straight up to heaven at the angels who most certainly waited there for her.

Then Jake Karney brought his two-and-a-half year old daughter, Phoebe, up to the casket. Jake knelt down and crossed himself big and dramatic, never once taking his eyes from his beloved wife, and then, as if suddenly possessed by demons, Phoebe began to wail and sob and hold her little hands out, hoping to grasp the corpse of her mother. She almost wriggled out of her father's arms and climbed into the casket with Evelyn herself.

Valley folks had never heard or seen anything like this, a tiny girl, barely out of infancy, grasping and groping for her mother that way, and calling out "Mama! Mama! Mama!" so hard that most of the women and some of the men, including Stan Jorgeson, generally considered both the toughest and meanest man in the valley, cried openly.

All through the month of May, all the time he worked alone in the dusty utility room in the barn, all the time he sawed and

159

measured and trimmed the pine into the proper and fitting shape of a casket, KJ thought of his little cousin Phoebe. Truly, the demon had never left her. Oh, she'd grown up, gone to the Consolidated country school where she'd graduated high school, and worked a summer at the Montgomery Ward store in the town of Anton, but the night before her nineteenth birthday she'd borrowed her boyfriend's Harley, something of a black demon itself as motorcycles went, and took it out on 149 three miles due south of Kepper bridge, and ran it head on into the path of a semi, a sixteen-wheeler to be exact, from which there had certainly been no deliverance. Unlike her mother's funeral, at Phoebe's the coffin had been kept closed.

KJ wondered what Phoebe would think of the casket he was making. He also wondered what Grandfather Kilpatrick would think of it. During the Depression, when most farmers starved, Grandpa Kilpatrick made decent money by turning out caskets for thirty-five dollars apiece. This was a story the Kilpatrick clan loved to tell, along with all sorts of ghost stories the more imaginative family members had put in the mouth of long-dead Grandpa to the Halloween delight of Kilpatrick kids everywhere.

Among his father's effects, KJ had found a letter that Grandpa had once written pa. Grandpa wanted pa to take up the same trade. The letter told him how to make a casket, it being a family superstition that one man in each generation must do so. Pine was the least expensive and, overall, most reliable of the woods. The contours of the casket should run to human-shape and for folks who wanted something fancy, it could be lined with white cotton and the cotton covered with raw white silk and nailed down with carpet tacks. The exterior should be painted with black paint and, for a very fancy effect, have a lid made from glass for those who wanted the body displayed at the all-night wake. Pretty simple, actually, the whole process.

Now all these long years later, him in his early thirties now, KJ spent a month building a coffin in the family utility room in the milking barn that stank of hot, pissy milk and the splashy fly-buzzed cow shit particular to milk cows.

Tonight he finished.

He put in the last of the carpet tacks, the hinges on the lid (an improvement on Grandpa's design) and a thick coat of shiny black paint.

It was done, sweet sawn wood shavings all over the floor, coiled as the Slinkys of his youth, the stink of the black paint harsh in his nostrils.

As he stood looking at the casket in the dusk room where Grandpa and pa after had worked, KJ felt a great sorrow for what was coming tonight. He had long sought a life like the other men in the valley knew, kids and a wife to be trusted, but in seven years Claudia had borne them no children, and had only fleetingly honored their marriage vows.

She sat in front of the TV set watching music videos and eating the boiled beef dinner she'd made earlier today. She was a good cook.

They had two La-Z-Boy recliners bought at Sears during a two-for-one sale. The blue one had become His. The tan one had become Hers.

He brought his plate in and sat down and started eating.

"God, I wish I had a pair like that black girl there," Claudia said.

Claudia, it seemed, liked nothing about herself. Not her face, which was appealing in a curiously insolent way; not her breasts, which were small but exceedingly charming; not her legs, which were short but finely wrought. She watched music videos as a means of comparison. She always found herself wanting.

"I'm bowling tonight, hon, remember."

"Right," he said.

"Be a little late probably. We're supposed to have that meeting with the league from over in Kendricks. You know, about the tournament next fall."

"Right."

She set her plate down on the floor, a signal to their sweet yellow collie, Daisy, to clean up what was left, and then pushed the recliner back and relaxed.

He sat in the dark room, in the soft flickering glow of the TV screen, in the hard harsh alien sound of rap music, looking at her.

She was the first girl who'd ever let him feel her breasts; the first girl who'd ever let him inside of her. When they were seventeen, and he was already hopelessly gone on her, he caught her one night in the shadows behind the high school, making love to a senior football star. He had stayed in bed for nearly two weeks, sick to his stomach at least three times a day. He did not help with chores. He lost eleven pounds in fourteen days.

He never told her about what he'd seen that terrible night nor what seeing it had done to him. He made up some mysterious malady to explain his time in bed. Eventually, they started seeing each other again and this continued on until they were twenty, which was when, at a dance, he found her out in the car with a musician she'd met a few weeks earlier. She had been straddling the kid in the back seat and making the familiar noise of her orgasm, so fulsome it was, innocent and rich as the sound of a baby's pleasure.

He waited until the boy had gone back in to the dance and she had started to drift back, moth to flame, to the amber light of the dance floor and the high tinny laughter of the night . . .

He stepped from the shadows and slapped her so hard across the mouth that his hand went dead, literally dead, on contact.

Nothing needed to be said. She knew he knew. He did not call her for two months nor did he take any of her phone calls, either.

At Christmas that year he was at the Wal-Mart buying fuzzy pink slippers for ma and flannel pajamas for pa when he saw her by accident and she looked so beautiful, her perfect cheeks tinted with the holiday air, that he nearly wept right there from his loss. She silently took his hand and three months later they were married.

That he knew of, she'd had six affairs in nine years. None lasted long. None, by her standards anyway, seemed to be serious.

Sometimes she smelled of cigarettes (she didn't smoke) and sometimes of whiskey (she didn't like anything stronger than beer) and sometimes she smelled of coming. And so then he knew. If any of this affected her emotionally, she did not show it. She was almost invariably cheery, almost invariably pleasant. No whispery phone calls; no sneaking off at odd hours. She knew how to conduct herself during an affair.

Until this spring, that is, when the man named Michael Redmond took over as manager of the Western Auto. He was so handsome, KJ almost hated to look at him that first chill March day, so handsome that as soon as KJ saw him he thought, with great and terrible foreknowledge, that soon enough Claudia would see him too and soon enough Claudia and handsome Michael Redmond would have an affair.

The affair began, near as KJ could tell, about three weeks later. Redmond had a wife but KJ knew just by looking at the man that that didn't matter, any more than it mattered to Claudia that she had a husband.

Something went wrong with this affair and went wrong right away. Claudia stayed in bed a lot and cried a lot and lost weight a lot. She paid almost no attention to KJ and then only to belittle him. Only on the nights she was to go out, fluttery and anxious as a school girl, was she her old cheery self.

Five weeks ago, he'd followed her. She'd gone to Bowl-R-Ama just the way she said, but she left early, scooching into the front seat of Michael Redmond's Pontiac Firebird and roaring away.

Redmond had quickly become friends with another local lover, a fleshy man named Chip Stevenson who kept a fishing cabin for his assignations. Redmond had taken Claudia to Chip's cabin that night. They went inside and turned the lights on and then after a few minutes turned the lights off. The lights stayed off for nearly an hour as KJ sat there, cold when the heater was off, hot when the heater was on, the windshield all silver from his breath, the night sky clear and starry and vast. Then the lights came on again and then went off again and then they hurried out of the cabin and into the Firebird, passing KJ two minutes later where he sat parked behind a shadowy copse of trees.

He followed her four more times. He knew that this affair was different from the other ones.

And so, apparently, did the rest of the town because now down at the co-op or at Fisher's Pharmacy or at Del's DX or at St. Patrick's Church or at Sud's Book n' Browse or at Lumberland or at Steiner's Grocery or at Wal-Mart, anywhere he went, there was pity in the eyes of those who beheld him, and a certain melancholy contempt as well.

Shortly after that, going up to the attic and his pa's effects, he found his grandpa's instructions for building the casket, and so he proceeded.

And tonight he finished.

"I baked you a nice chocolate cake," Claudia said, getting up from the recliner. She looked so happy, so excited that he felt ashamed for them both. "And there's some of that Kemper's vanilla ice cream you like so much in the freezer."

"Thanks."

"So," she said leaning over and giving him a quick dry kiss on the forehead, "if I'm a little late, don't worry."

Twenty minutes later, trailing perfume (and so he imagined) the sexual musk distinct to women, she left and joined the spring night so fertile with river and grass and birdsong and moonshadow and pure eternal desire for the man she loved so truly.

He waited five minutes, till he heard the sound of her seven-year-old Dodge station wagon fading, and then he went after her.

They were in the bowling alley for an hour-and-a-half.

KJ sat in the alley across the street, watching the parking lot.

When they came out, they came out together, her arm

through his. She threw her head back, long red hair glistening in the lights of the parking lot, and laughed.

Redmond took her in his arms and kissed her.

The kiss lasted a long time and during it, KJ took from the glove compartment the .38 that had belonged to his father.

Redmond, making a show of it, walked Claudia around the car and held the door for her. She slipped inside. A minute later, the Firebird blasted to life and set off out of town.

May was almost oppressively beautiful, the gold of moonlight on the fast running river, the burst of birdsong every few minutes in the green blooming trees, the sense of regeneration and immortality in the essence of all living things, wildflower and sweet soft kitten and human being alike.

They were going to the cabin.

KJ stayed a half mile behind them. He wanted to be one with the night, with life. He was instead one only with death.

Cabin windows glowed and fell dark even before KJ could park behind the copse of trees and start, half-jogging, across the dusty two-lane, the shacky cabin below, a fishing pole length from the moonlit river.

KJ heard her laugh on the night, his own wife. He closed his eyes, shuddered the terrible shudder that almost flung him into the grass. He remembered how sick he'd been in high school, the time he'd found her with that senior. He was afraid he was going to be that sick again.

Instead, he kept moving.

Crouched down, he came up from the small gulley in front of the cabin, and began to move, still crouching, toward the westward window of the one-room place.

Her laughter again; more a giggle, really.

And then his laughter, too. Redmond's.

The window screen smelled of dust and dead flies as KJ pressed his nose to it.

And then he saw them, two naked human shapes, shadows now, there on the squeaking cabin bed.

Redmond was on top and easy to hit, his long back arcing just as he sensed somebody watching, just as he turned to see

KJ—

KJ fired twice.

She was screaming even before the bullets reached her lover.

KJ ran around to the door then and kicked it open and went inside.

She was up and off the bed, Redmond sprawled unmoving at an angle across the sheets. KJ could smell blood and raw human shit.

"Jesus, KJ, Jesus, Oh Jesus, I just do these things they don't mean nothin'. Don't you know that KJ don't you know that?"

KJ went over and sat on a spindly straightback chair. He was out of breath. The cabin was dark. You could hear a barn owl somewhere, and closer the river rushing, rushing. KJ wished he could go with the river, all the way to the ocean, leaving memory and desire and pain behind, just rushing, rushing with the river.

"I didn't love him, KJ, I really didn't."

"It doesn't matter now."

"I just wanted you to know that."

"Shut up."

"And he was going to be the last one. I made myself that promise. The last one, KJ. True blue."

"I told you to shut up."

"It's just like having a virus or something, KJ. I burn and burn and burn with it but then I'm all right, then it's all over. This would have been all over, too."

She started sobbing, shaking, seeming not to notice she was naked.

They were quiet for a time, just the river, just the night, just the rolling prairie sweetness of spring . . .

"Can you see me?" KJ said.

"What KJ? Huh?" She was so scared she could barely form thoughts, barely speak.

"Can you see me, I said. Sitting here."

"Yes," she said. "Yes. I can see you, KJ."

"Good," he said.

"You going to kill me, KJ?"

"No," he said.

"He was going to be the last one, KJ, I promise. I promise."

He thought about saying something but it would just come out bitter and angry and wrong and somehow he didn't want to sound that way. Not for her sake; for his own.

He raised the .38.

He pointed it right between her naked breasts, the breasts she'd never been satisfied with.

"Oh Jesus Mary and Joseph, KJ," she said. "Oh Jesus Mary and Joseph."

He wished he could think of the right thing to say, just exactly the right thing, but he'd never been good with words. Never.

"Please, KJ, oh please KJ, please," she said over and over and over, her lover lying half dead half on half off the bed, forgotten utterly now. "Oh please KJ please don't kill me."

He raised the .38 a little higher.

Right to her heart.

Perfect shot.

"Can you see me?" he said. "Can you see me good?"

And then he turned the .38 abruptly around and brought it to his mouth and pulled the trigger.

After the police, after her mother, after her neighbor, after the minister, after a long time vomiting in the bathroom, she called the prim funeral director Blythe and he agreed to come out, arriving one hour later in his fine black Chrysler four-door.

He told her how sorry he was, though his gaze said that he knew her for the whore she was and the cause of the two mens' deaths, and then she took him out to the barn, him looking a little unhappy to be walking through cow shit, being a city man and all, and then, just as KJ's note had instructed, she took him to the utility room and she showed him the coffin in the grubby light of the lone hanging bulb.

"This is what he wants to be buried in," she said.

"This?"

167

"Yes."

"But he made it himself."

"Yes, yes he did," she said.

"But I'm not sure. I mean there are laws that—"

"There aren't any goddamn laws and you know it, you skinflint bastard. Don't worry, I'll buy a cheap coffin from you and pay you full price and then you can resell it to somebody else. But I want him buried in this one. Do you understand?"

On the way back to his fine black Chrysler, the funeral director stepped in a particularly squishy pile of cow shit and she couldn't help but take pleasure in this.

Then he was gone, all fading red tail lights and a plume of silver dust on the moonlit gravel road, and then there was just the night and the distant river, and after a time, not knowing what else to do, she went back to the barn and stood over the empty casket and ran her hand over the crude contours and lines of it.

Oh KJ, she thought. Oh KJ, in the long run I would've gotten over him; in the long run I really would have.

And then there was just the night, just the rolling prairie night, and the sad sudden silence of her life.

In my drinking days I often sat alone at the bar smoking cigarettes and eavesdropping on the conversations around me. One night I heard a rather vain Chicago ad man saying to his friend (another rather vain Chicago ad man), "You don't owe her anything. She's just your mistress." The line stayed with me for years and one day resulted in this Irwin Shawian vignette.

MY FRIEND BOBBY

I got there early but already the bar was crowded. This was mid-December, with winter break only a day away, and the students starting the festivities early.

Hard to believe I'd ever been one of them. Now that I was nearing forty, even the slickest of them looked transparent and clumsy.

The blond jock-type just now copping a cheap feel from his beautiful Tri-Delt girlfriend next to him in the booth. Is he already so drunk at 4:17 p.m. that he really doesn't think anybody knows what he's up to?

Or the three nerdy types flirting with the cute impatient waitress? Do these guys really think they have a chance?

Or the black guy in the corner in his nice Brooks Brothers suit. Probably talking perfect suburban English and contemplating a run for the student council next term. Does he think that white people can't see that curious mixture of contempt and sorrow in his eyes?

God, over the course of my college days, I was all of these types and more. The sexual braggart ala our friend with the wandering fingers, the shy and inept flirt ala the nerds, and even the angry but smiling outsider ala the young black man.

Different girls, different situations seemed to create different "me"s. By the time I finished college, I'd been several hundred different people.

"You think we were ever this stupid?"

I looked up and Bobby was there. Or Robert, as he now prefers to be called, now that he's CEO of a bank holding company that *Forbes* recently named one of the hundred hottest corporations in the country.

Bobby LeMat. Maybe the most successful student in my entire college class and he accomplished it all—girls, popularity with other boys, a certain Gatsby-like mystique—without throwing one football, kissing one TKE ass, or owning a single Corvette.

He accomplished it all with pure animal charm. He's handsome but he's more, too. He can make you feel as if you're the most special friend he's ever had.

He's certainly the most special friend *I've* ever had. He was the one who talked me into staying in school when I nearly flunked out my senior year; he was the one who sat up with me long drunken nights when my father was killed in an automobile crash; and he was the one who gave me courage enough to ask my wife Beth to marry me. Beth was several rungs up the social ladder. Bobby persuaded me that I loved her and that she loved me and that that's all that should matter. Our first of three sons was named Robert and Bobby became godfather to the other two. Beth is crazy about him.

He sat down. He still gets the looks, even from twenty-year-old co-eds. Despite a lot of working out, despite a lot of very careful dieting, he's starting to show age a little bit but from a distance the women still turn and look.

"How are you, my friend?"

"Not too bad, Bobby."

He always has this big smile and I always sound a little dour. I try not to but most of the time it's just how I am.

"How's the advertising business?" he said.

"You know how it is. The recession and all."

"You read the *Forbes* article?"

"One of the hundred hottest companies?"

"Right. And it's waiting for you there, too, if you'll just grab it, my friend."

"God, Bobby, that was great. The *Forbes* piece, I mean. I'm really happy for you."

He leaned forward and said, "David, you're missing my point. Recession is all up here." And with that he tapped his head. "You let the concept of recession loose inside your head and that was your first mistake." He sat back and grinned, natty in his dark double-breasted suit and white shirt and red necktie. "Recession isn't a concept to me. I won't let it be. And that's why my company's doing so well."

That was pure Bobby. Mind over matter. Always the positive slant on things.

Which is why I always turn to him when I've got a problem I need help with. You can have your ministers and priests and rabbis, you can have your counselors and shrinks, I'll take my friend Bobby any day. Financial trouble? Illness? Indecision? Twenty minutes across a booth from Bobby and you're able to deal with life again.

"So how are my kids?"

He always calls my sons "his kids." Beth loves it. "Fine."

"Great. And Beth?"

I hesitated. "She's great, too."

"So that's it. Beth."

I was just about to say something when a waitress came by, a very cute waitress, and Bobby went very smoothly into action. "A martini, very dry, for me; and a Cutty and water for my friend here."

She grinned at Bobby because he was grinning at her, and then she went away.

He said, "Is something wrong with Beth?"

"Not exactly, Bobby. Indirectly, I suppose she's involved in this but—" I took a deep breath. I knew how I was going to sound. So selfish and all. "It's Gwen."

"Your secretary? That tiny one with the nice little ass?"

"Right."

"I thought that was all over."

"Well, it was. For a while anyway. But you know how these things work sometimes. You see each other every day at work and—"

"—and one rainy night you ask her if she'd like to go have a drink with you for old time's sake and then all of a sudden it's midnight and you're all snug and warm in her bed and you're thinking, Holy Shit, this is starting all over again, isn't it?"

"Exactly."

"You know what my advice was, David."

"I know, I know. And I should've taken it."

"Only bop women you don't care about. And as I remember, you were starting to get kind of fond of little Gwen, weren't you?"

"She's real bright, Bobby. And real nice. And a good listener. And—"

"Trouble, my friend. Fastest way I know to bring down a marriage is to start having feelings for the women you're bopping on the side. Really starts complicating things at home with Mama. Suddenly Mama's body doesn't turn you on anymore and then she starts getting suspicious. And before you know it—"

"You don't ever have any feelings about the women you spend time with?"

The waitress was back with our drinks. He tipped her with several dollars and a wink. She winked back and went away. He watched her retreat, taking particular note, as I had earlier, of her calves and ankles. She had beautiful legs.

"Who's the most important person in my life, David?"

"Well, I—"

"Pam. My wife Pamela. That's who."

"Sure but—"

"So no matter who I sleep with here or who I sleep with there, it's always Pam I'm thinking about, and Pam I'm concerned with. Mama is number one right here." He thumped his heart. "And that's how it has to be. Mama is number one right here."

He took a deep taste of his martini and set the glass down and looked at me and said, "I assume you want my advice?"

"Right."

"Drop her. I'm talking about Gwen, of course."

"I want to but I can't."

"Sure you can."

"It's not that easy, Bobby. She's been diagnosed with cancer. And if I drop her—" I sighed. "She doesn't have anybody else, Bobby. Her folks live on the other side of the goddamn country and she's been in love with me for two years and so she hasn't developed any other friends. Not really, anyway."

"You don't owe her diddly, David."

"But she's sick, Bobby. Maybe real sick. And there's nobody to go see her at night."

He shook his head. "David, you are one crazy guy. You know that? I wish you could take a step back and hear what you're saying to me. You're saying that you think you owe your mistress something."

"Well, yeah, I guess that's what I'm saying."

"What the hell's a mistress for, anyway, David?"

"Well—"

"They're for fun. For relaxation. For R&R as we used to say in the Army. They're not for going through medical problems with, David. That's what wives are for. And you've got to get that straight."

"Sunday night in bed, I tried to make love to Beth and I couldn't. I couldn't even get a little teensy hard-on."

"See what I told you? Mama is number one right here because if she isn't—"

"And then we had this terrible argument that woke the boys up at two in the morning."

He stared straight at me. Right straight at me. "I've got dibs on your family, my friend. They're just like my own family."

"I know that, Bobby."

"And I also think I've earned the privilege of talking damned straight with you."

"You have, Bobby. That's why I asked you to meet me here."

"I want you to get this broad, this Gwen, out of your life and I want you to get her out of your life right now. You understand me?"

"But God, Bobby, she's going into the hospital next week."

"Won't her folks be here?"

"Well, yes—"

"Well, what? Then she's covered. Somebody will take her to the hospital and take her home from the hospital and then stay with her while she's recovering." He paused. "I'd say your problem is solved, David."

"But I care about her."

"You're saying she's number one in your heart?"

"No—I mean I'm not sure—but—"

"Mistresses are supposed to be fun, David. Look at it that way. And what the hell kind of fun is a mistress with cancer?"

I sighed. "I guess you're right."

"I'm not trying to be a hard-ass about this, my friend."

"I know."

"It's just that Mama has to come first."

"You're right again," I said.

"Yes, David, I am right. Incontestably right. Eg-fucking-xactly right."

"I won't call her tonight."

"Good."

"And I won't go up and see her at the hospital."

"Good."

"And I won't visit her when she's recuperating."

"Good."

"And she'll hate me by then."

"You should be so lucky, my friend."

"No, I know her. She'll be crushed because I didn't call her or visit her or even drop her a card. She'll be so crushed she'll probably go back to California with her parents, which they've been asking her to do for the last year."

"And you'll be one extremely fortunate sonofabitch. You'll have a nice cushy job as a VP at a major ad agency. And you'll have a desire for Mama in your pants again."

"God, that'd be so nice. To want her the way I used to. It's just that I feel so damned sorry for Gwen."

And then he stood up abruptly the way he always does, the meeting, as it were, adjourned.

Men who run one of the hottest corporations don't have a lot of time for chit-chat.

He clapped me on the shoulder and shook my hand. "Say hello to those kids of mine."

"I will, Bobby."

"Promise?"

"Promise."

"And take Mama out to some fancy restaurant this weekend. OK?"

"OK. And thanks, Bobby. Thanks an awful lot."

And then he was gone, moving toward the door somewhere beyond the crowd of students who were starting to pack this place.

I had one more drink and sat there and watched them for awhile, all the types they were, all the types I'd been, and wished I could be more like Bobby LeMat.

On the way out I passed a pay phone and for a terrible moment I stopped and thought of calling Gwen.

But then I started walking again, walking very fast, trying to forget it all, what it had all become with Gwen, so goddamned crazy—I walked straight past the phone and straight out the door, right out into the cold vast overwhelming midwestern night, just the way Bobby wanted me to.

One spring night these friends of mine called and said that their daughter had been murdered.

A few years later, it was said by our smug little social group that these people were not strong at all about their loss. And I suppose they weren't, but I can't say that any of the rest of us would have been strong, either.

Graham Greene once noted that H. Rider Haggard wept openly for his drowned son, even after the boy had been dead for thirty years. There is some grief you never recover from.

STALKER

1

Eleven years, two months, and five days later, we caught him. In an apartment house on the west edge of Des Moines. The man who had raped and murdered my daughter.

Inside the rental Pontiac, Slocum said, "I can fix it so we have to kill him." The dramatic effect of his words was lost somewhat when he waggled a bag of Dunkin' Donuts at me.

I shook my head, "No."

"No to the donuts. Or no to killing him?"

"Both."

"You're the boss."

I suppose I should tell you about Slocum. At least two hundred pounds overweight, given to western clothes too large for even his bulk (trying to hide that slope of belly, I suppose), Slocum is thirty-nine, wears a beard the angriest of Old Testament prophets would have envied, and carries at all times in his shoulder holster a Colt King Cobra, one of the most repellent-looking weapons I've ever seen. I don't suppose someone like me—former economics professor at the state university and antigun activist of the first form—ever quite gets used to the look and feel and smell of such weapons. Never quite.

I had been riding shotgun in an endless caravan of rented cars, charter airplanes, Greyhound buses, Amtrak passenger cars, and even a few motorboats for the past seven months, ever since that day in Chicago when I turned my life over to Slocum the way others turned their lives over to Jesus or Republicanism.

I entered his office, put twenty-five thousand dollars in cash on his desk, and said, "Everybody tells me you're the best. I hope that's true, Mr. Slocum."

He grinned at me with teeth that Red Man had turned the color of peach wine. "Fortunately for you, it is true. Now what is it you'd like me to do?" He turned down the Hank Williams, Jr. tape he'd been listening to and waved to me, with a massive beefy hand bearing two faded blue tattoos, to start talking.

I had worked with innumerable police departments, innumerable private investigators, two soldiers of fortune, and a psychic over the past eleven years in an effort to find the man who killed my daughter.

That cold, bright January day seven months ago, and as something of a last resort, I had turned to a man whose occupation sounded far too romantic to be any good to me: Slocum was a bounty hunter.

"Maybe you should wait here."

"Why?" I said.

"You know why."

"Because I don't like guns? Because I don't want to arrange it so we have to kill him?"

"It could be dangerous."

"You really think I care about that?"

He studied my face. "No, I guess you don't."

"I just want to see him when he gets caught. I just want to see his expression when he realizes he's going to go to prison for the rest of his life."

He grinned at me with his stained teeth. "I'd rather see him when he's been gut-shot. Still afraid to die but at the same time wanting to. You know? I gut-shot a gook in Nam once and watched him the whole time. It took him an hour. It was one long hour, believe me."

Staring at the three-story apartment house, I sighed. "Eleven years."

"I'm sorry for all you've gone through."

"I know you are, Slocum. That's one of the things a good liberal like me can't figure out about a man like you."

"What's that?"

"How you can enjoy killing people and still feel so much compassion for the human race in general."

He shrugged. "I'm not killing humanity in general, Robert. I'm killing animals." He took out the Cobra, grim gray metal almost glowing in the late June sunlight, checked it, and put it back. His eyes scanned the upper part of the red brick apartment house. Many of the screens were torn and a few shattered windows had been taped up. The lawn needed mowing and a tiny black baby walked around wearing a filthy too-small t-shirt and nothing else. Twenty years ago this had probably been a very nice middle-class place. Now it had the feel of an inner-city housing project.

"One thing," he said, as I started to open the door. He put a meaty hand on my shoulder for emphasis.

"Yes?"

"When this is all over—however it turns out—you're going to feel let down."

"You maybe; not me. All I've wanted for the past eleven years was finding Dexter. Now we have found him. Now I can start my life again."

"That's the thing," he said. "That's what you don't understand."

"What don't I understand?"

"This has changed you, Robert. You start hunting people—even when you've got a personal stake in it—and it changes you."

I laughed. "Right. I think this afternoon I'll go down to my friendly neighborhood recruiting office and sign up for Green Beret school."

Occasionally, he got irritated with me. Now seemed to be one of those times. "I'm just some big dumb redneck, right, Robert? What would I know about the subtleties of human psychology, right?"

181

"Look, Slocum, I'm sorry if—"
He patted his Cobra. "Let's go."

2

They found her in a grave that was really more of a wide
hole up in High Ridge forest where the scrub pines run heavy
down to the river. My daughter Debbie. The coroner estimated she had been there at least thirty days. At the time of
her death she'd been seventeen.

This is the way the official version ran: Debbie, leaving her
job at the Baskin-Robbins, was dragged into a car, taken into
the forest, raped, and killed. Only when I pressed him on the
subject did the coroner tell me the extent to which she had
been mutilated, the mutilation coming, so far as could be
determined, after she had died. At the funeral the coffin was
closed.

At the time I had a wife—small, tanned, intelligent in a hard
sensible way I often envied, quick to laugh, equally quick to
cry—and a son. Jeff was twelve the year his sister died. He was
seventeen when he died five years later.

When you're sitting home watching the sullen parade of
faceless murders flicker and die on your screen—the weeping
mother of the victim, the carefully spoken detective in charge,
the sexless doll-like face of the reporter signing off on the
story—you don't take into account the impact that the violent
death of a loved one has on a family. I do; after Debbie's death,
I made a study of the subject. Like so many things I've studied
in my life, I ended up with facts that neither enlightened nor
comforted. They were just facts.

My family's loss was measured in two ways—my wife's
depression (she came from a family that suffered mental illness
the way some families suffered freckles) and my son's wildness.

Not that I was aware of either of these problems as they
began to play out. When it became apparent to me that the
local police were never going to solve the murder—their entire

investigation centered on an elusive 1986 red Chevrolet—I virtually left home. Using a generous inheritance left to me by an uncle, I began—in tandem with the private eyes and soldiers of fortune and psychics I've already mentioned—to pursue my daughter's killer. I have no doubt that my pursuit was obsessive, and clinically so. Nights I would lie on the strange, cold, lonely bed of a strange, cold, lonely motel room thinking of tomorrow, always tomorrow, and how we were only hours away from a man we now knew to be one William K. Dexter, age thirty-seven, twice incarcerated for violent crimes, unduly attached to a very aged mother, perhaps guilty of two similar killings in two other midwestern states. I thought of nothing else—so much so that sometimes, lying there in the motel room, I wanted to take a butcher knife and cut into my brain until I found the place where memory dwelt—and cut it away. William K. Dexter was my only thought.

During this time, me gone, my wife began a series of affairs (I learned all this later) that only served to increase the senseless rage she felt (she seemed to resent the men because they could not give her peace)—she still woke up screaming Debbie's name. Her drinking increased also and she began shopping around for new shrinks the way you might shop around for a new car. A few times during her last two months we made love when I came home on the weekend from pursuing Dexter in one fashion or another—but afterward it was always the same. "You weren't a good father to her, Robert." "I know." "And I wasn't a good mother. We're such goddamned selfish people." And then the sobbing, sobbing to the point of passing out (always drunk of course) in a little-girl pile in the bathroom or the center of the hardwood bedroom floor.

Jeff found her. Just home from school, calling her name, not really expecting her to be there, he went upstairs to the TV room for the afternoon ritual of a dance show and there he found her. The last images of a soap opera flickering on the screen. A drink of bourbon in the Smurf glass she always found so inexplicably amusing. A cigarette guttering out in the ashtray. Dressed in one of Jeff's T-shirts with the rock-and-roll slogan on its front and a pair of designer jeans that pointed up the teenage sleekness of her body. Dead. Heart attack.

On the day of her funeral, up in the TV room where she'd died, I was having drinks of my own, wishing I had some facts to tell me what I should be feeling now . . . when Jeff came in and sat down next to me and put his arm around my neck the way he used to when he was three or four. "You can't cry, can you, Dad?" All I could do was sigh. He'd been watching me. "You should cry, Dad. You really should. You didn't even cry when Debbie was killed. Mom told me." He said all this in the young man's voice I still couldn't quite get used to—the voice he used so successfully with ninth-grade girls on the phone. He wasn't quite a man yet but he wasn't a kid, either. In a moment of panic I felt he was an imposter, that this was a joke; where was my little boy? "That's all I do, Dad. Is cry, I mean. I think it helps me. I really do."

So I'd tried, first there with Jeff in the TV room, later alone in my bedroom. But there were just dry choking sounds and no tears at all. At all. I would think of Debbie, her sweet soft radiance; and of my wife, the years when it had been good for us, her so tender and kind in the shadows of our hours together; and I wanted to cry for the loss I felt. But all I could see was the face of William K. Dexter. In some way, he had become more important to me even than the two people he'd taken from me.

Jeff died three years later, wrapped around a light pole on the edge of a country park, drugs and vodka found in the front seat of the car I'd bought him six months earlier.

Left alone at the wake, kneeling before his waxen corpse, an Our Father faint on my lips, I'd felt certain I could cry. It would be a tribute to Jeff; one he'd understand; some part of the process by which he'd forgive me for being gone so much, for pursuing William K. Dexter while Jeff was discovering drugs and alcohol and girls too young to know about nurturing. I put out my hand and touched his cheek, his cold waxen cheek, and I felt something die in me. It was the opposite of crying, of bursting forth with poisons that needed to be purged. Something was dead in me and would never be reborn.

It was not too long after this that I met Frank Slocum and it was not long after Slocum took the case that we began to close inexorably in on William K. Dexter.

And soon enough we were here, at the apartment house just outside Des Moines.

Eleven years, two months, and five days later.

3

The name on the hallway mailbox said Severn, George Severn. We knew better, of course.

Up carpeted stairs threadbare and stained, down a hallway thick with dusty sunlight, to a door marked 4-A.

"Behind me," Slocum whispered, waving me to the wall.

For a moment, the only noises belonged to the apartment building; the thrum of electricity snaking through the walls; the creak of roof in summer wind; a toilet exploding somewhere on the floor below us.

Slocum put a hefty finger to his thick mouth, stabbing through a thistle of beard to do so. Sssh.

Slocum stood back from the door himself. His Cobra was in his hand, ready. He reached around the long way and set big knuckles against the cheap faded pine of the door.

On the other side of the door, I heard chair legs scrape against tile.

Somebody in there.

William K. Dexter.

Chair legs scraped again; footsteps. They did not come all the way to the door, however, rather stopped at what I imagined was probably the center of the living room.

"Yeah?"

Slocum put his finger to his lips again. Reached around once more and knocked.

"I said 'Yeah.' Who the hell is it?"

He was curious about who was in the hall, this George

Severn was, but not curious enough to open the door and find out.

One more knock. Quick rap really; nothing more.

Inside, you could sense Severn's aggravation.

"Goddammit," he said and took a few loud steps toward the door but then stopped.

Creak of floor; flutter of robin wings as bird settled on hallway window; creak of floor again from inside the apartment.

Slocum held up a halting hand. Then he pantomimed Don't Move with his lips. He waited for my reaction. I nodded.

He looked funny, a man as big as he was, doing a very broad, cartoon version of a man walking away. Huge noisy steps so that it sounded as if he were very quickly retreating. But he did all this in place. He did it for thirty seconds and then he eased himself flat back against the wall. He took his Cobra and put it man-high on the edge of the door frame.

Severn didn't come out in thirty seconds but he did come out in about a minute.

For eleven years I'd wondered what he'd look like. Photos deceive. I always pictured him as formidable. He would have to be, I'd reasoned; the savage way he'd mutilated her ... He was a skinny fortyish man in a stained white T-shirt and Levis that looked a little too big. He wore the wide sideburns of a hillbilly trucker and the scowl of a mean drunk. He stank of sleep and whiskey. He carried a butcher knife that appeared to be new. It still had the lime-green price sticker on the black handle.

When he came out of his apartment, he made the mistake of looking straight ahead.

Slocum did two things at the same time: slammed the Cobra's nose hard against Severn's temple and yanked a handful of hair so hard, Severn's knees buckled. "You're dead, man, in case you haven't figured it out already," Slocum said. He seemed enraged; he was a little frightening to watch.

He grabbed some more hair and then he pushed Severn all the way back into his apartment.

186

4

Slocum got him on a straight-backed chair, hit him so hard in the mouth that you could hear teeth go, and then handcuffed him, still in the chair, to the aged formica dining-room table.

Slocum then cocked his foot back and kicked Severn clean and hard in the ribs. Almost immediately, Severn's mouth started boiling with red mucus that didn't seem quite thick enough to be blood.

Slocum next went over to Severn and ripped his T-shirt away from his shoulder. Without a word, Slocum motioned me over.

With his Cobra, Slocum pointed to a faded tattoo on Severn's right shoulder. It read: *Mindy* with a rose next to it. Not many men had such a tattoo on their right shoulder. It was identical to the one listed in all of Severn's police records.

Slocum slapped him with stunning ferocity directly across the mouth, so hard that both Severn and his chair were lifted from the floor.

For the first time, I moved. Not to hit Severn myself but to put a halting hand on Slocum's arm. "That's enough."

"We've got the right guy!" It was easy to see he was crazed in some profound animal way I'd never seen in anybody before.

"I know we do."

"The guy who killed your daughter!"

"I know," I said, "but, —"

"But what?"

I sighed. "But I don't want to be like him and if we sat here and beat him, that's exactly what we'd be. Animals—just like him."

Slocum's expression was a mixture of contempt and disbelief. I could see whatever respect he'd had for me—or perhaps it had been nothing more than mere pity—was gone now. He looked at me the same way I looked at him—as some alien species.

"Please, Slocum," I said.

He got one more in, a good solid right hand to the left side of Severn's head. Severn's eyes rolled and he went out. From the smell, you could tell he'd wet his pants.

I kept calling him Severn. But of course he wasn't Severn. He was William K. Dexter.

Slocum went over to the ancient Kelvinator, took out a can of Hamms and opened it with a great deal of violence, and then slammed the refrigerator door.

"You think he's all right?" I said.

"What the hell's that supposed to mean?"

"It means did you kill him?"

"Kill him?" He laughed. The contempt was back in his voice. "Kill him? No, but I should have. I keep thinking of your daughter, man. All the things you've told me about her. Not a perfect kid—no kid is—but a real gentle little girl. A girl you supposedly loved. Your frigging daughter, man. Your frigging daughter." He sloshed his beer in the general direction of Dexter. "I should get out my hunting knife and cut his balls off. That's what I should do. And that's just for openers. Just for openers."

He started pacing around, then, Slocum did, and I could gauge his rage. I suppose at that moment he wanted to kill us both—Dexter for being an animal, me for being a weakling— neither of us the type of person Slocum wanted in his universe.

The apartment was small and crammed with threadbare and wobbly furniture. Everything had been burned with cigarettes and disfigured with beer-can rings. The sour smell of bad cooking lay on the air; sunlight poured through filthy windows; and even from here you could smell the rancid odors of the bathroom. On the bureau lay two photographs, one of a plump woman in a shabby housedress standing with her arm around Dexter, obviously his mother; and a much younger Dexter squinting into the sun outside a gray metal barracks where he had served briefly as an army private before being pushed out on a mental.

Peeking into the bedroom, I found the centerfolds he'd pinned up. They weren't the centerfolds of the quality men's magazines where the women were beautiful to begin with and made even more so with careful lighting and gauzy effects; no, these were the women of the street, hard-eyed, flabby-bodied, some even tattooed like Dexter himself. They covered the walls on either side of his sad little cot where he slept in a room littered with empty beer cans and hard-crusted pizza boxes. Many of the centerfolds he'd defaced, drawing penises in black ballpoint aimed at their vaginas or their mouths, or putting huge blood-dripping knives into their breasts or eyes or even their vaginas. All I could think of was Debbie and what he'd done to her that long ago night . . .

A terrible, oppressive nausea filled me as I backed out of the bedroom and groped for the couch so I could sit down.

"What's the matter?" Slocum said.

"Shut up."

"What?"

"Shut the fuck up!"

I sank to the couch—the sunlight through the greasy window making me ever warmer— and cupped my hands in my face and swallowed again and again until I felt the vomit in my throat and esophagus and stomach recede.

I was shaking, chilled now with sweat.

"Can you wake him up?"

"What?"

"Can you wake him up?"

"Sure," Slocum said, "Why?"

"Because I want to talk to him."

Slocum gulped the last of his beer, tossed the can into a garbage sack overflowing with coffee grounds and tomato rinds, and then went over to the sink. He took down a big glass with the Flintstones on it and filled it with water, then took the glass over to where he had Dexter handcuffed. With a certain degree of obvious pleasure, he threw the water across Dexter's head. He threw the glass—as if it were now contaminated—into the corner where it shattered into three large jagged pieces.

He grabbed Dexter by the hair and jerked his head back.

Groaning, Dexter came awake.

"Now what?" Slocum said, turning to me.

"Now I want to talk to him."

"Talk to him," Slocum said. "Right."

He pointed a large hand at Dexter as if he were a master of ceremonies introducing the next act.

It wasn't easy, getting up off that couch and going over to him. In a curious way, I was terrified of him. If I pushed him hard enough, he would tell me the exact truth about the night. The truth in detail. What she had looked like and sounded like—her screams as he raped her; her screams as she died—and then I would have my facts . . . but facts so horrible I would not be able to live with them. How many times—despite myself—I had tried to recreate that night. But there would be no solace in this particular truth; no solace at all.

I stood over him. "Have you figured out who I am yet?"

He stared up at me. He started crying. "Hey, man, I never did nothing to you."

"You raped and killed a girl named Debbie eleven years ago."

"I don't know what you're talking about, man. Honest. You got the wrong guy."

I knew that by the way I studied his face—every piece of beard stubble, the green matter collected in the corners of his eyes, the dandruff flaked off at the front of his receding hairline—that I was trying to learn something about him, something that would grant me peace after all these years.

A madman, this Dexter, and so not quite responsible for what he'd done and perhaps even deserving of pity in my good liberal soul.

But he didn't seem insane, at least not insane enough to move me in any way. He was just a cheap trapped frightened animal.

"Really, man; really I don't know what the hell you're talking about."

"I've been tracking you for eleven years now—"

"Jesus, man; listen—"

"You're going to hate prison, Dexter. Or maybe they'll even execute you. Did you ever read anything about the injections they give? They make it sound so humane but it's the waiting, Dexter. It's the waiting—"

"Please," he said, "please," and he writhed against his handcuffs, scraping the table across the floor in the process.

"Eleven years, Dexter," I said.

I could hear my voice, what was happening to it—all my feelings about Dexter were merging into my memories of those defaced centerfolds in his bedroom—and Slocum must have known it too, with his animal wisdom, known at just what moment I would be right for it

because just then and just so
the Cobra came into my hands and I
shot Dexter once in the face and once in the
chest and I

5

Slocum explained to me—though I really wasn't listening—that they were called by various names (toss guns or throw away guns) but they were carried by police officers in case they wanted to show that the person they'd just killed had been armed.

From a holster strapped to his ankle, Slocum took a .38, wiped it clean of prints, and set it next to Dexter's hand.

Below and to the side of us the apartment house was a frenzy of shouts and cries—fear and panic—and already in the distance sirens exploded red on the soft blue air of the summer day.

6

That evening I cried.

I sat in a good room in a good hotel with the air-conditioning going strong, a fine dinner and many fine drinks in my belly, and I cried.

Wept, really.

Whatever had kept me from crying for my daughter and then my wife and then my son was gone now and so I could love and mourn them in a way I'd never been able to. I thought of each of them—their particular ways of laughing, their particular sets of pleasures and dreams, their particular fears and apprehensions—and it was as if they joined me there in that chill antiseptic hotel room, Debbie in her blue sweater and jeans, my wife in her white linen sheath, Jeff in his Kiss T-shirt and chinos—came round in the way the medieval church taught that angels gathered around the bed of a dying person . . . only I wasn't dying.

My family was there to tell me that I was to live again. To seek some sort of peace and normalcy after the forced march of these past eleven years.

"I love you so much," I said aloud to each of them, and wept all the more; "I love you so much."

And then I slept.

7

"I talked to the district attorney," Slocum said in the coffee shop the following morning. "He says it's very unlikely there will be any charges."

"He really thought Dexter was armed?"

"Wouldn't you? A piece of trash like Dexter?"

I stared at him. "You know something terrible?"

"What?"

"I don't feel guilty."

He let go with one of those cigarette-raspy laughs of his. "Good."

Then it was his turn to stare at me, there in the hubbub of clattering dishes and good sweet coffee smells and bacon sizzling on the grill. "So what now?"

"See if I can get my job back."

"At the university?"

"Umm-hmm."

He kept staring. "You don't feel any guilt do you?"

"No. I mean, I know I should. Whatever else, he was a human being. But—"

He smiled his hard Old Testament smile. "Now don't you go giving me any of those mousy little liberal 'buts,' all right?"

"All right."

"You just go back and live your life and make it a good one."

"I owe you one hell of a lot, Slocum."

He put forth a slab of hand and a genuine look of affection in his eyes. "Just make it a good one," he said. "Promise?"

"Promise."

"And no guilt?"

"No guilt."

He grinned. "I knew I could make a man out you."

8

Her name was Anne Stevens and she was to dominate my first year back at the university. Having met at the faculty picnic—hot August giving way to the fierce melancholy of Indian summer—we began what we both hoped (her divorced; me not quite human yet) would be a pleasant but slow-moving relationship. We were careful to not introduce real passion, for instance, until we both felt certain we could handle it, about the time the first of the Christmas decorations blew in the gray wind of Harcourt Square.

School itself took some adjusting. First, there was the fact that the students seemed less bright and inquisitive, more conservative than the students I remembered. Second, the faculty had some doubts about me; given my experiences over the past eleven years, they wondered how I would fit into a setting whose goals were at best abstract. I wondered, too . . .

After the first time we made love—Anne's place, un-planned, satisfying if slightly embarrassing—I went home and stared at the photograph of my wife I keep on my bureau. In whispers, I apologized for what I'd done. If I'd been a better husband I would have no guilt now. But I had not, alas, been a better husband at all . . .

In the spring, a magazine took a piece on inflation I wrote and the academic dean made a considerable fuss over this fact. Also in the spring Anne and I told each other that we loved each other in a variety of ways, emotionally, sexually, spiritually. We set June 23 as our wedding day.

It was on May 5 that I saw the item in the state newspaper. For the following three weeks I did my best to forget it, troubling as it was. Anne began to notice a difference in my behavior, and to talk about it. I just kept thinking of the newspaper item and of something Slocum had said that day when I killed Dexter.

In the middle of a May night—the breeze sweet with the newly blooming world—I typed out a six-page letter to Anne, packed two bags, stopped by a 7-11 and filled the Volvo and dropped Anne's letter in a mailbox, and then set out on the Interstate.

Two mornings later, I walked up a dusty flight of stairs inside an apartment house. A Hank Williams, Jr. record filled the air.

To be heard above the music, I had to pound.

I half-expected what would happen, that when the door finally opened a gun would be shoved in my face. It was.

A Cobra.

I didn't say anything. I just handed him the news clipping. He waved me in—he lived in a place not dissimilar from the one Dexter had lived in—read the clipping as he opened an 8:48 A.M. beer.

Finished reading it, he let it glide to the coffee table that was covered with gun magazines.

"So?"

"So I want to help him. I don't want him to go through what I did."

"You know him or something?"

"No."

"Just some guy whose daughter was raped and killed and the suspect hasn't been apprehended."

"Right."

"And you want what?"

"I've got money and I've got time. I quit my job."

"But what do you want?"

"I want us to go after him. Remember how you said that I'd changed and that I didn't even know it?"

"Yeah, I remember."

"Well, you were right. I have changed."

He stood up and started laughing, his considerable belly shaking beneath his Valvoline T-shirt. "Well, I'll be god-damned, Robert. I'll be goddamned. I did make a man out of you, after all. So how about having a beer with me?"

At first—it not being nine A.M. yet—I hesitated. But then I nodded my head and said, "Yeah, Slocum. That sounds good. That really sounds good."

Child sexual abuse is much discussed these days but sometimes in all the furor—and all the resultant psychobabble—we forget that some scars never heal.

THE MONSTER

He sat a long time in the sunny June parking lot looking up at the seven story brick hospital. The same hospital in which he'd been born thirty-six years ago, the same hospital in which he'd likely die when the time came, hopefully decades hence. It would give his life a rough symmetry.

He was still not sure what he was going to say or do when he went up to Room 715. How long he'd rehearsed it. How many variations he'd wrung. But now that the time was actually here . . .

In the lobby, waiting for an elevator, he noted the age of the white-garbed nuns who worked in the hospital. Only rarely did you see young nuns these days. Just aged, worn ones who could, despite their years and the grief they'd seen within these hospital walls, offer you something like a sincere smile. A testament to their faith.

On the third floor, surgery floor, the elevator stopped and let on a middle-aged mother and a teenaged boy. The mother was weeping softly into a white cloth handkerchief. The boy kept glancing at Kelly, looking embarrassed. Teenaged boys had such pride, such a precarious sense of their masculinity, that they did not want to appear vulnerable even when a loved one was gravely ill or dying. The mother and son got off on floor five, where there was a lounge and where you could look across the city from a fine, wide window.

A plump black lady in a mauve-colored uniform was waxing and polishing the seventh floor hallway. In the sunlight, the tiles appeared to be made of molten gold. At the nurses station, Kelly checked to see if Room 715 could still have visitors. The nurse said yes but that it was getting a little overcrowded.

Most of the people standing in the hallway and inside the room Kelly recognized from television and newspapers. Politicians. The men and women who ran the city. They offered him quick smiles and somewhat puzzled glances. He did not exude power the way they did; obviously they wondered who he was.

For the next hour, he stayed with the few people he did recognize, people from the old neighborhood who remembered him from days when he'd lived there and his father had sold insurance for Prudential. How old they looked now, these adults of his youth; their faces spiderworks of wrinkles, the color of their eyes faded, their bones sharp and vulnerable. Too soon they'd be here in such rooms, dying, dying.

He did not go into the room very far. He did not want the man in the bed to see him. He wanted to wait until they were alone.

There was a great deal of laughter. It put him in mind of one of the Las Vegas conventions he went to every year for the small travel agency he ran. He could hear the man in the bed laughing, too. Everybody here seemed determined to deny what was really going on.

Finally, a hard-eyed nurse, trying to be nicer than was her natural inclination, appeared on crisply squeaking white shoes and told everybody that it was time to leave.

Kelly went down the hall to one of the men's rooms and stayed there for fifteen minutes, wanting to be sure that the old man would be alone when Kelly got back to his room.

The man's name was O'Banyon. Even in death (cancer of the liver) there was a charm and power undeniable to the handsome face and strong if beefy body. Not even the forty pounds he lost over the last three months could quell his natural and somewhat theatrical presence. He had been a first-string football player at the state university, a decorated veteran of Korea, and a leading golfer at various country clubs.

All these things had led him to politics and helped him succeed. So had his wife, who came from money. Now he was sixty-six and dying and obviously trying to make some sense—give some purpose—to all these (and so many more) disparate facts that made up his life.

He didn't recognize Kelly. This almost made Kelly smile. How many long years Kelly had dreaded and hated this man. How many nightmares the man had inspired. How much pain and doubt and useless rage this man had wrought in Kelly.

And so finally Kelly confronted him . . . and the man didn't even know who the hell Kelly was.

Kelly walked up next to the man's bed and said, "You really don't remember me, do you?"

O'Banyon's room looked like a florist's. So many bouquets; so many plants. Red and blue and yellow in the sunlight. Cheerful *Get Well* cards covering all the available space not taken up by flowers. There was even a fake yellow telegram from the Governor ordering O'Banyon to get well.

"I'm a little drugged-up right now, I'm afraid," O'Banyon said. His bed had been cranked up so he could sit up straight. He narrowed his eyes and stared at Kelly. "Being on the city council, I meet a lot of people and it's not always easy to remember—" And then he stopped talking. And then it was clear that he had recognized Kelly at last.

What was in his gaze now? Fear? Dread? "You're Bobby Kelly."

"Robert these days. I haven't been Bobby since you were our next door neighbor."

O'Banyon seemed almost afraid of silence now. Just kept pushing words forth nervously. "How's your Dad?"

"He died ten years ago."

"Oh, I'm sorry. I guess I haven't done a very good job of keeping up. And your Mom?"

"Doing well."

"Good; good; she was always a very nice woman. Liked her a lot." He was bantering, babbling.

Kelly said, there in the lazing sunlight, there in the cheery

199

impersonal death room, "When I was six years old, you molested me. I don't suppose you've forgotten about that, as
much as you'd probably like to."

Now it was definitely fear Kelly saw in O'Banyon's eyes.
Definitely.

"And it wasn't just me," Kelly went on. "There were three
other boys in the neighborhood you molested, too." Kelly
shook his head. "When I heard you were dying, I wanted to
come up here and gloat. To laugh in your face. Because I've
never been able to forget what happened. I used to think it
was my fault, that there was something wrong with me, that in
some way I caused you to molest me. For a long time I even
worried that I was queer, that because you'd done what you'd
done I was marked in some way, like being bitten by a vampire
or something. I couldn't even talk about it to my wife. When
I'd think about it, I'd feel sick and ashamed. I wanted to find
you and kill you, even after all those years. And when I heard
you were dying—"

Kelly let his gaze stray to the family photo standing upright
on the ledge next to the bed. It showed Grandpa O'Banyon
with his four kids and his ten grandkids. How healthy and
normal they all looked. "You should have asked for help," Kelly
said. "That's the part I resent. You were sick and you knew
you were sick but you didn't ask for help. You just kept right
on doing it. To me and other little boys, too."

O'Banyon at last found his voice. "I don't know what
you're talking about."

Kelly laughed harshly. "My God, you're going to pretend
you're innocent even when there's nobody else in the room?
Don't worry. I'm not going to tell anybody. I'm still ashamed
of it. That's the terrible part. I still feel as if I were responsible
for it somehow. Even though I was only six years old."

"Then what the hell did you come up here for? They must
have told you I was dying. They give me two months at the
outside. Inoperable. Does that make you happy?" O'Banyon
was shouting, just the way a powerful city councilman would
be used to shouting when something displeased him.

The hard-eyed nurse on the squeaky soles poked her head into the room and said, "Is everything all right, gentlemen?"

"Everything's fine," O'Banyon said, but of course his harsh voice conveyed just the opposite.

The nurse looked from one man to the other. To Kelly she said, "I'll give you five more minutes, then I really want you to leave. All right?"

Kelly nodded.

For a long time after the nurse left, neither man said anything. Kelly walked over to the window. In a private room such as this, a hospital could almost be pleasant. At the window, he looked across the city. How much it was changing. Many of the neighborhoods he'd lived in had been brought down by urban renewal. The new neighborhoods were shiny and fine to be sure but they lacked some essential warmth, that soul and poetry unknown to urban planners and housing developers alike.

"You're not here for money, are you?" O'Banyon said.

Kelly smiled and turned back to the man. "No, not here for money, O'Banyon."

"Then why did you come up here?"

Kelly shrugged. "Because since I've been six years old, I've wanted to tell you how much I resented what you did to me, and how much I hate you." He looked at O'Banyon's family and then back at the man in the bed. "But you know something? I can't even hate you now. At least not the way I want to. I look at you and see you're dying and I don't take any pleasure from it. I want to, O'Banyon; I want to laugh in your face for all the little boys you molested. But I can't. It's too late for that, now, you sonofabitch." Tears sounded in Kelly's voice. "All I can feel is that you can't hurt anybody else because you won't be alive much longer. The terrible thing is that there'll be somebody else to take your place; somebody just as selfish and just as sick."

O'Banyon's face was red with anger. "You've had your say, Kelly. Now get the hell out of here."

Kelly smiled again, bitterly. "At least you haven't said you were sorry. At least you didn't make it worse with hypocrisy, O'Banyon. For that I thank you."

And then O'Banyon collapsed. Internally. His face went white and his right arm began to twitch and he sank back in his bed and looked, now, ninety years old. His eyes closed and he began shaking his head from side to side, going over and over some ancient grief Kelly could only guess at.

"Get out of here," O'Banyon whispered, trying to infuse his voice with force and fury. But now he was just a sick old man. "Get out of here."

Kelly stared at him one last time. The monster. The man in the darkness. The source of shame and doubt and helpless rage.

Squeaking soles announced the arrival of the nurse. Peeking in the door, she said, "It's time."

O'Banyon kept his eyes closed. His face was even chalkier than it had been, his right arm continuing to twitch.

"It's time," the nurse said again.

Kelly left.

Forty-five minutes later, Kelly pulled his car into the driveway of his suburban home. From the backyard, he heard the summer squeals of his five-year-old Todd.

Kelly went to the fence and leaned over it and watched Todd awkwardly try to hit the wiffle ball with the wiffle ball bat. Kelly had never exactly been a hymn to athletic prowess and neither had Todd. But they both tried hard and that was what really counted.

Kelly's wife Jane came over from hanging white sheets on the clothesline. They both liked the way wind-dried sheets smelled so fresh. She slid her arms around his waist and stood there watching Todd with him.

"He's so precious," Jane said.

"He sure is." Kelly smiled as Todd got hold of a good one and batted it several feet in the air.

"I just worry about him sometimes. All the things that can hurt little children. Running out into the street or catching a terrible virus of some kind or—"

"Or monsters," Kelly said.

"Monsters?" Jane said, trying to see if he was kidding or not. "You mean like Dracula or Frankenstein?"

"No, hon, I mean real monsters. The kind who live next door and mow their lawns on Saturday afternoons and worry about keeping up the payments on their American Express cards. Real monsters."

Before Jane could ask her husband what he meant by that, he was gone, inside the fence with Todd, pitching his son slow easy ones so Todd could belt them out of the park.

By noon, the temperature was in the warm, breezy eighties and Jane served them tuna fish sandwiches with potato chips and big dill pickles. The three of them ate at the picnic table on the veranda.

Before they started eating, Kelly raised his glass of strawberry Kool-Aid and insisted that they do likewise. Then he clinked their glasses in a formal toast.

"What're we toasting?" Jane said.

"Why, I thought you could guess," Kelly said, mock scolding her. "I'm toasting how much I love you two and how good I feel today."

"How come today, Daddy? How come you feel so good today?" Todd wanted to know.

Kelly tousled his son's hair and said, "Because today I killed a monster."

"Oooo, Daddy," Todd said. "That's neat."

And as they began to eat, a warm soft breeze came and brought with it the scent of buttercups and the sight of butterflies.

And Kelly sat there and finished his lunch and watched the cloudless blue prairie sky and knew that he really had killed a monster today. He really had.

In the days when I wrote and produced documentaries and commercials, I spent a week interviewing mothers of infants who were essentially mutants. One such mother told me, in great sad rage, that she and her child were utterly alone in the universe and that nobody, not even her husband, could understand their pain and despair. There was enormous useless violence in her, and a kind of furious dignity, too. I never forgot her or the angry way in which she showed me photographs of her son, as if daring me to look away or express cheap pity.

One snowy Sunday, years later, I read in the Obituaries column that the woman had been killed in a car accident. I wrote this story for her.

THE UGLY FILE

The cold rain didn't improve the looks of the housing development, one of those sprawling valleys of pastel-colored tract houses that had sprung from the loins of greedy contractors right at the end of WW II, fresh as flowers during that exultant time but now dead and faded.

I spent fifteen minutes trying to find the right address. Houses and streets formed a blinding maze of sameness.

I got lucky by taking what I feared was a wrong turn. A few minutes later I pulled my new station wagon up to the curb, got out, tugged my hat and raincoat on snugly, and then started unloading.

Usually, Merle, my assistant, is on most shoots. He unloads and sets up all the lighting, unloads and sets up all the photographic umbrellas, and unloads and sets up all the electric sensors that trip the strobe lights. But Merle went on this kind of shoot once before and he said never again, "not even if you fire my ass." He was too good an assistant to give up so now I did these particular jobs alone.

My name is Roy Hubbard. I picked up my profession of photography in Nam, where I was on the staff of a captain whose greatest thrill was taking photos of bloody and dismembered bodies. He didn't care if the bodies belonged to us or them just as long as they had been somehow disfigured or dismembered.

In an odd way, I suppose, being the captain's assistant prepared me for the client I was working for today, and had been working for, on and off, for the past two months. The best-paying client I've ever had, I should mention here. I don't want you to think that I take any special pleasure, or get any special kick, out of gigs like this. I don't. But when you've got a family to feed, and you live in a city with as many competing photography firms as this one has, you pretty much take what's offered you.

The air smelled of wet dark earth turning from winter to spring. Another four or five weeks and you'd see cardinals and jays sitting on the blooming green branches of trees.

The house was shabby even by the standards of the neighborhood, the brown grass littered with bright cheap forgotten plastic toys and empty Diet Pepsi cans and wild rain-sodden scraps of newspaper inserts. The small picture window to the right of the front door was taped lengthwise from some long ago crack, and the white siding ran with rust from the drain spouts. The front door was missing its top glass panel. Cardboard had been set in there.

I knocked, ducking beneath the slight overhang of the roof to escape the rain.

The woman who answered was probably no older than twenty-five but her eyes and the sag of her shoulders said that her age should not be measured by calendar years alone.

"Mrs. Cunningham?"

"Hi," she said, and her tiny white hands fluttered about like doves. "I didn't get to clean the place up very good."

"That's fine."

"And the two oldest kids have the flu so they're still in their pajamas and — "

"Everything'll be fine, Mrs. Cunningham." When you're a photographer who deals a lot with mothers and children, you have to learn a certain calm, doctorly manner.

She opened the door and I went inside.

The living room, and what I could see of the dining room, was basically a continuation of the front yard—a mine field of cheap toys scattered everywhere, and inexpensive furniture of the sort you buy by the room instead of the piece strewn with magazines and pieces of the newspaper and the odd piece of children's clothing.

Over all was a sour smell, one part the rain-sodden wood of the exterior house, one part the lunch she had just fixed, one part the house cleaning this place hadn't had in a good long while.

The two kids with the flu, boy and girl respectively, were parked in a corner of the long, stained couch. Even from here I knew that one of them had diapers in need of changing. They showed no interest in me or my equipment. Out of dirty faces and dead blue eyes they watched one cartoon character beat another with a hammer on a TV whose sound dial was turned very near the top.

"Cindy's in her room," Mrs. Cunningham explained.

Her dark hair was in a pert little pony tail. The rest of her chunky self was packed into a faded blue sweat shirt and sweat pants. In high school she had probably been nice and trim. But high school was an eternity behind her now.

I carried my gear and followed her down a short hallway. We passed two messy bedrooms and a bathroom and finally we came to a door that was closed.

"Have you ever seen anybody like Cindy before?"

"I guess not, Mrs. Cunningham."

"Well, it's kind of shocking. Some people can't really look at her at all. They just sort of glance at her and look away real quick. You know?"

"I'll be fine."

"I mean, it doesn't offend me when people don't want to look at her. If she wasn't my daughter, I probably wouldn't want to look at her, either. Being perfectly honest, I mean."

"I'm ready, Mrs. Cunningham."

She watched me a moment and said, "You have kids?"

"Two little girls."

"And they're both fine?"

"We were lucky."

For a moment, I thought she might cry. "You don't know how lucky, Mr. Hubbard."

She opened the door and we went into the bedroom.

It was a small room, painted a fresh, lively pink. The furnishings in here—the bassinet, the bureau, the rocking horse in the corner—were more expensive than the stuff in the rest of the house. And the smell was better. Johnson's Baby Oil and Johnson's Baby Powder are always pleasant on the nose. There was a reverence in the appointments of this room, as if the Cunninghams had consciously decided to let the yard and the rest of the house go to hell. But this room—

Mrs. Cunningham led me over to the bassinet and then said, "Are you ready?"

"I'll be fine, Mrs. Cunningham. Really."

"Well," she said, "here you are then."

I went over and peered into the bassinet. The first look is always rough. But I didn't want to upset the lady so I smiled down at her baby as if Cindy looked just like every other baby girl I'd ever seen.

I even touched my finger to the baby's belly and tickled her a little. "Hi, Cindy."

After I had finished my first three or four assignments for this particular client, I went to the library one day and spent an hour or so reading about birth defects. The ones most of us are familiar with are clubfoots and cleft palates and harelips and things like that. The treatable problems, that is. From there you work up to spina bifida and cretinism. And from there—

What I didn't know until that day in the library is that there are literally hundreds of ways in which infants can be deformed, right up to and including the genetic curse of The Elephant Man. As soon as I started running into words such as achondroplastic dwarfism and supernumerary chromosomes, I quit reading. I had no idea what those words meant.

Nor did I have any idea of what exactly you would call Cindy's malformation. She had only one tiny arm and that was so short that her three fingers did not quite reach her rib cage. It put me in mind of a flipper on an otter. She had two legs but only one foot and only three digits on that. But her face was the most terrible part of it all, a tiny little slit of a mouth and virtually no nose and only one good eye. The other was almond-shaped and in the right position but the eyeball itself was the deep, startling color of blood.

"We been tryin' to keep her at home here," Mrs. Cunningham said, "but she can be a lot of trouble. The other two kids make fun of her all the time and my husband can't sleep right because he keeps havin' these dreams of her smotherin' because she don't have much of a nose. And the neighbor kids are always tryin' to sneak in and get a look at her."

All the time she talked, I kept staring down at poor Cindy. My reaction was always the same when I saw these children. I wanted to find out who was in charge of a universe that would permit something like this and then tear his fucking throat out.

"You ready to start now?"

"Ready," I said.

She was nice enough to help me get my equipment set up. The pictures went quickly. I shot Cindy from several angles, including several straight-on. For some reason, that's the one the client seems to like best. Straight-on. So you can see everything.

I used VPS large format professional film and a Pentax camera because what I was doing here was essentially making many portraits of Cindy, just the way I do when I make a portrait of an important community leader.

Half an hour later, I was packed up and moving through Mrs. Cunningham's front door.

"You tell that man—that Mr. Byerly who called—that we sure do appreciate that $2000 check he sent."

"I'll be sure to tell him," I said, walking out into the rain.

"You're gonna get wet."

"I'll be fine. Goodbye, Mrs. Cunningham."

Back at the shop, I asked Merle if there had been any calls and he said nothing important. Then, "How'd it go?"

"No problems," I said.

"Another addition to the ugly file, huh?" Then he nodded

to the three filing cabinets I'd bought years back at a government auction. The top drawer of the center cabinet contained the photos and negatives of all the deformed children I'd been shooting for Byerly.

"I still don't think that's funny, Merle."

"'The ugly file?'" He'd been calling it that for a couple weeks now and I'd warned him that I wasn't amused. I have one of those tempers that it's not smart to push on too hard or too long.

"Uh-huh," I said.

"If you can't laugh about it then you have to cry about it."

"That's a cop-out. People always say that when they want to say something nasty and get away with it. I don't want you to call it that any more, you fucking understand me, Merle?"

I could feel the anger coming. I guess I've got more of it than I know what to do with, especially after I've been around some poor god damned kid like Cindy.

"Hey, boss, lighten up. Shit, man, I won't say it any more, OK?"

"I'm going to hold you to that."

I took the film of Cindy into the dark room. It took six hours to process it all through the chemicals and get the good, clear proofs I wanted.

At some point during the process, Merle knocked on the door and said, "I'm goin' home now, all right?"

"See you tomorrow," I said through the closed door.

"Hey, I'm sorry I pissed you off. You know, about those pictures."

"Forget about it, Merle. It's over. Everything's fine."

"Thanks. See you tomorrow."

"Right."

When I came out of the dark room, the windows were filled with night. I put the proofs in a manila envelope with my logo and return address on it and then went out the door and down the stairs to the parking lot and my station wagon.

The night was like October now, raw and windy. I drove over to the freeway and took it straight out to Mannion Springs, the wealthiest of all the wealthy local suburbs.

On sunny afternoons, Mary and I pack up the girls some-times and drive through Mannion Springs and look at all the houses and daydream aloud of what it would be like to live in a place where you had honest-to-God maids and honest-to-God butlers the way some of these places do.

I thought of Mary now, and how much I loved her, more the longer we were married, and suddenly I felt this terrible, almost oppressive loneliness, and then I thought of little Cindy in that bassinet this afternoon and I just wanted to start crying and I couldn't even tell you why for sure.

The Byerly place is what they call a shingle Victorian. It has dormers of every kind and description—hipped, eyebrow and gabled. The place is huge but has far fewer windows than you'd expect to find in a house this size. You wonder if sunlight can ever get into it.

I'd called Byerly before leaving the office. He was expect-ing me.

I parked in the wide asphalt drive that swept around the grounds. By the time I reached the front porch, Byerly was in the arched doorway, dressed in a good dark suit.

I walked right up to him and handed him the envelope with the photos in it.

"Thank you," he said. "You'll send me a bill?"

"Sure," I said. I was going to add "That's my favorite part of the job, sending out the bill" but he wasn't the kind of guy you joke with. And if you ever saw him, you'd know why.

Everything about him tells you he's one of those men who used to be called aristocratic. He's handsome, he's slim, he's athletic, and he seems to be very, very confident in everything he does—until you look at his eyes, at the sorrow and weariness of them, at the trapped gaze of a small and broken boy hiding in there.

Of course, on my last trip out here I learned why he looks this way. Byerly was out and the maid answered the door and we started talking and then she told me all about it, in whispers of course, because Byerly's wife was upstairs and would not have appreciated being discussed this way.

Four years ago, Mrs. Byerly gave birth to their only child, a son. The family physician said that he had never seen a deformity of this magnitude. The child had a head only slightly larger than an apple and no eyes and no arms whatsover. And it made noises that sickened even the most doctorly of doctors . . .

The physician even hinted that the baby might be destroyed, for the sake of the entire family . . .

Mrs. Byerly had a nervous breakdown and went into a mental hospital for nearly a year. She refused to let her baby be taken to a state institution. Mr. Byerly and three shifts of nurses took care of the boy.

When Mrs. Byerly got out of the hospital everybody pretended that she was doing just fine and wasn't really crazy at all. But then Mrs. Byerly got her husband to hire me to take pictures of deformed babies for her. She seemed to draw courage from knowing that she and her son were not alone in their terrible grief . . .

All I could think of was those signals we send deep into outer space to see if some other species will hear them and let us know that we're not alone, that this isn't just some frigging joke, this nowhere planet spinning in the darkness . . .

When the maid told me all this, it broke my heart for Mrs. Byerly and then I didn't feel so awkward about taking the pictures any more. Her husband had his personal physician check out the area for the kind of babies we were looking for and Byerly would call the mother and offer to pay her a lot of money . . . and then I'd go over there and take the pictures of the kid . . .

Now, just as I was about to turn around and walk off the porch, Byerly said, "I understand that you spent some time here two weeks ago talking to one of the maids."

"Yes."

"I'd prefer that you never do that again. My wife is very uncomfortable about our personal affairs being made public."

He sounded as I had sounded with Merle earlier today.

Right on the verge of being very angry. The thing was, I didn't blame him. I wouldn't want people whispering about me and my wife, either.

"I apologize, Mr. Byerly. I shouldn't have done that."

"My wife has suffered enough." The anger had left him. He sounded drained. "She's suffered way too much, in fact."

And with that, I heard a child cry out from upstairs.

A child—yet not a child—a strangled, mournful cry that shook me to hear.

"Good night," he said.

He shut the door very quickly, leaving me to the wind and rain and night.

After awhile, I walked down the wide steps to my car and got inside and drove straight home.

As soon as I was inside, I kissed my wife and then took her by the hand and led her upstairs to the room our two little girls share.

We stood in the doorway, looking at Jenny and Sara. They were asleep.

Each was possessed of two eyes, two arms, two legs; and each was possessed of song and delight and wonderment and tenderness and glee.

And I held my wife tighter than I ever had, and felt an almost giddy gratitude for the health of our little family.

Not until much later, near midnight it was, my wife asleep next to me in the warmth of our bed—not until much later did I think again of Mrs. Byerly and her photos in the upstairs bedroom of that dark and shunned Victorian house, up there with her child trying to make frantic sense of the silent and eternal universe that makes no sense at all.

There isn't much to say about this very short story. It speaks for itself.

BLESS US OH LORD

I usually think of Midwestern Thanksgivings as cold, snowy days. But as we gathered around the table this afternoon, my parents and my wife Laura and our two children Rob and Kate, I noticed that the blue sky and sunlight in the window looked more like an April day than one in late November.

"Would you like to say grace today?" my mother said to four-year-old Kate.

Kate of the coppery hair and slow secretive smile nodded and started in immediately. She got the usual number of words wrong and everybody smiled the usual number of times and then the meal began.

Dad is a retired steel worker. I remember, as a boy, watching fascinated as he'd quickly work his way through a plate heaped with turkey, sweet potatoes, dressing, cranberry sauce and two big chunks of the honey wheat bread mom always makes for Thanksgiving and Christmas. And then go right back for seconds of everything and eat all that up right away, too.

He's sixty-seven now and probably thirty pounds over what he should be and his eyesight is fading and the only exercise he gets is taking out the garbage once a day—but he hasn't, unfortunately, lost that steelworker's appetite.

Mom on the other hand, thin as she was in her wedding pictures, eats a small helping of everything and then announces, in a sort of official way, "I'm stuffed."

"So how goes the lawyer business?" Dad asked after everybody had finished passing everything around.

Dad never tires of reminding everybody that his youngest son did something very few young men in our working class neighborhood did—went on to become a lawyer, and a reasonably successful one, too, with downtown quarters in one of the shiny new office buildings right on the river, and two BMWs in the family, even if one of them is fourteen years old.

"Pretty well, I guess," I said.

Laura smiled and laid her fingers gently on my wrist. "Some day this son of yours has to start speaking up for himself. He's doing very well. In fact, Bill Grier—one of the three partners—told your son here that within two years he'll be asked to be a partner, too."

"Did you hear that, Margaret?" Dad said to Mom.

"I heard," she said, grinning because Dad was grinning.

Dad's folks were Czechs. His father and mother landed in a ship in Galveston and trekked all the way up to Michigan on the whispered rumor of steel mill work. Dad was the first one in his family to learn English well. So I understood his pride in me.

Laura patted me again and went back to her food. I felt one of those odd gleeful moments that married people get when they realize, every once in a while, that they're more in love with their mates now than they were even back when things were all backseat passion and spring flowers.

Of course, back then, I'd been a little nervous about bringing Laura around the house. Mom and Dad are very nice people, you understand, but Laura's father is a very wealthy investment banker and I wasn't sure how she'd respond to the icons and mores of the working class—you know, the lurid and oversweet paintings of Jesus in the living room and the big booming excitement Dad brings to his pro wrestling matches on the tube.

But she did just fine. She fell in love with my Mom right away and if she was at first a little intimidated by the hard Slav passions of my father, she was still able to see the decent and gentle man abiding in his heart.

As I thought of all this, I looked around the table and felt almost tearful. God, I loved these people, they gave my life meaning and worth and dignity, every single one of them.

And then Mom said it, as I knew she inevitably would. "It's a little funny without Davey here, isn't it?"

Laura glanced across the table at me then quickly went back to her cranberry sauce.

Dad touched Mom's hand right away and said, "Now, Mom, Davey would want us to enjoy ourselves and you know it."

Mom was already starting to cry. She got up from the table and whispered "Excuse me" and left the dining room for the tiny bathroom off the kitchen.

Dad put his fork down and said, "She'll be all right in a minute or two."

"I know," I said.

My six-year-old son Rob said, "Is Gramma sad about Uncle Davey, Grandpa?"

And Dad, looking pretty sad himself, nodded and said, "Yes, she is, honey. Now you go ahead and finish your meal."

Rob didn't need much urging to do that.

A minute later, Mom was back at the table. "Sorry," she said.

Laura leaned over and kissed Mom on the cheek.

We went back to eating our Thanksgiving meal.

Davey was my younger brother. Five years younger. He was everything I was not—socially poised, talented in the arts, a heartbreaker with the ladies. I was plodding, unimaginative and no Robert Redford, believe me.

I had only one advantage over Davey. I never became a heroin addict. This happened sometime during his twenty-first year, back at the time the last strident chords of all those sixties protest guitars could be heard fading into the dusk.

He never recovered from this addiction. I don't know if you've ever known any family that's gone through addiction but in some ways the person who suffers least is the person who is addicted. He or she can hide behind the drugs or the alcohol.

He doesn't have to watch himself slowly die, nor watch his loved ones die right along with him, or watch them go through their meager life savings trying to help him.

Davey was a heroin addict for fourteen years. During that time he was arrested a total of sixteen times, served three long stretches in county jail (he avoided prison only because I called in a few favors), went through six different drug rehab programs, got into two car accidents—one that nearly killed him, one that nearly killed a six-year-old girl—and went through two marriages and countless clamorous relationships, usually with women who were also heroin addicts (a certain primness keeps me from calling my brother a "junkie," I suppose).

And most of the time, despite the marriages, despite the relationships, despite the occasional re-hab programs, he stayed at home with my folks.

Those happy retirement years they'd long dreamed of never came because Davey gave them no rest. One night a strange and exotic creature came to the front door and informed Dad that if Davey didn't pay him the drug money he owed him in the next twenty-four hours, Davey would be a dead man. Another night Davey pounded another man nearly to death on the front lawn.

Too many times, Dad had to go down to the city jail late at night to bail Davey out. Too many times, Mom had to go to the doctor to get increased dosages of tranquilizers and sleeping pills.

Davey was six months shy of age forty and it appeared that given his steely Czech constitution, he was going to live a lot longer—not forego the heroin, you understand—live maybe another full decade, a full decade of watching him grind Mom and Dad down with all his hopeless grief.

Then a few months ago, early September, a hotel clerk found him in this shabby room frequently used as a "shooting gallery." He was dead. He'd overdosed.

Mom and Dad were still working through the shock.

"Is there pink ice cream, Grandma?" Kate asked.

Grandma smiled at me. Baskin-Robbins has a bubble-gum

flavored ice cream and Mom has made it Kate's special treat whenever she visits.

"There's plenty of pink ice cream," Grandma said. "Especially for good girls like you."

And right then, seeing Kate and my mother beaming at each other, I knew I'd done the right thing sneaking up to the hotel room where Davey sometimes went with other junkies, and then giving him another shot when he was still in delirium and blind ecstasy from the first. He was still my brother, lying there dying before me, but I was doing my whole family a favor. I wanted Mom and Dad to have a few good years anyway.

"Hey, Mr. Counselor," Dad said, getting my attention again. "Looks like you could use some more turkey."

I laughed and patted my burgeoning little middle-class belly. "Correction," I said. "I could use a lot more turkey."

An editor called me one day and said he'd like a "different" kind of private-eye story and did I think I could come up with one? I'd been planning to write "Turn Away" for months and the invitation gave me a reason to do it. After reading the story, the editor called and said he was making it the lead piece in the anthology but that "it really isn't a private detective story at all. It's a mainstream story about a private detective." And you know, I think he was right.

TURN AWAY

On Thursday she was there again. (This was on a soap opera he'd picked up by accident looking for a western movie to watch since he was all caught up on his work.) Parnell had seen her Monday but not Tuesday then not Wednesday either. But Thursday she was there again. He didn't know her name, hell it didn't matter, she was just this maybe twenty-two twenty-three year old who looked a lot like a nurse from Enid, Oklahoma he'd dated a couple of times (Les Elgart had been playing on the Loop) six seven months after returning from WWII.

Now this young look-alike was on a soap opera and he was watching.

A frigging soap opera.

He was getting all dazzled up by her, just as he had on Monday, when the knock came sharp and three times, almost like a code.

He wasn't wearing the slippers he'd gotten recently at K-mart so he had to find them, and he was drinking straight from a quart of Hamms so he had to put it down. When you were the manager of an apartment building, even one as marginal as The Alma, you had to go to the door with at least a little "decorousness," the word Sgt. Meister, his boss, had always used back in Parnell's cop days.

It was 11:23 A.M. and most of the Alma's tenants were at work. Except for the ADC mothers who had plenty of work of their own kind what with some of the assholes down at Social

221

Services (Parnell had once gone down there with the Jamaican woman in 201 and threatened to punch out the little bastard who was holding up her check), not to mention the sheer simple burden of knowing the sweet innocent little child you loved was someday going to end up just as blown-out and bitter and useless as yourself.

He went to the door, shuffling in his new slippers which he'd bought two sizes too big because of his bunions.

The guy who stood there was no resident of the Alma. Not with his razor-cut black hair and his three-piece banker's suit and the kind of melancholy in his pale blue eyes that was almost sweet and not at all violent. He had a fancy mustache spoiled by the fact that his pink lips were a woman's.

"Mr. Parnell?"

Parnell nodded.

The man, who was maybe thirty-five, put out a hand. Parnell took it, all the while thinking of the soap opera behind him and the girl who looked like the one from Enid, Oklahoma. (Occasionally he bought whack-off magazines but the girls either looked too easy or too arrogant so he always had to close his eyes anyway and think of somebody he'd known in the past.) He wanted to see her, fuck this guy. Saturday he would be sixty-one and about all he had to look forward to was a phone call from his kid up the Oregon coast. His kid, who, God rest her soul, was his mother's son and not Parnell's, always ran a stopwatch while they talked so as to save on the phone bill. Hi Dad Happy Birthday and It's Been Really Nice Talking To You. I-Love-You-Bye.

"What can I do for you?" Parnell said. Then as he stood there watching the traffic go up and down Cortland Boulevard in baking July sunlight, Parnell realized that the guy was somehow familiar to him.

The guy said, "You know my father."

"Jesus H. Christ—"

"—Bud Garrett—"

"—Bud. I'll be goddamned." He'd already shaken the kid's hand and he couldn't do that again so he kind of patted him on the shoulder and said, "Come on in."

"I'm Richard Garrett."

"I'm glad to meet you, Richard."

He took the guy inside. Richard looked around at the odds and ends of furniture that didn't match and at all the pictures of dead people and immediately put a smile on his face as if he just couldn't remember when he'd been so enchanted with a place before, which meant of course that he saw the place for the dump Parnell knew it to be.

"How about a beer?" Parnell said, hoping he had something besides the generic stuff he'd bought at the 7-11 a few months ago.

"I'm fine, thanks."

Richard sat on the edge of the couch with the air of somebody waiting for his flight to be announced. He was all ready to jump up. He kept his eyes downcast and he kept fiddling with his wedding ring. Parnell watched him. Sometimes it turned out that way. Richard's old man had been on the force with Parnell. They'd been best friends. Garrett, Sr. was a big man, six-three and fleshy but strong, a brawler and occasionally a mean one when the hootch didn't settle in him quite right. But his son . . . Sometimes it turned out that way. He was manly enough, Parnell supposed, but there was an air of being trapped in himself, of petulance, that put Parnell off.

Three or four minutes of silence went by. The soap opera ended with Parnell getting another glance of the young lady. Then a "CBS Newsbreak" came on. Then some commercials. Richard didn't seem to notice that neither of them had said anything for a long time. Sunlight made bars through the venetian blinds. The refrigerator thrummed. Upstairs but distantly a kid bawled.

Parnell didn't realize it at first, not until Richard sniffed, that Bud Garrett's son was either crying or doing something damn close to it.

"Hey, Richard, what's the problem?" Parnell said, making sure to keep his voice soft.

"My, my Dad."

"Is something wrong?"

"Yes."

"What?"

Richard looked up with his pale blue eyes. "He's dying."

"Jesus."

Richard cleared his throat. "It's how he's dying that's so bad."

"Cancer?"

Richard said, "Yes. Liver. He's dying by inches."

"Shit."

Richard nodded. Then he fell once more into his own thoughts. Parnell let him stay there a while, thinking about Bud Garrett. Bud had left the force on a whim that all the cops said would fail. He started a rent-a-car business with a small inheritance he'd come into. That was twenty years ago. Now Bud Garrett lived up in Woodland Hills and drove the big Mercedes and went to Europe once a year. Bud and Parnell had tried to remain friends but beer and champagne didn't mix. When the Mrs. had died Bud had sent a lavish display of flowers to the funeral and a note that Parnell knew to be sincere but they hadn't had any real contact in years.

"Shit," Parnell said again.

Richard looked up, shaking his head as if trying to escape the aftereffects of drugs. "I want to hire you."

"Hire me? As what?"

"You're a personal investigator aren't you?"

"Not anymore. I mean I kept my ticket—it doesn't cost that much to renew it—but hell I haven't had a job in five years." He waved a beefy hand around the apartment. "I manage these apartments."

From inside his blue pin-striped suit Richard took a sleek wallet. He quickly counted out five one hundred dollar bills and put them on the blond coffee table next to the stack of Luke Short paperbacks. "I really want you to help me."

"Help you do what?"

"Kill my father."

Now Parnell shook his head. "Jesus, kid, are you nuts or

what?"

Richard stood up. "Are you busy right now?"

Parnell looked around the room again. "I guess not."

"Then why don't you come with me?"

"Where?"

When the elevator doors opened to let them out on the sixth floor of the hospital, Parnell said, "I want to be sure that you understand me."

He took Richard by the sleeve and held him and stared into his pale blue eyes. "You know why I'm coming here, right?"

"Right."

"I'm coming to see your father because we're old friends. Because I cared about him a great deal and because I still do. But that's the only reason."

"Right."

Parnell frowned. "You still think I'm going to help you, don't you?"

"I just want you to see him."

On the way to Bud Garrett's room they passed an especially good-looking nurse. Parnell felt guilty about recognizing her beauty. His old friend was dying just down the hall and here Parnell was worrying about some nurse.

Parnell went around the corner of the door. The room was dark. It smelled sweet from flowers and fetid from flesh literally rotting.

Then he looked at the frail yellow man in the bed. Even in the shadows you could see his skin was yellow.

"I'll be damned," the man said.

It was like watching a skeleton talk by some trick of magic.

Parnell went over and tried to smile his ass off but all he could muster was just a little one. He wanted to cry until he collapsed. You sonofabitch, Parnell thought, enraged. He just wasn't sure who he was enraged with. Death or God or himself—or maybe even Bud himself for reminding Parnell of just how terrible and scary it could get near the end.

"I'll be damned," Bud Garrett said again.

He put out his hand and Parnell took it. Held it for a long time.

"He's a good boy, isn't he?" Garrett said, nodding to Richard.

"He sure is."

"I had to raise him after his mother died. I did a good job, if I say so myself."

"A damn good job, Bud."

This was a big private room that more resembled a hotel suite. There was a divan and a console tv and a dry bar. There was a Picasso lithograph and a walk-in closet and a deck to walk out on. There was a double-sized water bed with enough controls to drive a space ship and a big stereo and a bookcase filled with hardcovers. Most people Parnell knew dreamed of living in such a place. Bud Garrett was dying in it.

"He told you," Garrett said.

"What?" Parnell spun around to face Richard, knowing suddenly the worst truth of all.

"He told you."

"Jesus, Bud, you sent him, didn't you?"

"Yes. Yes, I did."

"Why?"

Parnell looked at Garrett again. How could somebody who used to have a weight problem and who could throw around the toughest drunk the barrio ever produced get to be like this. Nearly every time he talked he winced. And all the time he smelled. Bad.

"I sent for you because none of us is perfect," Bud said.

"I don't understand."

"He's afraid."

"Richard?"

"Yes."

"I don't blame him. I'd be afraid too." Parnell paused and stared at Bud. "You asked him to kill you, didn't you?"

"Yes. It's his responsibility to do it."

Richard stepped up to his father's bedside and said, "I agree with that, Mr. Parnell. It is my responsibility. I just need a little help is all."

"Doing what?"

"If I buy cyanide, it will eventually be traced to me and I'll be tried for murder. If you buy it, nobody will ever connect you with my father."

Parnell shook his head. "That's bullshit. That isn't what you want me for. There are a million ways you could get cyanide without having it traced back."

Bud Garrett said, "I told him about you. I told him you could help give him strength."

"I don't agree with any of this, Bud. You should die when it's your time to die. I'm a Catholic."

Bud laughed hoarsely. "So am I, you asshole." He coughed and said, "The pain's bad. I'm beyond any help they can give me. But it could go on for a long time." Then, just as his son had an hour ago, Bud Garrett began crying almost imperceptibly. "I'm scared, Parnell. I don't know what's on the other side but it can't be any worse than this." He reached out his hand and for a long time Parnell just stared at it but then he touched it.

"Jesus," Parnell said. "It's pretty fucking confusing, Bud. It's pretty fucking confusing."

Richard took Parnell out to dinner that night. It was a nice place. The table cloths were starchy white and the waiters all wore shiny shoes. Candles glowed inside red glass.

They'd had four drinks apiece, during which Richard told Parnell about his two sons (six and eight respectively) and about the perils and rewards of the rent-a-car business and about how much he liked windsurfing even though he really wasn't much good at it.

Just after the arrival of the fourth drink, Richard took something from his pocket and laid it on the table.

It was a cold capsule.

"You know how the Tylenol Killer in Chicago operated?" Richard asked.

Parnell nodded.

"Same thing," Richard said. "I took the cyanide and put it in a capsule."

"Christ. I don't know about it."

"You're scared too, aren't you?"

"Yeah, I am."

Richard sipped his whiskey-and-soda. With his regimental striped tie he might have been sitting in a country club. "May I ask you something?"

"Maybe."

"Do you believe in God?"

"Sure."

"Then if you believe in God, you must believe in goodness, correct?"

Parnell frowned. "I'm not much of an intellectual, Richard."

"But if you believe in God, you must believe in goodness, right?"

"Right."

"Do you think what's happening to my father is good?"

"Of course I don't."

"Then you must also believe that God isn't doing this to him—right?"

"Right."

Richard held up the capsule. Stared at it. "All I want you to do is give me a ride to the hospital. Then just wait in the car down in the parking lot."

"I won't do it."

Richard signaled for another round.

"I won't god damn do it," Parnell said.

By the time they left the restaurant Richard was too drunk to drive. Parnell got behind the wheel of the new Audi. "Why don't you tell me where you live? I'll take you home and take a cab from there."

"I want to go to the hospital."

"No way, Richard."

Richard slammed his fist against the dashboard. "You

fucking owe him that, man!" he screamed.

Parnell was shocked, and a bit impressed, with Richard's violent side. If nothing else, he saw how much Richard loved his old man.

"Richard, listen."

Richard sat in a heap against the opposite door. His tears were dry ones, choking ones. "Don't give me any of your speeches." He wiped snot from his nose on his sleeve. "My Dad always told me what a tough guy Parnell was." He turned to Parnell, anger in him again. "Well, I'm not tough, Parnell, and so I need to borrow some of your toughness so I can get that man out of his pain and grant him his one last fucking wish. DO YOU GOD DAMN UNDERSTAND ME?"

He smashed his fist on the dashboard again.

Parnell turned on the ignition and drove them away.

When they reached the hospital, Parnell found a parking spot and pulled in. The mercury vapor lights made him feel as though he were on Mars. Bugs smashed against the windshield.

"I'll wait here for you," Parnell said.

Richard looked over at him. "You won't call the cops?"

"No."

"And you won't come up and try to stop me?"

"No."

Richard studied Parnell's face. "Why did you change your mind?"

"Because I'm like him."

"Like my father?"

"Yeah. A coward. I wouldn't want the pain either. I'd be just as afraid."

All Richard said, and this he barely whispered, was "Thanks."

While he sat there Parnell listened to country western music and then a serious political call-in show and then a call-in show where a lady talked about Venusians who wanted to pork her and then some salsa music and then a religious minister who sounded like Foghorn Leghorn in the old Warner Brothers cartoons.

By then Richard came back.

He got in the car and slammed the door shut and said, completely sober now, "Let's go."

Parnell got out of there.

They went ten long blocks before Parnell said, "You didn't do it, did you?"

Richard got hysterical. "You sonofabitch! You sonofabitch!"

Parnell had to pull the car over to the curb. He hit Richard once, a fast clean right hand, not enough to make him unconscious but enough to calm him down.

"You didn't do it, did you?"

"He's my father, Parnell. I don't know what to do. I love him so much I don't want to see him suffer. But I love him so much I don't want to see him die, either."

Parnell let the kid sob. He thought of his old friend Bud Garrett and what a good goddamn fun buddy he'd been and then he started crying, too.

When Parnell came down Richard was behind the steering wheel.

Parnell got in the car and looked around the empty parking lot and said, "Drive."

"Any place especially?"

"Out along the East River road. Your old man and I used to fish off that little bridge there."

Richard drove them. From inside his sportcoat Parnell took the pint of Jim Beam.

When they got to the bridge Parnell said, "Give me five minutes alone and then you can come over, ok?"

Richard was starting to sob again.

Parnell got out of the car and went over to the bridge. In the hot night you could hear the hydroelectric dam half a mile downstream and smell the fish and feel the mosquitoes feasting their way through the evening.

He thought of what Bud Garrett had said, "Put it in some

whiskey for me, will you?"

So Parnell had obliged.

He stood now on the bridge looking up at the yellow circle of moon thinking about dead people, his wife and many of his WWII friends, the rookie cop who'd died of a sudden tumor, his wife with her rosary-wrapped hands. Hell, there was probably even a chance that nurse from Enid, Oklahoma was dead.

"What do you think's on the other side?" Bud Garrett had asked just half-an-hour ago. He'd almost sounded excited. As if he were a farm kid about to ship out with the Merchant Marines.

"I don't know," Parnell had said.

"It scare you, Parnell?"

"Yeah," Parnell had said. "Yeah it does."

Then Bud Garrett had laughed. "Don't tell the kid that. I always told him that nothin' scared you."

Richard came up the bridge after a time. At first he stood maybe a hundred feet away from Parnell. He leaned his elbows on the concrete and looked out at the water and the moon. Parnell watched him, knowing it was all Richard, or anybody, could do.

Look out at the water and the moon and think about dead people and how you yourself would soon enough be dead.

Richard turned to Parnell then and said, his tears gone completely now, sounding for the first time like Parnell's sort of man, "You know, Parnell, my father was right. You're a brave sonofabitch. You really are."

Parnell knew it was important for Richard to believe that— that there were actually people in the world who didn't fear things the way most people did—so Parnell didn't answer him at all.

He just took his pint out and had himself a swig and looked some more at the moon and the water.

The most frightening thing I ever saw was a five-year-old boy—a friend of mine—trying to stop his father from killing his mother. The man kept beating and beating and beating his wife in the face. My friend and I flung ourselves on his father's back but it was no use. My father, downstairs, heard us screaming and ran to the apartment upstairs.

My father grabbed the man just in time. The woman was unconscious on the floor. Her husband had started to kick her in the ribs.

All during the beating, my friend's seven-year-old sister stood in the corner, watching. The girl was considered "slow" because she rarely spoke. When I was older, I was told why she didn't speak. Her father regularly forced her into his bed and since then she'd kept pretty much to herself.

She became even quieter as we got older, pretty but already dead, at least spiritually. Physical death came when she was eighteen, of drugs, most likely suicide.

THE COMING OF NIGHT,
THE PASSING OF DAY

Penny knew Mr. Rigler's schedule pretty well. After all, Mr.
Rigler's eleven-year-old daughter Louise happened to be
Penny's best friend.

So Penny knew just when to do it, just when to walk down
the alley, just when to climb the slanting covered stairs that led
up to the rear apartment, just when to find Mr. Rigler in the
wide, sagging double bed where he slept off the hangovers he
inflicted on himself after working the night shift at Raylon
Manufacturing.

Penny—dressed in a white blouse and jeans and a pair of
Keds (Mom always saying, "Jesus Christ, kid, you think I'm
made outta fucking money?" whenever Penny brought up the
subject of Reeboks)—Penny moved through the noonday heat
pretty and shy as one of the soft blue butterflies she liked to lie
on the grass sometimes and watch.

On her back was the red nylon pack she carried to school
every day. Inside it always smelled of the baloney sandwiches
and Ho-Hos Mom always packed for her lunch.

She turned off the gravel alley and into the small junkyard
of rusting cars that belonged to Mr. Rigler. He was always

promising his wife and daughter that he was going to clean up the backyard someday—"Get ridda them eyesores once and for all"—but that was sort of like his promise that he was someday going to stop beating his wife and daughter, too. He hadn't kept that promise, either.

A week ago Mr. Rigler had broken Louise's arm in three places. He'd first hit her in the mouth with his fist and then shoved her over an ottoman. She'd tripped and smashed her arm. Mr. Rigler was pretty drunk, of course. There was so much shouting and yelling that half the block ran into the alley to see what was going on and then two cop cars came screaming down the street and the cops jumped out and they pushed Mr. Rigler around pretty hard, even though he was so drunk he could hardly stand up, and then Mrs. Rigler (who'd been screaming for them to arrest him) started crying and saying how it was all an accident and the cops looked real frustrated and mad and said you mean you aren't going to press charges, and Mrs. Rigler kept crying and holding on to her husband like he was some kind of prize she didn't want to lose and saying no, she wouldn't press charges because it was all an accident and if those fuckin' cops knew what was good for them they'd get off her fuckin' property and right now. So the cops had left and Mrs. Rigler had taken Louise to the emergency ward.

Next day, Louise came over and showed Penny her cast and talked about how weird it felt to have something like this on your arm and how much her arm hurt and how she'd had to get five different x-rays and how cute the young doctor was. Then she'd started crying, the way she usually did after her father had beaten her or her mother, started sobbing and Penny had taken her into her arms and held her and said over and over that sonofabitch that sonofabitch and then Louise had said why couldn't something happen to her father the way it had to Mr. Menetti, who used to beat his wife and child just the same way. But then one day they found Mr. Menetti burned char black in his bed. Seems he'd been drunk and smoking and dropped his cigarette and the whole bed had gone up in flames.

Fortunately, the afternoon with Louise had gotten a little better. They both liked to smoke cigarettes so Penny got out the Winston Lights she stole one-at-a-time from her mother and they sat in front of the TV and watched MTV and drank Pepsi and told kind of semi-dirty jokes and laughed and gossiped about boys at school and generally had a good time until Bob came home.

Bob was Mom's newest boyfriend. He'd lived with them for a year now. He was a used car salesman, one of the few men on the block to wear a necktie to work, which Mom thought was real cool for some reason. He had black wavy hair and very white teeth and you could tell by the way he looked at you that he really thought he was pretty hot stuff. On all his sport coats you could see a fine white powder of dust from walking around the car lot all day.

Penny hated Bob but Mom loved him. After she'd been dumped by her last boyfriend, Mom had tried to kill herself with tranquilizers. She'd ended up getting her stomach pumped and staying in a mental hospital for three weeks while Penny lived with her aunt. Mom hadn't really snapped out of it for a whole year, till she met Bob. Now Mom was her old self again. "Oh, hon, if Bob'd ever leave me, I just don't know what I'd do," Mom would always say after she and Bob had had a fight. And Penny would get scared. Maybe next time Mom actually would kill herself.

She thought of all these things in an instant as she watched Bob's slow, sly smile.

Now, he stood there staring down at Penny so long that Louise finally got up and said it was time she git and so she got and Bob said then, "Your Mom's not gonna be home for another couple hours."

But Penny didn't want to think about Bob now. She wanted to think about Mr. Rigler. The way she'd thought about Mr. Menetti before him and Mr. Stufflebeam before him (Mr. Stufflebeam was another who frequently used his fists on his family).

She went up the stairs quickly.

The covered porch smelled of heat and spaghetti from last night. From the downstairs apartment came the sounds of dorky country music and a little baby crying. In this kind of heat babies usually cried.

At the screen door, she knocked once and then listened very carefully. She didn't hear anybody talking or moving around. Louise, she knew, was across the city at a movie with her cousin. Mrs. Rigler was at the restaurant where she was a short-order cook.

And Mr. Rigler was sleeping off his drunk. He'd get up at two, shave, shower, fix himself something to eat, and then head for the factory in an old Ford that was nearly as junky as those dying beasts he kept in the backyard.

"Mr. Rigler?" she called.

She could hear a window air-conditioner roaring and rattling in the distance. But nothing else.

"Mr. Rigler?"

She waited a full two minutes and then went inside.

The apartment smelled of cigarettes and beer and spaghetti. Dirty dishes packed the sink. Without both arms, Louise could hardly do housework.

Penny went through the kitchen into the living room where aged overstuffed furniture was all covered with decorator sheets so they'd look newer.

The bedrooms and the bathroom were down a hall.

She was halfway down the hall when she picked up his snoring. He was really out.

When she reached the door, she peeked in and saw him on the bed. He wore a sleeveless t-shirt. You could see his huge hairy belly riding up and down beneath it as he breathed. His face was dark with stubble. The panther tattoo on his fleshy right arm looked as faded as the flesh itself. He smelled of beer and onions and cigarettes and farts. Penny's stomach grabbed momentarily.

She stood watching him. Just watching him. She wasn't even sure why.

She thought of Louise's arm. The way it must hurt. She thought about the time Louise's Mom had gotten her collarbone broken. And the time he'd given her not one but two black eyes.

He was the same kind of man Mr. Menetti had been. The same kind of man Mr. Stufflebeam had been.

"You sonofabitch," she said to the man who lay there in the silence in the bedroom. "You fucking sonofabitch."

Then she got to work.

Penny was back in her apartment watching a "Happy Days" rerun—she dreamed of a world as nice as the one Richie Cunningham lived in—when she heard the first truck rumbling down the brick street, siren singing.

They'd hurry in there with their axes and their hoses but it would be too late. Just as it had been too late with Mr. Menetti and Mr. Stufflebeam. Asphyxiation, was the word that had been in all the newspaper articles.

After a time, she went out on the fire escape and looked across five back yards to where the two red fire trucks filled the alley. Maybe as many as forty or fifty neighbors had come out to watch.

The ambulance came next, a big white box, two attendants rushing over to the back stairs.

After a time, Penny went in and opened a Pepsi and turned on MTV. She really liked the new Whitney Houston video. She hoped they'd play that before three o'clock, which was when she had to be out of the apartment. Before Bob got home.

At two-thirty, she was in the bedroom, tugging on a fresh Madonna t-shirt, when she heard the front door open and shut.

It could have been Mom but she knew better.

She knew damned well who it was.

By the time she was finished pulling on the t-shirt, he was leaning in the doorway, a smirk on his mouth and a cigarette in his hand.

"Hey, babe, how's it goin'?"

"I'm on my way out."

"Oh, yeah? To where?"

"The park."

"Your Mom don't like for you to go to the park."

"Yeah," Penny said, staring right at Bob and knowing he'd get her meaning. "She's afraid a child molester will get me."

He was still smiling, even when he took two quick steps across the room to her, even when he slapped her hard across the mouth.

"That crack about the child molester s'posed to be funny, you little bitch?"

She fought her tears. She didn't ever want him to see her cry. Ever.

"Huh? That s'posed to be funny?"

She didn't want to say anything, either, but she hated him too much and words were her only weapon. "I could tell her. I could tell her what you been doin' to me in the bathroom."

At first, Bob visibly paled. This was the first time she'd ever threatened him this way. And there was great satisfaction in watching him lose his self-confidence and look scared.

But he quickly recovered himself. She could see cunning now in his stupid blue gaze; he was Bob the used car salesman once again.

"You know what she'd do if you told her about us?"

"She'd throw you out," Penny said. "That's what she'd do."

"Yeah. Yeah, she probably would. But you know what she'd do then?"

He drew a long, white finger slowly across his throat. "She'd kill herself. 'Cause I'm the only hope she's got. The only damned hope she's got in the whole wide world. She's never had no other man stay with her as long as I have, not even your old man, that sorry sonofabitch."

She started to say something but he held up his hand for silence.

"I'm goin' in the bathroom and I want you in there in five minutes."

"No."

He stared at her. "Five minutes, you understand me, you

little bitch?"

She shook her head.

He grinned. He was the old Bob again. "Five minutes, babe. Then I'll take you out to the mall and buy you a new blouse. How'd that be?"

She had the satisfaction of watching him panic again.

She took three steps back to the nightstand and picked up the phone.

She didn't threaten, this time. She simply dialed her Mom's work number and before he could slap the phone from her hand, she said, "This is Penny Baker. I'd like to speak to my Mom please. Thank you."

"You little bitch—"

"Hi, Mom."

She almost laughed. Bob almost looked funny. He'd totally lost it. Was starting to pace back and forth, running a trembling hand through his hair.

"Hi, honey, everything all right?"

"I just wanted to talk to you, Mom."

"Hon, I'm kinda busy right now. Is it real important?"

"It's about Bob."

He made a big fist and shook it at her.

"Bob?" Mom said. "What about him, hon?"

"Just that—"

But Mom didn't wait. "Nothin' happened to him, did it?"

"No, Mom I—"

"Oh, God, hon, I have nightmares all the time about somethin' happening to him. Getting hit by a car in a crosswalk or gettin' mugged somewhere or—"

Penny heard the need, then, heard it more clearly than ever before, the child-like need her mother felt for Bob. Bob hadn't been exaggerating when he'd said that her mother would kill herself if he left.

"You gonna tell me, hon?" Mom said, still sounding crazy with fear.

"Tell you?"

"Why you called, hon? Jesus, Pen, this is scaring the shit

out of me."

"I just called to—"

"—yes?—"

"Tell you that Bob—"

And now Bob moved closer. She could smell his sweat and his aftershave. And in his eyes now she could see pleading; *oh, please, Penny, don't tell her; please don't tell her.*

"Tell me what, hon? Jesus, please just say it."

"That Bob's going to take me to the mall."

And then Mom started laughing. "God, hon, that's what you wanted to tell me?"

Bob knew enough not to approach her.

He just stood there a few feet away from her and held his hands up to God as if in supplication and gratitude.

"That's all you wanted to tell me?"

"Yes," Penny said. "That's all I wanted to tell you."

A few minutes later, Bob was in the bathroom. The water was running and the medicine cabinet closing. He liked to get himself all cleaned up for her down there, he always said.

Penny lay on the bed. She listened to a distant lawn mower on the summer afternoon.

The water in the bathroom stopped running.

After a time, the door opened and he said, "You can come in here now."

She didn't get up. Not at first.

She lay there for a time and thought of Mr. Rigler and Mr. Menetti and Mr. Stufflebeam.

The smoke and the fire and the too-late screams.

She saw Bob lying on such a bed now. And heard his own too-late screams.

"You don't want to keep old Bob waitin' now, do you, babe?" he called again.

Oh, yes, someday it would happen; somehow. Bob on the bed with his too-late screams.

And then she got up and went into the bathroom.

We kill so many people off in our stories that I worry we have no sense of real death, or the true spiritual cost of dying.

In this story, I wanted to give death at least a little dominion.

THE LONG SILENCE AFTER

The flight from Baltimore was bumpy. Not that Neely cared much. Not now.

At Hertz he asked for a city map. The counter woman, sweet in her chignon and early evening exhaustion, smiled sadly. As if she knew why he'd come here. She gave him the map and a brand new Buick that did not yet smell as if somebody had barfed in it and then covered up the stench with Air-Wick.

He had one more stop to make. The Fed-Ex office near O'Hare. A package waited there for him. He did not unwrap it until he got back to the car.

Inside the red white and blue wrapping, inside the well-lined box, he found what he'd sent himself here last night; a snub-nosed .38. From the adjacent small box he took the cartridges. He would never have gotten this stuff through airport security.

Finally now, he was ready.

He spent four hours driving. Street names meant nothing. Sometimes faces were white, sometimes black. He wanted a certain section. Three times he stopped at gas stations and described the area. How there was this drugstore on one corner and a Triple-XXX theater directly across the street and (cheap irony here) a big stone Catholic church a couple blocks down.

Finally, one guy said, Oh, yeah, and told him where he'd

find it in relationship to Rogers Park (which was where he was now).

Around nine, just before he saw the drugstore and the XXX-theater, it started raining. Cold March rain. Beading on the windshield, giving all the neon the look of watercolors.

He found a parking garage. A black guy who had a big chaw of chewing tobacco kept spitting all the time he was taking the keys. And kind of glaring. Fucking suburban white dudes. Motherfuckers anyway.

In the front of the XXX-theater was a small shop where you could rent videos and buy various "appliances" (as they are called). He was never comfortable in such places. Probably his strict Lutheran upbringing. These are places of sin.

The man behind the counter had bad teeth and a wandering left eye. Somehow that was fitting in a place like this.

He described the woman he was looking for but the counterman immediately shook his head. "Don't know her, pal."

He described the woman a little more but the man shook his head again. "Sorry," he said exhaling Pall Mall smoke through the brown stubs of his teeth.

He didn't expect to get lucky right off, and he sure didn't. He started at the west end of the street and worked down it: three bars, a massage parlor, a used clothing store, a tiny soup kitchen run by two old nuns, and a bar with a runway for strippers.

And nothing.

Sorry, my friend. Sorry, buddy. Sorry, Jack.

Never seen/heard of her. You know, pal?

And so then he started on the women themselves.

Because of the rain, which was steady and cold, they stood in doorways instead of along the curbsides. The thirty-four degree temperature kept them from any cute stuff. No whistling down drivers. No shaking their asses. No jumping into the streets.

Just huddling in doorways instead. And kind of shivering. And it was the same with them: no help.

He'd describe her and they'd shrug or shake their heads or pretend they were thinking a long moment and go "Nope, 'fraid not, friend."

Only one of them got smart-mouth. She said, "She musta been somethin' really special, huh?" and all the time was rubbing her knuckles against his crotch.

Inside his nice respectable topcoat, the .38 was burning a fucking hole.

Around midnight he stopped in this small diner for coffee and a sandwich. He was tired, he already had sniffles from the cold steady rain, and he had a headache, too. He bought his food and a little aluminum deal of Bufferin and took them right down.

And then he asked the counter guy—having no hopes really, just asking the guy kind of automatically—and the guy looked at him and said, "Yeah. Betty."

"Yes. That's right. Her name was Betty."

Through the fog of four years, through the fog of a liquored-up night: yes, goddamit that's right, Betty was her name. Betty.

He asked, "Is she still around?"

The counter man, long hairy tattoed arms, leaned forward and gave him a kind of queer look. "Oh, yeah, she's still around."

The counter man sounded as if he expected the man to know what he was hinting at.

"You know where I can find her?"

The counter man shook his head. "I don't know if that'd be right, mister."

"How come?"

He shrugged. "Well, she's sort of a friend of mine."

"I see."

And from inside his respectable suburban topcoat, he took

his long leather wallet and peeled off a twenty and laid it on the counter and felt like fucking Sam Spade. "I'd really like to talk to her tonight."

The counter man stared at the twenty. He licked dry lips with an obscene pink tongue. "I see what you mean."

"How about it?"

"She really is kind of a friend of mine."

So Sam Spade went back into action. He laid another crisp twenty on the original crisp twenty.

The tongue came out again. This time he couldn't watch the counter man. He pretended to be real interested in the coffee inside his cheap chipped cup.

So of course the counter man gave him her address and told him how to get there.

Fog. Rain. The sound of his footsteps. You could smell the rotting lumber of this ancient neighborhood now that it was soaked. Little shabby houses packed so close together you couldn't ride a bicycle between some of them. One-story brick jobs mostly that used to be packed with Slavs. But the Slavs have good factory jobs now so they had moved out and eager scared blacks had taken their place.

Hers was lime green stucco. Behind a heavy drape a faint light shone.

He gripped the gun.

On the sidewalk he stepped in two piles of dogshit. And now the next-door dog—as if to confirm his own existence—started barking.

He went up the narrow walk to her place.

He stood under the overhang. The concrete porch had long ago pulled away from the house and was wobbly. He felt as if he were trying to stand up on a capsizing row boat.

The door opened. A woman stood there. "Yes?"

His memory of her was that she'd been much heavier. Much.

He said, "Betty?"

"Right."

"Betty Malloy?"

"Right again." She sounded tired, even weak. "But not the old Betty Malloy."

"Beg pardon?"

"I ain't what I used to be."

Cryptic as her words were, he thought that they still made sense.

"I'd like to come in."

"Listen, I don't do that no more, all right?"

"I'd like to come in anyway."

"Why?"

He sighed. If he pulled the gun here, she might get the chance to slam the door and save herself.

He had to get inside.

He put his hand on the knob of the screen door.

It was latched.

Sonofabitch.

"I need to use your phone," he said.

"Who are you?"

In some naive way, he'd expected her to remember who he was. But of course she wouldn't.

"Could I use your phone?"

"For what?"

"To call Triple-A."

"Something's wrong with your car?"

"The battery went dead."

"Where's your car?"

"What?"

"I asked where your car was. I don't see no new car. And you definitely look like the kind of guy who'd be driving a new car."

So he decided screw it and pulled the gun.

He put it right up against the screen door.

She didn't cry out or slam the door or anything. She just stood there. The gun had mesmerized her.

"You gotta be crazy, mister."

"Unlatch the door."

"I ain't got no money, man. I ain't got nothing you'd want. Believe me."

"Just unlatch the fucking door or I start shooting."

"My God, mister, I don't know what this could be about. I really don't."

But she unlatched the door and he went inside.

He closed and locked both doors behind him.

He turned around and looked at the small living room she stood in. The first thing he noticed was that she had not one but two velvet paintings of Jesus above the worn and frayed couch. There was a 17-inch color tv set playing a late movie with Sandra Dee. There was a pressed wood coffee table with only three legs, a stack of paperback books substituting for the missing leg.

She sat on the couch.

He pointed the gun at her.

She said, sounding exhausted now, "You look crazy, mister. I can't help but tell you the truth. You really look crazy."

And now he had some idea of how much weight she'd lost. Maybe forty, fifty pounds. And her facial skin was pulled drum-tight over her cheekbones. And her pallor was gray.

There was a bad odor in the place, too, and he didn't have to ask what it was.

"You fucking bitch," he said, waving the gun at her. She'd been right. He heard his words. He was crazy.

She looked up at him from sad and weary eyes. "I'm so tired, mister, just from walking over to the door that I can't— What do you want anyway?"

"You know this is pretty goddamn funny."

"What is?"

He started pacing. For a time he didn't talk. Just paced. She watched him. The floorboards creaked as he walked over them.

"You destroy me and you don't even remember who I am? That's pretty goddamned good."

And then she said, seeming to know everything suddenly, "Oh, shit, mister. Now I know why you come here. And all I can say is I'm sorry."

He turned on her, seized with his fury. "I've got a wife and two children. I've got a good business. I'm not gay or some junkie or—"

She said, and now her breathing was ragged, and she looked suddenly spent: "How long have you known?"

But he didn't want to answer questions.

He wanted to shake the gun in her face, the gun that signified how trapped and outraged he felt.

And so he shook it. He went right up to her and shook it in her face and said, "You fucking bitch, couldn't you have had yourself checked out before you went on the streets?"

Because that was how it had happened. Him visiting Chicago for an insurance convention. Some executive friend of his from Milwaukee who really liked slumming bringing him down here for a little "black poontang" and—

And a week ago his family doctor, just as incredulous as he was, told him. "David, Jesus Christ, these tests can be wrong sometimes but right now it looks as if—"

Only once in eighteen years of marriage had he been unfaithful.

In Chicago.

Insurance convention.

Black woman.

And now he stood above her. "I can't tell you how badly I want to blow your fucking head off, you bitch."

She looked up at him and said, "Maybe you'd be doing me a favor. I got maybe six months to go myself, mister, and this is some hard way to die, let me tell you." Again she sounded completely spent.

"The worst thing is, I may have infected my wife."

"I know," she said. "My old man left me when he found out. But it's probably too late for him, too."

"You fucking bitch!" he said, no longer able to control himself.

He brought the gun down hard across her jaw.

Almost immediately she started sobbing.

And then he couldn't hit her anymore.

He heard in her tears the inevitable tears of his wife and children when they found out.

And he couldn't hit her at all any more.

She just sat there and sobbed, her whole body trembling, weaker with each moment.

He said, "I'm sorry."

She just kept crying.

He started pacing again.

"I can't believe this. I keep thinking that there's no way I could—"

He shook his head and looked over at her. She was daubing at her nose with an aqua piece of Kleenex.

"Do you get help?"

She nodded. She wouldn't look at him anymore. "The welfare folks. They send out people."

"I'm sorry I was so angry."

"I know."

"And I'm sorry I hit you."

"I know that too."

"I'm just so fucking scared and so fucking angry."

Now she looked at him again. "The anger goes after awhile. You get too tired to be angry anymore."

"I don't know how I'm going to tell my wife."

"You'll do it, mister. That's the only thing I figured out about this thing. You do what you've got to do. You really do."

He dumped the gun in the pocket of his respectable topcoat. And then he took out his wallet and flicked off a hundred dollars in twenties.

"You really must be crazy, mister," she said. "Leavin' me money like that."

"Yes," he said. "I really must be crazy."

She started crying again.

He closed the doors quietly behind him. Even halfway down the walk, even in the fog and even in the rain, he could still hear her crying.

There was a three o'clock flight to Baltimore. He wasn't

sure he had nerve enough to tell her yet but he knew he would have to. He owed her so much; he certainly owed her the truth.

He walked faster now, and soon he disappeared completely inside the fog. He was just footsteps now; footsteps.

Ray Bradbury's "The Dwarf" has long been one of my favorite stories, one of those rare works of art that can truthfully be called perfect. But just as memorable as the sad and doomed dwarf himself is the young woman Aimee. It's not easy to create a person who is innately good because you run the risk of drawing somebody who is little more than a plaster saint, one of the those "virtuous" women of the old slicks. But Bradbury made her real, painfully so, and honorable and fine and true.

I never forgot Aimee and so when Bill Nolan asked me to write a story in honor of Bradbury, I decided to make it about her. I wanted to meet Aimee again—walk with her in the hot carnival night—and I decided this was the best way.

THE WIND FROM MIDNIGHT

Even with the windows open, the Greyhound bus was hot inside as it roared through the rural California night.

Plump ladies in sweat-soaked summer dresses furiously worked paper fans that bore the names of funeral parlors. Plump men in sleeveless t-shirts sat talking of disappointing baseball scores ("Them Goddamn Red Sox just don't have it this year; nossir they don't") and the Republican convention that had just nominated Dwight Eisenhower. Most of the men aboard liked Ike and liked him quite a bit. These men smoked Lucky Strikes and Chesterfields and Fatimas and more than a few of them snuck quick silver flasks from their hip pockets.

In the middle of the bus was a slender, pretty woman who inexplicably burst into tears every twenty miles or so. It was assumed by all who watched her that she was having man trouble of some sort. A woman this pretty wouldn't carry on so otherwise. She'd been deserted and was heading home to Mama was the consensus aboard the Greyhound.

Traveling with the pretty woman was a sweet-faced little girl who was obviously the daughter. She was maybe five or six and wore a faded white dress that reminded some of First Communion and patent-leather shoes that reminded others of Shirley Temple. For the most part she was well-behaved, the little girl, stroking and petting her mama when she cried, and sitting prim and obedient when mama was just looking sadly out the window.

But fifty miles ago the little girl had gone back to use the restroom—she'd had a big nickel Pepsi and it had gone right through her—and there she'd seen the tiny woman sitting all by herself in one corner of the vast back seat.

All the little girl could think of—and this was what she whispered to her mama later—was a doll that had come to life.

Before the bus pulled into the oceanside town for a rest stop, the little girl found exactly four excuses to run back there and get another good peek at the tiny woman.

She just couldn't believe what she was seeing.

A lot of passengers hurried to get off the bus so they could stand around the front of the depot and get a good look at her. In the rolling darkness of the Greyhound, they hadn't really gotten much of a glimpse and they were just naturally curious, these kind of people.

She didn't disappoint them.

She was just as tiny as she'd seemed and in her plain white blouse and her navy linen skirt and her dark seamed hose and her cute little pumps with the two-inch heels she looked like a five-year-old who was all dressed up in her Mama's clothes.

Back on the bus they'd argued in whispers whether she was a dwarf or a midget. There was some scientific difference between the two but damned if anybody could remember exactly what that was.

From inside the depot came smells of hamburgers and onions and french fries and cigar smoke, all stale on the still summer air. Also from inside came the sounds of Miss Kay Starr singing "The Wheel of Fortune." Skinny white cowboys clung like moths to the lights of the depot entrance as did old black men the color of soot and snappy young sailors in their dress whites and hayseed grins.

This was the scene the tiny woman confronted. And in moments she was gone from it.

The cabbie knew where the carnival was, of course. There would be only one in a burg like this.

He drove his rattling '47 Plymouth out to the pier where the midway and all the rides looked like the toys of a baby giant.

He drove her right up to the entrance and said, "That'll be eighty-five cents, miss."

She opened her purse and sank a tiny hand into its deep waiting darkness.

She gave him a dollar's worth of quarters and said, "That's for you."

"Why, thank you."

She opened the door. The dome light came on. He noticed for the first time that she was nice-looking. Not gorgeous or anything like that. But nice-looking. Silken dark hair in a page boy. Blue eyes that would have been beautiful if they weren't tainted with sorrow. And a full mouth so erotic it made him uncomfortable. Why if a normal-sized man was to try anything with a tiny woman like this—

He put the thought from his mind.

As she started to leave the cab, he just blurted it out. "I suppose you know what happened here a month ago. About the—little guy, I mean."

She just looked at him.

"He stole a gun from one of the carnies here and raced back to his hotel room and killed himself." The cabbie figured that the tiny woman would want to know about it, her being just like the little guy and all. To show he was friendly, the cabbie always told colored people stories about colored people in just the same way.

The cabbie's head was turned in profile, waiting for the woman to respond.

But the only sound, faint among the *crack* of air rifles and the roar of the rollercoaster and the high piping pitch of the calliope, was the cab door being quietly closed.

A lady with a beard, a man with a vagina. A chance to get your fortune told by a gypsy woman with a knife scar on her left cheek. A sobbing little blonde boy looking frantically for his lost mother. A man just off the midway slapping hard a woman he called a fucking whore bitch. An old man in a straw hat gaping fixedly at a chunky stripper the barker kept pointing to with a long wooden cane.

Linnette saw all these things and realized why her brother had always liked carnivals. She liked them for the same reason. Because in all the spectacle—beautiful and ugly, happy and sad alike—tiny people tended to get overlooked. There was so much to see and do and feel and desire that normal people barely gave tiny people a glance.

And that's why, for many of his thirty-one years, her brother had been drawn to midways.

He told her about this one, of course, many times. How he came here after a long day at the typewriter. How he liked to sit on a bench up near the shooting gallery and watch the women go by and try and imagine what they'd be like if he had had the chance to meet them. He was such a romantic, her brother, in his heart a matinee-idol worthy of Valentino and Gable.

She'd learned all this from his infrequent phone calls. He always called at dinner time on Sunday evening because of the rates and he always talked nine minutes exactly. He always asked her how things were going at the library where she worked and she always asked him if he was ever going to write that important novel she knew he had in him.

They were brother and sister, and more, of course, which was why, when he'd put that gun to his head there in the dim little coffin of a room where he lived and wrote—

She tried not to think of these things now.

She worked her way through the crowd, moving slowly toward the steady *cracking* sounds of the shooting gallery. A Mr. Kelly was who she was looking for.

A woman given to worry and anxiety, she kept checking the new white number ten envelope in her purse. One hundred dollars in crisp green currency. Certainly that should be enough for Mr. Kelly.

Aimee was taking a cigarette break when she happened to see Linnette. She'd spent the last month trying to forget about the dwarf and the part Ralph Banghart, the man who ran the

MIRROR MAZE, had played in the death of the dwarf.

And the part Aimee had played, too.

Maybe if she'd never gotten involved, never tried to help the poor little guy—

Aimee lit her next Cavalier with the dying ember of her previous Cavalier.

Standing next to the tent she worked, Aimee reached down to retrieve the Coke she'd set in the grass.

And just as she bent over, she felt big male hands slip over her slender hips. "Booo!"

She jerked away from him immediately. She saw him now as this diseased person. Whatever ugliness he had inside him, she didn't want to catch.

"I told you, Ralph, I don't ever want you touching me again."

"Aw, babe, I just—"

She slapped him. And hard enough that his head jerked back and a grunt of pain sounded in his throat.

"Hey—"

"You still don't give a damn that little guy killed himself, do you?"

Ralph rubbed his sore cheek. "I didn't kill him."

"Sure you did. You're just not man enough to admit it. If you hadn't played that practical joke on him—"

"If the little bastard couldn't take a joke—"

She raised her hand to slap him again. Grinning, he started to duck away.

She spit at him. This, he didn't have time to duck away from. She got him right on the nose.

"I don't want you to come anywhere goddamn near me, do you understand?" Aimee said, knowing she was shrieking and not caring.

Ralph, looked around, embarrassed now that people were starting to watch, shook his head and muttered some curses, and left, daubing off the spittle with his white soiled handkerchief.

Aimee tossed her cigarette into the summer dry grass and

started looking around for the dwarf woman again.

She just had this sense that the woman had somehow known the little guy who'd killed himself.

Aimee just had to find her and talk to her. Just had to.

She started searching.

Mr. Kelly turned out to be a big man with an anchor tattoo on his right forearm and beads of silver sweat standing in rows on his pink bald pate.

At the moment he was showing a woman with huge breasts how to operate an air rifle. Mr. Kelly kept nudging her accidentally-on-purpose with his elbow. If the woman minded, she didn't complain. But then the woman's boyfriend came back from somewhere and he looked to be about the same size but younger and trimmer than Mr. Kelly so Mr. Kelly withdrew his elbow and let the boyfriend take over the shooting lessons.

Then Mr. Kelly turned to Linnette. "What can I do for ya, small fry?"

Linnette always told herself that insults didn't matter. Sticks and stones and all that. And most of the time they didn't. But every once in a while, as right now for instance, they pierced the heart like a fatal sliver of glass.

"My name is Linnette Dobbins."

"So? My name is Frank Kelly."

"A month or so ago my brother stole a gun from you and—"

Smiles made most people look pleasant. But Mr. Kelly's smile only served to make him look knowing and dirty. "Oh, the dwarf." He looked her up and down. "Sure. I should've figured that out for myself."

"The police informed me that they've given you the gun back."

"Yeah. What about it?"

"I'd like to buy it from you."

"Buy it from me? What the hell're you talkin' about, small fry?"

Mr. Kelly was just about to go on when a new pair of lovers bellied up to the gallery counter and waited for instructions.

Without excusing himself, Mr. Kelly went over to the lovers, picked up an air rifle and started demonstrating how to win the gal here a nice little teddy bear.

"A dwarf, you say?"

Aimee nodded.

"Jeeze, Aimee, I think I'd remember if I'd seen a dwarf woman wanderin' around the midway."

"Thanks, Hank."

Hank then got kind of flustered and said, "You think we're ever gonna go to a movie sometime Aimee, like I asked you that time?"

She touched his shoulder tenderly and gave him a sweet quick smile. "I'm sure thinking about it, Hank. I really am." Hank was such a nice guy. She just wished he were her type.

And then she was off again, moving frantically around the midway, asking various carnies if they'd seen a woman who was a dwarf.

Hank's was the tenth booth she'd stopped at.

Nobody had seen the woman. Nobody.

"So why would you want the gun your brother killed himself with, small fry?"

From her purse, Linnette took the plain white number ten envelope and handed it up to Mr. Kelly.

"What's this?" he said.

"Look inside."

He opened the envelope flap and peeked in. He ran a pudgy finger through the bills. He whistled. "Hundred bucks."

"Right."

"For a beat up old service revolver. Hell, small fry, you don't know much about guns. You could buy a gun like that in a pawn shop for five bucks."

"The money's all yours."

"Just for this one gun?"

"That's right, Mr. Kelly. Just for this one gun."

He whistled again. The money had made him friendlier.

259

This time his smile lacked malevolence. "Boy, small fry, I almost hate to take your money."

"But you will?"

He gave her a big cornball grin now and she saw in it the fact that he was just as much a hayseed as the rubes he bilked every night. The difference was, he didn't know he was a hayseed.

"You damn bet ya I will," he said, and trotted to the back of the tent to get the gun.

"I'll need some bullets for it, too," Linnette called after him.

He turned around and looked at her. "Bullets? What for?"

"Given the price I'm paying, Mr. Kelly, I'd say that was my business."

He looked at her for a long time and then his cornball grin opened his face up again. "Well, small fry, I guess I can't argue with you on that one now, can I? Bullets it is."

The carnival employed a security man named Bulicek. It was said that he was a former cop who'd gotten caught running a penny ante protection racket on his beat and had been summarily discharged. Here, he always smelled of whiskey and Sen-Sen to cut the stink of the whiskey. He strutted around in his blue uniform with big half-moons of sweat under each arm and a creaking leather holster riding around his considerable girth. His best friend in the carny was Kelly at the shooting gallery, which figured.

Aimee avoided Bulicek because he always managed to put his hands on her in some way whenever they talked. But now she had no choice.

She'd visited seven more carnies since Hank and nobody had seen a woman dwarf.

Bulicek was just coming out of the big whitewashed building that was half men's and half women's.

He smiled when he saw her. She could feel his paws on her already.

"I'm looking for somebody," she said.

"So am I. And I found her." Bulicek knew every bad movie

line in the world.

"A woman who's a dwarf. She's somewhere on the midway. Have you seen her?"

Bulicek shrugged. "What do I get if I tell ya?"

"You get the privilege of doing your job." She tried to keep the anger from her voice. She needed his cooperation.

"And nothing else?" His eyes found a nice place on her body to settle momentarily.

"Nothing else."

He raised his eyes and shook his head and took out a package of cigarettes.

Some teenagers with ducks ass haircuts and black leather jackets—even in this kind of heat for crissakes—wandered by and Bulicek, he-man that he was, gave them the bad eye.

When he turned back to Aimee, she was shocked by his sudden anger. "You think you could talk to me one time, Miss High and Mighty, without making me feel I'm a piece of dogshit?"

"You think you could talk to me one time without copping a cheap feel?"

He surprised her by saying, "I shouldn't do that, Aimee, and I'm sorry. You wanna try and get along?"

She laughed from embarrassment. "God, you're really serious aren't you?"

"Yeah, I am." He put out a hand. "You wanna be friends, Aimee?"

This time the laugh was pure pleasure. "Sure, Bulicek. I'd like to be friends. I really would. You show me some respect and I'll show you some, too."

They shook hands.

"Now, about the dwarf you was askin' about?"

"Yeah? You saw her?" Aimee couldn't keep the excitement from her voice.

Bulicek pointed down the midway. "Seen her 'bout fifteen minutes ago at Kelly's."

Aimee thanked him and started running.

* * *

Linnette had a different taxi driver this time.

This guy was heavy and Mexican. The radio played low, Mexican songs from a station across the border. The guy sure wore a lot of after-shave.

Linnette sat with the gun inside her purse and her purse on her lap.

She looked out the window at the passing streets. Easy to imagine her brother walking across these streets, always the focus of the curious stare and the cold quick smirk. Maybe it was harder for men, she thought. They were expected to be big and strong and—

She opened her purse. The sound was loud in the taxi. She saw the driver's eyes flick up to his rearview and study her. Then his eyes flicked away.

She rode the rest of the way with her hand inside her purse, gripping the gun.

She closed her eyes and tried to imagine her brother's hand on the handle, on the trigger.

She hoped that there was a God somewhere and that all of this made sense somehow, that some people should be born of normal height and others, freaks, be born with no arms or legs or eyes.

Or be born dwarfs.

"Here you are, lady."

He pulled over to the curb and told her the fare.

Once again, she found her money swiftly and paid him off.

He reached over and opened the door for her, studying her all the time. Did it ever occur to him—fat and Mexican and not very well educated—that he looked just as strange to her as she did to him? But no, he wouldn't be the kind of man who'd have an insight like that.

She got out of the cab and he drove away.

Even in a bleak little town like this one, the Ganges Arms was grim. FIREPROOF was much larger than Ganges on the neon sign outside, and the drunk throwing up over by the curb told her more than she wanted to know about the type of man who lived up there.

She couldn't imagine how her brother had managed to survive here six years.

She went inside. The lobby was small and filled with ancient couches that dust rose from like shabby ghosts. A long-dead potted plant filled one corner while a cigarette vending machine filled the other. In the back somewhere a toilet flushed with the roar of an avalanche. A black-and-white tv screen flickered with images of Milton Berle in a dress.

A big woman in a faded housedress that revealed fleshy arms and some kind of terrible rash on her elbows was behind the desk. The woman had a beauty mark that was huge and hairy, like a little animal clinging to her cheek.

She grinned when she saw Linnette.

"You don't have to tell me, sweetie."

"Tell you?"

"Sure. Who you are."

"You know who I am?"

"Sure. You're the little guy's sister. He talked about you all the time."

She leaned over the counter, coughing a cigarette hack that sounded sickeningly phlegmy, and said, "Linnette, right?"

"Right."

The woman grimaced. "Sorry about the little guy."

"Thank you."

"I was the one who found him. He wasn't pretty, believe me."

"Oh."

"And I was the first one who read the note." She shook her head again and put a cigarette in her mouth. "He was pretty gimped up inside, poor little guy."

"Yes; yes he was."

The woman stared at her, not as if Linnette were a freak, but rather curious about why she might be here.

"I was just traveling through," Linnette said quietly. "I thought I might stay here tonight." She hesitated. "Sleep in my brother's room, perhaps."

Now the woman really stared at her. "You sure, hon?"

"Sure?"

"About wantin' to take his room and all? Frankly, it'd give me the creeps."

Linnette opened her purse, reached in for her bills. "I'd just like to see where he lived and worked is all. I'm sure it will be a nice experience."

The woman shrugged beefy shoulders. "You're the boss, hon. You're the boss."

Kelly was arguing with a drunk who claimed that the shooting gallery was rigged. The drunk had been bragging to his girl about what a marksman he'd become in Korea and wanted to do a little showing off. All he'd managed to do was humiliate himself.

Aimee waited as patiently as she could for a few minutes and then she interrupted the drunk—whose girlfriend was now trying to tug him away from making any more of a scene—and said, "Kelly, I'm looking for a woman who's a dwarf. Bulicek said he saw her here."

The drunk turned and looked at Aimee as if she'd just said she'd seen a Martian.

Aimee's remark unsettled the drunk enough that his girlfriend was now able to draw him away, and get themselves lost on the midway.

"Yeah. She was here. So what?"

"Did you talk to her?"

"Yeah."

"About what?"

"What the hell's your interest, Aimee?"

"Kelly, I don't have time to explain. Just please help me, all right?"

Kelly sighed. "Okay, kid, what do you want?"

"What'd she say to you?"

"She said she wanted to buy a gun."

"A gun? What kind of gun?"

"The gun her brother stole from me."

"My God."

"What's wrong?"

"Don't you see?"

"See what, kid? Calm down."

"If she wanted to buy the gun her brother stole from you then maybe she plans to use it on herself just the way her brother did."

Kelly said, "Shit. You know, I never thought of that."

"So you gave her the gun?"

Kelly seemed a little embarrassed now. "Yeah. Gave it to her for a hundred bucks."

"A hundred? But Kelly that isn't worth more than—"

"That's what she offered me for it. So that's what I took, kid. I never said I was no saint."

"Where did she go?"

"Hell, how would I know?"

"God, Kelly, didn't you notice the direction she was going?"

He shrugged. "Down near the entrance, I guess." He looked chastened that he hadn't paid attention.

"Thanks, Kelly. I appreciate it."

And before he could say another word, she was gone, running fast toward the front of the midway.

There was a card table sitting next to the room's only window. It had the uncertain legs of a young colt. He'd put his portable typewriter on it—the one she'd bought him for his birthday ten years ago—and worked long into the night.

The room had a bureau with somebody's initials knifed into the top, a mirror mottled with age, wallpaper stained with moisture, a double bed with a paint-chipped metal headboard, and linoleum so old it was worn to wood in patches.

She tried not to think of all the sad lives that had been lived out here. Men without women; men without hope.

She made sure the door was locked behind her and then came into the room.

She could feel him here, now. She had always believed in ghosts—were ghosts any more unlikely than men and women

265

who only grew to be three-and-a-half feet tall?—and so she spoke out loud to him for the first time since being told of his suicide.

"I hope you know how much I love you, brother," she said, moving across the small, box-like room to the card table, running her fingers across the small indentations the Smith-Corona had made on the surface.

She decided against turning the overhead light on.

The on-and-off red of the neon was good enough.

"I miss you, brother. I hope you know that, too."

She heard the *clack* of a ghostly typewriter; saw her brother's sweet round face smiling up at her after he'd finished a particularly good sentence; listened to the soft sad laughter that only she'd been able to elicit from him.

"I wish you would have called me, brother. I wish you would have told me what you had in mind. You know why?"

She said nothing for a time.

Distant ragged traffic sounds from the highway; the even fainter music of the midway further away in the darkness.

"Because I would have joined you, brother. I would have joined you."

She set her purse on the card table. She unclasped the leather halves and then reached in.

The gun waited there.

She brought out the gun with the reverence of a priest bringing forth something that has been consecrated to God.

She brought out the gun and held it for a time, in silhouette, against the window with the flashing red neon.

And then, slowly, inevitably, she brought the gun to her temple.

And eased the hammer back.

At the entrance, Aimee asked fourteen people if they'd seen the woman. None had. But the fifteenth did, and pointed to a rusted beast of a taxi cab just now pulling in.

Aimee ran to the cab and pushed her head in the front window before the driver even stopped completely.

"The dwarf woman. Where did you take her?"

"Who the hell are you?"

"The woman, where did you take her?" Aimee knew she was screaming. She didn't care.

"Goddamn, lady. You're fucking nuts." But despite his tough words, the cab driver saw that she was going to stay here until she had her answer. He said, "I took her to the Ganges Arms. Why the hell're you so interested, anyway?"

"Then take me there, too," Aimee said, flinging open the back door and diving in. "Take me there, too!"

She went over and sat on the bed.

That would make it easier for everybody. The mess would be confined to the mattress. A mattress you could just throw out.

She lay back on the bed.

Her shoes fell off, one at a time, making sharp noises as they struck the floor.

Two-inch heels, she thought. How pathetic of me. Wanting so desperately to be like other people.

She closed her eyes and let the sorrow come over her. Sorrow for her brother and herself; sorrow for their lives.

She saw him again at his typewriter; heard keys striking the eternal silence.

"I wish you would have told me, brother. I wish you would have. It would have been easier for you. We could have comforted each other."

She raised the hand carrying the gun, brought the gun to her temple once again.

The hammer was still back.

"Can't you go any faster?"

"Maybe you think this is an Indy race car or somethin', huh, lady?"

"God, please; please just go as fast as you can."

"Jes-uz," the cab driver said. "Jes-uz."

She said a prayer, nothing formal, just words that said she

hoped there was a God and that he or she or it or whatever form it took would understand why she was doing this and how much she longed to be with her brother again and that both God and her brother would receive her with open arms.

She tightened her finger on the trigger and then—

—the knock came.

"Hon?"

Oh, my Lord.

"Hon, you awake in there?"

Finding her voice. Clearing her throat. "Yes?"

"Brought you some Kool-Aid. That's what I drink all summer. Raspberry Kool-Aid. Quenches my thirst a lot better than regular pop, you know? Anyway, I brought you a glass. You wanna come get it?"

Did she have any choice?

Linnette lay the gun down on the bed and pulled the purse over the gun.

She got up and straightened her skirt and went to the door.

A long angle of dirty yellow light fell across her from the hallway.

The woman was a lot heavier than she'd looked downstairs. Linnette liked her.

The woman bore a large glass of Kool-Aid in her right hand and a cigarette in her left. She kept flicking her ashes on the hallway floor.

"You like Raspberry?"

"Thank you very much."

"Sometimes I like cherry but tonight I'm just in a kind of raspberry mood. You know?"

"I really appreciate this."

The woman nodded to the stairs. "You get lonely, you can always come down and keep me company."

"I think I'll try and get some sleep first but if I don't doze off, I'll probably be down."

The woman looked past Linnette into the room. "You got everything you need?"

"I'm fine."

"If your brother's room starts to bother you, just let me know. You can always change rooms for no extra cost."

"Thanks."

The woman smiled. "Enjoy the Kool-Aid." She checked the man's wristwatch she wore on her thick wrist. "Hey, time for Blackie."

"Blackie?"

"Boston Blackie. You ever watch him?"

"I guess not."

"Great show; really, great show."

"Well, thank you."

"You're welcome. And remember about keeping me company."

"Oh, I will. I promise."

"Well, good night."

"Good night," Linnette said, and then quietly closed the door.

Ten minutes later, the cabbie pulled up in front of the hotel.

As always, the street reminded Aimee of a painting by Thomas Hart Benton she'd once seen in a Chicago gallery, a street where even the street lamps looked twisted and grotesque.

Aimee flung a five dollar bill in the front seat and said, "I appreciate you speeding."

The cabbie picked up the fin, examined it as if he suspected it might be counterfeit, and then said, "Good luck with whatever your problem is, lady."

Aimee was out of the cab, hurrying into the lobby.

She went right to the desk and to the heavyset clerk who was leaning on her elbows and watching Kent Taylor as "Boston Blackie."

The woman sighed bitterly, as if she'd just been forced to give up her first born, and said, "Help you?"

"I'm looking for a woman who just came in here."

"What kind of woman?"

"A dwarf."

The desk clerk looked Aimee over more carefully. "What about her?"

"It's important that I talk to her right away."

"Why?"

"Because—because she's a friend of mine and I think she's going to do something very foolish."

"Like what?"

"For God's sake," Aimee said. "I know she's here. Tell me what room's she in before it's too late."

The desk clerk was just about to respond when the gunshot sounded on the floor above.

Aimee had never heard anything so loud in her life.

The echo seemed to go on for hours.

"What room is she in?" Aimee screamed.

"208!" the woman said.

Aimee reached the staircase in moments, and started running up the steps two at a time.

An old man in boxer shorts and a sunken, hairy chest stood in the hallway in front of 208 looking sleepy and scared.

"What the Sam hell's going on?"

Aimee said nothing, just pushed past him to the door. She turned the knob. Locked.

Aimee heard the desk clerk lumbering up the stairs behind her.

Aimee turned and ran toward the steps again. She pushed out her hand and laid the palm up and open.

"The key. Hurry."

The desk clerk, her entire body heaving from her exertion, dropped the key in Aimee's hand. The desk clerk tried to say something but she had no wind.

Aimee ran back to 208, inserted the key. Pushed the door open.

The first thing was the darkness; the second, the acrid odor of gunpowder. The third was the hellish neon red that shone through the dirty sheer curtains.

Aimee was afraid of what she was going to see.

Could she really handle seeing somebody who'd shot herself at point blank range?

Aimee took two steps over the threshold.

And then heard the noise.

At first, she wasn't sure what it was. Only after she took a few more steps into the dark tiny room did she recognize what she was hearing.

A woman lying face down in the bed, the sound of her sobbing muffled into the mattress.

Just now the desk clerk came panting into the yellow frame of the door and said, "She dead?"

"No," Aimee said quietly to the woman. "No, she's not dead."

And then Aimee silently closed the door behind her and went to sit with Linnette on the bed.

Aimee had been with carnivals since she was fourteen years old, when she'd run off from a Kentucky farm and from a pa who saw nothing wrong with doing with her what he'd done with her other two sisters. She was now twenty-eight. In the intervening years she'd wondered many times what it would be like to have a child of her own and tonight she thought she was finding out, at least in a curious sort of way.

It was not respectful, she was sure, to think of Linnette as a child just because Linnette was so little, but as Aimee sat there for three-and-a-half hours in the dark, breathless from holding Linnette in her lap and rocking her as she would an infant, the thought was inevitable. And then the wind from midnight came, and things cooled off at least a little bit.

Aimee didn't say much, really—what could she say?—she just hugged Linnette and let her cry and let her talk and let her cry some more and it was so sad that Aimee herself started crying sometimes, thinking of how cruel people could be to anybody who was different in any way, and thinking of that sonofabitch Ralph Banghart spying on the little guy in the house of mirrors, and thinking of how terrified the little guy had been when he fell prey to Ralph's practical joke. Life was just so sad sometimes when you saw what happened to people, and usually to innocent people at that, people that life had been cruel enough to already.

So that's why she mostly listened, Aimee, because when something was as overwhelming as the little guy's life had been—

Sometimes the desk clerk made the long and taxing trip up the stairs and knocked with a single knuckle and said, "You okay in there, hon?"

And Aimee would say, "We're fine, we're fine," not knowing exactly who "you" meant.

And then the desk clerk would go away and Aimee would start rocking Linnette again and listening to her and wanting to tell Linnette that she felt terrible about the little guy's death.

And then it occurred to Aimee that maybe by sitting here like this and listening to Linnette and rocking her, maybe she was in some way making up for playing a small part in the little guy's suicide.

"Sometimes I just get so scared," Linnette said just as dawn was breaking coral colored across the sky.

And Aimee knew just what Linnette was talking about because Aimee got scared like that, too, sometimes.

The Greyhound arrived twenty-three minutes late that afternoon.

Aimee and Linnette stood in the depot entrance with a group of other people. There was a farm girl who kept saying how excited she was to be going to Fresno and a Marine who kept saying it was going to be good to see Iowa again and an old woman who kept saying she hoped they kept the windows closed because even on a 92 degree day like this one she'd get a chill.

"You ever get up to Sacramento?" Linnette asked.

"Sometimes."

"You could always call me at the library and we could have lunch."

"That sounds like fun, Linnette. It really does."

Linnette took Aimee's hand and gave it a squeeze. "You really helped me last night. I'll never forget it, Aimee. I really won't."

Just then the bus pulled in with a *whoosh* of air brakes and a puff of black diesel smoke.

In one of the front windows a five-year-old boy was looking out and when he saw Linnette, he started jumping up and down and pointing, and then a couple of moments later another five-year-old face appeared in the same window and now there were two boys looking and pointing and laughing at Linnette.

Maybe the worst part of it all, Aimee thought, was that they didn't even really mean to be cruel.

And then the bus door was flung open and a Greyhound driver looking dapper in a newly-starched uniform stepped down and helped several old ladies off the bus.

"I wish he could have known you, Aimee," Linnette said. "He sure would have liked you. He sure would've."

And then, for once, it was Aimee who started the crying and she wasn't even sure why. It just seemed right somehow, she thought, as she helped the little woman take the first big step up into the bus.

A minute later, Linnette was sitting in the middle of the bus, next to a window seat. Her eyes barely reached the window ledge.

Behind Aimee, the door burst open and the two five-year-olds came running out of the depot, carrying cups of Pepsi.

They looked up and saw Linnette in the window. They started pointing and giggling immediately.

Aimee grabbed the closest one by the ear, giving it enough of a twist to inflict some real pain.

"That's one fine lady aboard that bus there, you hear me? And you treat her like a fine lady, too, or you're going to get your butts spanked! Do you understand me?" Aimee said.

Then she let go of the boy's ear.

"You understand me?" she repeated.

The boys looked at each other and then back to Aimee.

They seemed scared of her, which was what she wanted them to be.

"Yes, ma'm," both boys said in unison. "We understand."

"Good. Now you get up there on that bus and behave yourselves."

"Yes, ma'm," the boys said again, and climbed aboard the bus, not looking back at her even once.

Aimee waited till the Greyhound pulled out with a roar of engine and a poof of sooty smoke.

She waved at Linnette and Linnette waved back. "Good-bye," Aimee said, and was afraid she was going to start crying.

When the bus was gone, Aimee walked over to the taxi stand. A young man who looked like a child was driving.

Aimee told him to take her to the carnival and then she settled back in the seat and looked out the window.

After a time, it began to rain, a hot summer rain, and the rest of the day and all the next long night, Aimee tried to keep herself from thinking about certain things. She tried so very hard.

When I was in the tenth grade, a friend of mine got drunk one night, drank too much whiskey with an ex-con, and then rode along as the ex-con stuck up a gas station with a shotgun.

The poor kid who'd been working the graveyard shift took three bullets in the chest, and was dead by the time the police arrived.

In my old neighborhood, prison was not an unknown fate. To some kids, serving time was even a badge of honor.

But there was no honor for those left behind. Even in the neighborhood, the wives and the children of convicts knew they were just as much outcasts as their husbands and fathers.

A woman I worked with in the eighties saw her own husband go off to prison and on the days she visited him, fear and dread in her eyes, I realized that, three decades later, nothing had changed. Nothing had changed at all.

PRISONERS

I am in my sister's small room with its posters of Madonna and Tiffany. Sis is fourteen. Already tall, already pretty. Dressed in jeans and a blue t-shirt. Boys call and come over constantly. She wants nothing to do with boys.

Her back is to me. She will not turn around. I sit on the edge of her bed, touching my hand to her shoulder. She smells warm, of sleep. I say, "Sis listen to me."

She says nothing. She almost always says nothing.

"He wants to see you Sis."

Nothing.

"When he called last weekend—you were all he talked about. He even started crying when you wouldn't come to the phone Sis. He really did."

Nothing.

"Please, Sis. Please put on some good clothes and get ready 'cause we've got to leave in ten minutes. We've got to get there on time and you know it." I lean over so I can see her face.

She tucks her face into her pillow.

She doesn't want me to see that she is crying.

"Now you go and get ready Sis. You go and get ready, all right?"

"I don't know who she thinks she is," Ma says when I go downstairs. "Too good to go and see her own father."

As she talks Ma is packing a big brown grocery sack. Into it go a cornucopia of goodies—three cartons of Lucky Strike filters, three packages of Hershey bars, two bottles of Ban roll-on deodorant, three Louis L'Amour paperbacks as well as all the stuff that's there already.

Ma looks up at me. I've seen pictures of her when she was a young woman. She was a beauty. But that was before she started putting on weight and her hair started thinning and she stopped caring about how she dressed and all. "She going to go with us?"

"She says not."

"Just who does she think she is?"

"Calm down Ma. If she doesn't want to go, we'll just go ahead without her."

"What do we tell your Dad?"

"Tell him she's got the flu?"

"The way she had the flu the last six times?"

"She's gone a few times."

"Yeah twice out of the whole year he's been there."

"Well."

"How do you think he feels? He gets all excited thinking he's going to see her and then she doesn't show up. How do you think he feels? She's his own flesh and blood."

I sigh. Ma's none too healthy and getting worked up this way doesn't do her any good. "I better go and call Riley."

"That's it. Go call Riley. Leave me here alone to worry about what we're going to tell your Dad."

"You know how Riley is. He appreciates a call."

"You don't care about me no more than your selfish sister does."

I go out to the living room where the phone sits on the end table I picked up at Goodwill last Christmastime. A lot of people don't like to shop at Goodwill, embarrassed about going in there and all. The only thing I don't like is the smell. All those old clothes hanging. Sometimes I wonder if you opened up a grave if it wouldn't smell like Goodwill.

I call K-Mart, which is where I work as a manager trainee while I'm finishing off my retail degree at the junior college. My girlfriend Karen works at K-Mart too. "Riley?"

"Hey, Tom."

"How're things going in my department?" A couple
months ago Riley, who is the assistant manager over the whole
store, put me in charge of the automotive department.

"Good great."

"Good. I was worried." Karen always says she's proud
'cause I worry so much about my job. Karen says it proves I'm
responsible. Karen says one of the reasons she loves me so
much is 'cause I'm responsible. I guess I'd rather have her love
me for my blue eyes or something but of course I don't say
anything because Karen can get crabby about strange things
sometimes.

"You go and see your old man today, huh?" Riley says.

"Yeah."

"Hell of a way to spend your day off."

"It's not so bad. You get used to it."

"Any word on when he gets out?"

"Be a year or so yet. Being his second time in and all."

"You're a hell of a kid Tom I ever tell you that before?"

"Yeah you did Riley and I appreciate it." Riley is a year
older than me but sometimes he likes to pretend he's my uncle
or something. But he means well and, like I told him, I
appreciate it. Like when Dad's name was in the paper for the
burglary and everything. The people at K-Mart all saw it and
started treating me funny. But not Riley. He'd walk up and
down the aisles with me and even put his arm on my shoulder
like we were the best buddies in the whole world or something.
In the coffee room this fat woman made a crack about it and
Riley got mad and said, "Why don't you shut your fucking
mouth, Shirley?" Nobody said anything more about my Dad
after that. Of course poor Sis had it a lot worse than me at
Catholic school. She had it real bad. Some of those kids really
got vicious. A lot of nights I'd lay awake thinking of all the
things I wanted to do to those kids. I'd do it with my hands
too, wouldn't even use weapons.

"Well say hi to your Mom."

"Thanks Riley. I'll be sure to."

"She's a hell of a nice lady." Riley and his girl came over one night when Ma'd had about three beers and was in a really good mood. They got along really well. He had her laughing at his jokes all night. Riley knows a lot of jokes. A lot of them.

"I sure hope we make our goal today."

"You just relax Tom and forget about the store. OK?"

"I'll try."

"Don't try Tom. Do it." He laughs, being my uncle again. "That's an order."

In the kitchen, done with packing her paper bag, Ma says, "I shouldn't have said that."

"Said what?" I say.

"About you being like your sister."

"Aw Ma. I didn't take that seriously."

"We couldn't have afforded to stay in this house if you hadn't been promoted to assistant manager. Not many boys would turn over their whole paychecks to their Mas." She doesn't mention her sister who is married to a banker who is what bankers aren't supposed to be, generous. I help but he helps a lot.

She starts crying.

I take her to me, hold her. Ma needs to cry a lot. Like she fills up with tears and will drown if she can't get rid of them. When I hold her I always think of the pictures of her as a young woman, of all the terrible things that have cost her her beauty.

When she's settled down some I say, "I'll go talk to Sis."

But just as I say that I hear the old boards of the house creak and there in the doorway, dressed in a white blouse and a blue skirt and blue hose and the blue flats I bought her for her last birthday, is Sis.

Ma sees her too and starts crying all over again. "Oh God hon thanks so much for changing your mind."

Then Ma puts her arms out wide and she goes over to Sis and throws her arms around her and gets her locked inside this big hug.

I can see Sis' blue eyes staring at me over Ma's shoulder.

* * *

In the soft fog of the April morning I see watercolor brown cows on the curve of the green hills and red barns faint in the rain. I used to want to be a farmer till I took a two week job summer of junior year where I cleaned out dairy barns and it took me weeks to get the odor of wet hay and cowshit and hot pissy milk from my nostrils and then I didn't want to be a farmer ever again.

"You all right hon?" Ma asks Sis.

But Sis doesn't answer. Just stares out the window at the watercolor brown cows.

"Ungrateful little brat" Ma says under her breath.

If Sis hears this she doesn't let on. She just stares out the window.

"Hon slow down" Ma says to me. "This road's got a lot of curves in it."

And so it does.

Twenty-three curves—I've counted them many times—and you're on top of a hill looking down into a valley where the prison lies.

Curious, I once went to the library and read up on the prison. According to the historical society it's the oldest prison still standing in the Midwest, built of limestone dragged by prisoners from a nearby quarry. In 1948 the west wing had a fire that killed 18 blacks (they were segregated in those days) and in 1957 there was a riot that got a guard castrated with a busted pop bottle and two inmates shot dead in the back by other guards who were never brought to trial.

From the two-lane asphalt road that winds into the prison you see the steep limestone walls and the towers where uniformed guards toting riot guns look down at you as you sweep west to park in the visitors' parking lot.

As we walk through the rain to the prison, hurrying as the fat drops splatter on our heads, Ma says, "I forgot. Don't say anything about your cousin Bessie."

281

"Oh. Right."

"Stuff about cancer always makes your Dad depressed. You know it runs in his family a lot."

She glances over her shoulder at Sis shambling along. Sis had not worn a coat. The rain doesn't seem to bother her. She is staring out at something still as if her face was nothing more than a mask which hides her real self. "You hear me?" Ma asks Sis.

If Sis hears she doesn't say anything.

"How're you doing this morning Jimmy?" Ma asks the fat guard who lets us into the waiting room.

His stomach wriggles beneath his threadbare uniform shirt like something troubled struggling to be born.

He grunts something none of us can understand. He obviously doesn't believe in being nice to Ma no matter how nice Ma is to him. Would break prison decorum apparently the sonofabitch. But if you think he is cold to us—and most people in the prison are—you should see how they are to the families of queers or with men who did things to children.

The cold is in my bones already. Except for July and August prison is always cold to me. The bars are cold. The walls are cold. When you go into the bathroom and run the water your fingers tingle. The prisoners are always sneezing and coughing. Ma always brings Dad lots of Contac and Listerine even though I told her about this article that said Listerine isn't anything except a mouthwash.

In the waiting room—which is nothing more than the yellow-painted room with battered old wooden chairs—a turn-key named Stan comes in and leads you right up to the visiting room, the only problem being that separating you from the visiting room is a set of bars. Stan turns the key that raises these bars and then you get inside and he lowers the bars behind you. For a minute or so you're locked in between two walls and two sets of bars. You get a sense of what it's like to be in a cell. The first couple times this happened I got scared. My chest started heaving and I couldn't catch my breath, sort of like the nightmares I have sometimes.

Stan then raises the second set of bars and you're one room away from the visiting room or VR as the prisoners call it. In prison you always lower the first set of bars before you raise the next one. That way nobody escapes.

In this second room, not much bigger than a closet with a stand-up clumsy metal detector near the door leading to the VR, Stan asks Ma and Sis for their purses and me for my wallet. He asks if any of us have got any open packs of cigarettes and if so to hand them over. Prisoners and visitors alike can carry only full packs of cigarettes into the VR. Open packs are easy to hide stuff in.

You pass through the metal detector and straight into the VR room.

The first thing you notice is how all of the furniture is in color coded sets—loungers and vinyl molded chairs makes up a set—orange green blue or red. Like that. This is so Mona the guard in here can tell you where to sit just by saying a color such as "Blue" which means you go sit in the blue seat. Mona makes Stan look like a really friendly guy. She's fat with hair cut man short and a voice man deep. She wears her holster and gun with real obvious pleasure. One time Ma didn't understand what color she said and Mona's hand dropped to her service revolver like she was going to whip it out or something. Mona doesn't like to repeat herself. Mona is the one the black prisoner knocked unconscious a year ago. The black guy is married to this white girl which right away you can imagine Mona not liking at all so she's looking for any excuse to hassle him so the black guy one time gets down on his hands and knees to play with his little baby and Mona comes over and says you can only play with the kids in the Toy Room (TR) and he says can't you make an exception and Mona sly like bumps him hard on the shoulder and he just flashes the way prisoners sometimes do and jumps up from the floor and not caring that she's a woman or not just drops her with a right hand and the way the story is told now anyway by prisoners and their families, everybody in VR instead of rushing to help her break out into applause just like it's a movie or something. Standing ovation. The black guy was in the hole for six months but was quoted afterward as saying it was worth it.

Most of the time it's not like that at all. Nothing exciting I mean. Most of the time it's just depressing.

Mostly it's women here to see husbands. They usually bring their kids so there's a lot of noise. Crying laughing chasing around. You can tell if there's trouble with a parole— the guy not getting out when he's supposed to—because that's when the arguments always start, the wife having built her hopes up and then the husband saying there's nothing he can do I'm sorry honey nothing I can do and sometimes the woman will really start crying or arguing, I even saw a woman slap her husband once, the worst being of course when some little kid starts crying and says, "Daddy I want you to come home!" That's usually when the prisoner himself starts crying.

As for touching or fondling, there's none of it. You can kiss your husband for thirty seconds and most guards will hassle you even before your time's up if you try it open mouth or anything. Mona in particular is a real bitch about something like this. Apparently Mona doesn't like the idea of men and women kissing.

Another story you hear a lot up here is how this one prisoner cut a hole in his pocket so he could stand by the Coke machine and have his wife put her hand down his pocket and jack him off while they just appeared to be innocently standing there, though that may be one of those stories the prisoners just like to tell.

The people who really have it worst are those who are in the hole or some other kind of solitary. On the west wall there's this long screen for them. They have to sit behind the screen the whole time. They can't touch their kids or anything. All they can do is look.

I can hear Ma's breath take up sharp when they bring Dad in.

He's still a handsome man—thin, dark curly hair with no

gray, and more solid than ever since he works out in the prison weight room all the time. He always walks jaunty as if to say that wearing a gray uniform and living in an interlocking set of cages has not yet broken him. But you can see in his blue eyes that they broke him a long time ago.

"Hiya everybody" he says trying to sound real happy.

Ma throws her arms around him and they hold each other. Sis and I sit down on the two chairs. I look at Sis. She stares at the floor.

Dad comes over then and says, "You two sure look great."

"So do you" I say. "You must be still lifting those weights."

"Bench pressed two-twenty-five this week."

"Man" I say and look at Sis again. I nudge her with my elbow.

She won't look up.

Dad stares at her. You can see how sad he is about her not looking up. Soft he says, "It's all right."

Ma and Dad sit down then and we go through the usual stuff, how things are going at home and at my job and in junior college, and how things are going in prison. When he first got there, they put Dad in with this colored guy—he was Jamaican—but then they found out he had AIDs so they moved Dad out right away. Now he's with this guy who was in Viet Nam and got one side of his face burned. Dad says once you get used to looking at him he's a nice guy with two kids of his own and not queer in any way or into drugs at all. In prison the drugs get pretty bad.

We talk a half hour before Dad looks at Sis again. "So how's my little girl."

She still won't look up.

"Ellen" Ma says "you talk to your Dad and right now."

Sis raises her head. She looks right at Dad but doesn't seem to see him at all. Ellen can do that. It's really spooky.

Dad puts his hand out and touches her.

Sis jerks her hand away. It's the most animated I've seen her in weeks.

"You give your Dad a hug and you give him a hug right

now" Ma says to Sis.

Sis, still staring at Dad, shakes her head.

"It's all right" Dad says. "It's all right. She just doesn't like to come up here and I don't blame her at all. This isn't a nice place to visit at all." He smiles. "Believe me I wouldn't be here if they didn't make me."

Ma asks "Any word on your parole?"

"My lawyer says two years away. Maybe three, 'cause it's a second offense and all." Dad sighs and takes Ma's hand. "I know it's hard for you to believe hon—I mean practically every guy in here says the same thing—but I didn't break into that store that night. I really didn't. I was just walking along the river."

"I do believe you hon" Ma says "and so does Tom and so does Sis. Right kids?"

I nod. Sis has gone back to staring at the floor.

"'Cause I served time before for breaking and entering the cops just automatically assumed it was me" Dad says. He shakes his head. The sadness is back in his eyes. "I don't have no idea how my billfold got on the floor of that place." He sounds miserable and now he doesn't look jaunty or young. He looks old and gray.

He looks back at Sis. "You still gettin' straight A's hon?"

She looks up at him. But doesn't nod or anything.

"She sure is" Ma says. "Sister Rosemary says Ellen is the best student she's got. Imagine that."

Dad starts to reach out to Sis again but then takes his hand back.

Over in the red section this couple start arguing. The woman is crying and this little girl maybe six is holding real tight to her Dad who looks like he's going to start crying too. That bitch Mona has put on her mirror sunglasses again so you can't tell what she's thinking but you can see from the angle of her face that she's watching the three of them in the red section. Probably enjoying herself.

"Your lawyer sure it'll be two years?" Ma says.

"Or three."

"I sure do miss you hon" Ma says.

"I sure do miss you too hon."

"Don't know what I'd do without Tom to lean on." She makes a point of not mentioning Sis who she's obviously still mad at because Sis won't speak to Dad.

"He's sure a fine young man" Dad says. "Wish I woulda been that responsible when I was his age. Wouldn't be in here today if I'da been."

Sis gets up and leaves the room. Says nothing. Doesn't even look at anybody exactly. Just leaves. Mona directs her to the ladies room.

"I'm sorry she treats you this way hon" Ma says. "She thinks she's too good to come see her Dad in prison."

"It's all right" Dad says looking sad again. He watches Sis leave the visiting room.

"I'm gonna have a good talk with her when we leave here hon" Ma says.

"Oh don't be too hard on her. Tough for a proud girl her age to come up here."

"Not too hard for Tom."

"Tom's different. Tom's mature. Tom's responsible. When Ellen gets Tom's age I'm sure she'll be mature and responsible too."

Half hour goes by before Sis comes back. Almost time to leave. She walks over and sits down.

"You give your Dad a hug now" Ma says.

Sis looks at Dad. She stands up then and goes over and puts her arms out. Dad stands up grinning and takes her to him and hugs her tighter than I've ever seen him hug anybody. It's funny because right then and there he starts crying. Just holding Sis so tight. Crying.

"I love you hon" Dad says to her. "I love you hon and I'm sorry for all the mistakes I've made and I'll never make them again I promise you."

Ma starts crying too.

Sis says nothing.

When Dad lets her go I look at her eyes. They're the same

as they were before. She's staring right at him but she doesn't seem to see him somehow.

Mona picks up the microphone that blasts through the speakers hung from the ceiling. She doesn't need a speaker in a room this size but she obviously likes how loud it is and how it hurts your ears.

"Visiting hours are over. You've got fifteen seconds to say goodbye and then inmates have to start filing over to the door."

"I miss you so much hon" Ma says and throws her arms around Dad.

He hugs Ma but over his shoulder he's looking at Sis. She is standing up. She has her head down again.

Dad looks so sad so sad.

"I'd like to know just who the hell you think you are treatin' your own father that way" Ma says on the way back to town.

The rain and the fog are real bad now so I have to concentrate on my driving. On the opposite side of the road cars appear quickly in the fog and then vanish. It's almost unreal.

The wipers are slapping loud and everything smells damp the rubber of the car and the vinyl seat covers and the ashtray from Ma's menthol cigarettes. Damp.

"You hear me young lady?" Ma says.

Sis is in the back seat again alone. Staring out the window. At the fog I guess.

"Come on Ma, she hugged him" I say.

"Yeah when I practically had to twist her arm to do it." Ma shakes her head. "Her own flesh and blood."

Sometimes I want to get really mad and let it out but I know it would just hurt Ma to remind her what Dad was doing to Ellen those years after he came out of prison the first time. I know for a fact he was doing it because I walked in on them one day little eleven-year-old Ellen there on the bed underneath my naked dad, staring off as he grunted and moved around inside her, staring off just the way she does now.

Staring off.

Ma knew about it all along of course but she wouldn't do anything about it. Wouldn't admit it probably not even to herself. In psychology, which I took last year at the junior college, that's called denial. I even brought it up a couple times but she just said I had a filthy mind and don't ever say nothing like that again.

Which is why I broke into that store that night and left Dad's billfold behind. Because I knew they'd arrest him and then he couldn't force Ellen into the bed anymore. Not that I blame Dad entirely. Prison makes you crazy no doubt about it and he was in there four years the first time. But even so I love Sis too much.

"Own flesh and blood" Ma says again lighting up one of her menthols and shaking her head.

I look into the rearview mirror at Sis's eyes. "Wish I could make you smile" I say to her. "Wish I could make you smile."

But she just stares out the window.

She hasn't smiled for a long time of course.

Not for a long time.

(For Gail Cross)

AFTERWORD

Dean R. Koontz

1. The Origins of the Relationship
Ed Gorman and I met on the telephone and spent scores of hours in conversation spread over almost two years before we finally met face to face. No, it wasn't one of those sleazy pay-by-the-minute "party-line" dating services gone awry. It started as an interview for his magazine, *Mystery Scene*, but we spent so much time laughing that we began having bull sessions on a regular basis.

He has a marvelous sense of humor and a dry wit. Oh, sure, he can produce faux flatulence with his hand in his armpit every bit as convincingly as Princess Di can, and like the Pope he never goes anywhere without plastic vomit and a dribble glass, but it's the more *refined* side of Ed that I find the most amusing.

2. How I Wound Up in Cedar Rapids
In 1989, my wife Gerda and I drove across country to do some book research, to visit some relatives and old friends, to receive an honorary doctorate at my alma mater in Pennsylvania—and to give a proper test to our new radar detector. The

detector worked swell: we left the Los Angeles area at eight o'clock on a Thursday morning and were in eastern Arkansas in time for dinner. We ate at our motel, and the food wasn't all that good, but everyone thought we were enjoying the hell out of ourselves because crossing six states under four Gs of acceleration contorts your face muscles into a wide grin that remains fixed for eight to ten hours after you get out of the car.

The research was conducted successfully. The visits with friends and relatives were a delight. The address I delivered to the graduating class was well received. I was awarded the honorary doctorate—whereafter I had to decide whether to be a podiatrist or cardiovascular surgeon, a very difficult choice in a world where heart disease and sore feet tragically afflict millions.

Soon we were driving west from Pennsylvania, on our way home, our tasks completed and our lofty goals fulfilled. Our radar detector was clipped to the sun visor, Ohio and Illinois and Indiana were passing in a pretty blur rather like that of the star swarms beyond the portals of the Enterprise when Captain Kirk tells Scotty to put the ship up to warp speed, and we were proud to be participating in that great American pastime— Avoiding Police Detection. Driving in opposition to the direction of Earth's rotation, therefore having to set the car clock back an hour every once in a while, we might have made it to California before we left for the journey east, in time to warn ourselves against that damn salad-bar restaurant outside of Memphis—except we planned to take a side trip to Cedar Rapids, Iowa, to meet Ed and his wife Carol.

3. The First Night of that Historic Visit

After leaving Interstate 80, we passed through gently rising plains and rich farmland, all of it so bland that we began to be afraid that we had died and gone to the twenty-third circle of Hell (Dante had it wrong; he undercounted), where the punishment for the sinner is terminal boredom. We couldn't get anything on the radio but Merle Haggard tunes.

Late in the afternoon, we reached Cedar Rapids, which

proved to be a surprisingly pleasant place, attractive to more than the eye. As we crossed the city line, the air was redolent of brown sugar, raisins, coconut, and other delicious aromas, because one of the giant food-processing companies was evidently cooking up a few hundred thousand granola bars. How pleasant, we thought, to live in a place where the air was daily perfumed with such delicious scents. It would be like living in the witch's fragrant gingerbread house after Hansel and Grettel had disposed of her and there was no longer a danger of becoming a human popover in the crone's oven.

That evening we went to dinner with Ed and Carol at a lovely restaurant in our hotel. We had a great good time. Carol, who is also a writer—primarily of young-adult fiction—is an attractive blonde with delicate features, very personable and very much a lady. Ed surprised us by wearing shoes. Not to say that shoes were the only thing he was wearing. He had socks, too, and a nice suit, and I think he was also wearing a shirt, though my memory might well be faulty regarding that detail.

There was almost *too* much conviviality for one evening. Ed started telling jokes about Zoroastrianism, involving the God Ahura Mazda, of which he has an infinite store—always a sure sign that he is having too good a time and might begin to hyperventilate or even pass a kidney stone out of sheer exuberance. They usually begin, "Ahura Mazda, Jehova, and Buddha were all in a rowboat together," or something like that. For his sake, we decided to call it an evening and meet again first thing in the morning. Carol asked if there was anything special we'd like to do or see around town (like watch corn growing), and we said that we had heard there was a large Czechoslovakian community in Cedar Rapids; as this was an ethnic group about which we knew little, we thought it might be interesting to visit any shops that dealt in Czech arts, crafts, foods, assault weapons imported from the East Bloc, and that sort of thing. We all hugged, and after Ed told one more Zoroastrianism joke— "Ahura Mazda was having lunch with two attorneys and a proctologist"—we parted for the night.

4. *On the Edge of Sleep*

Lying in our hotel-room bed that night, on the edge of sleep, Gerda and I spoke of what a lovely evening it had been.

"They're both so nice," Gerda said.

"It's so nice that someone you like on the phone turns out to be someone you also like in person," I said.

"I had such a nice time," Gerda said.

"That's nice," I said.

"Those Zoroastrianism jokes were hilarious."

"He was wearing shoes," I noted.

"I was a little worried when he hyperventilated."

"Yeah, I was afraid it was going to build up to a kidney-stone expulsion," I said.

"But it didn't," Gerda said, "and that's nice."

"Yes, that's very nice," I agreed.

"Tomorrow is going to be a very nice day."

"Very nice," I agreed, anticipating the morning with enormous pleasure.

5. *A Very Nice Day*

Overnight, Ed and Carol discovered a museum of Czechoslovakian arts and crafts in Cedar Rapids, and in the morning we happily embarked on a cultural expedition. The museum proved to be on a—how shall I say this as nicely as possible?—on a rather *frayed* edge of town. When we got out of Ed's car, I was hit by the most powerful stench I'd ever encountered in more than forty years of varied experience. This was a stink so profound that it not only brought tears to my eyes and forced me to clamp a handkerchief over my nose but brought me instantly to the brink of regurgitation that would have made the explosively vomiting girl in *The Exorcist* seem like a mere dribbler. When I looked at Gerda, I saw she had also resorted to a handkerchief over the nose. Though you might have noticed that comic hyperbole is an element of the style in which I've chosen to write this piece, you must understand that as regards this odor, I am not exaggerating in the least. This vile miasma was capable of searing the paint off a car and blinding small animals, yet Ed and Carol led us toward the museum, chatting and laughing, apparently oblivious of the hellish fetor that had nearly rendered us unconscious.

Finally, after I had clawed desperately at Ed's arm for ten or fifteen unsteady steps, I caught his attention. Choking and wheezing in disgust, I said, "Ed, for the love of God, man, what is that horrible odor?"

"Odor?" Ed said. Puzzled he stopped, turned, sniffing delicately at the air, as if seeking the elusive scent of a frail tropical flower.

"Surely you smell it," I protested. "It's so bad I'm beginning to bleed from the ears!"

"Oh, *that*," Ed said. He pointed toward some huge buildings fully five hundred yards away. "That's a slaughterhouse. They must be in the middle of a hog kill, judging by the smell. It's the stink of blood, feces, urine, internal organs, all mixed up together."

"It doesn't bother you?"

"Not really. When you've smelled it often enough over the years, you get used to it."

Gagging but determined to be manly about this, I managed to follow them into the Czech museum, where the odor miraculously did not penetrate. The museum turned out to be one of the most fascinating we'd ever toured, humble quarters but a spectacular and charming collection of all things Czech.

We spent longer there than we had anticipated, and when we stepped outside again, the air was clean, the stench gone without a trace. All the paint had melted off the Gormans' car, and a couple of hundred birds had perished in flight and now littered the ground, but otherwise there was no indication that the air had ever been anything but sweet.

I thought of the delicious aroma of granola-bar manufacturing, which had marked our arrival. That was at the front door. The steaming malodor of the slaughterhouse indicated what went on at the back door. Suddenly Cedar Rapids seemed less innocent, even sinister, and I began to understand for the first time how Ed could live in such sunny, bucolic environs with the gracious and lovely Carol always nearby—and nevertheless be inspired to write about the dark side of the human heart.

6. *Ed Gorman, Writer*

Aside from being a great guy, Ed Gorman can write circles around a whole slew of authors who are more famous than he is. Hell, he could write hexagons around them if he wanted.

He has a knack for creating dialogue that sounds natural and true. His metaphors and similes are spare and elegant. His characters are multifaceted and often too human for their own good. His style is so clean and sharp you could almost perform surgery with it; *he* does, using it like a scalpel to lay bare the inner workings of the human mind and heart.

His Jack Dwyer mysteries—especially *The Autumn Dead* and the beautifully moody and poignant *A Cry of Shadows*—are as compelling and stylistically sophisticated as any detective stories I've ever read.

If Ed has a shortcoming as a writer, it is that he wants to do *everything*. He likes Westerns, so periodically he writes an oater—always a damned good oater, too. He likes horror stories, so now and then, writing as Daniel Ransom, he produces a horror story. He likes totally serious, almost somber detective fiction but also lighter-hearted detective fiction; he has written both types well. He likes suspense, science fiction ... well, you get the idea. Having such a catholic taste is healthy; it contributes to his freshness of viewpoint. But when a writer actually produces work in multiple genres, he dilutes his impact with readers and has more difficulty building a reputation. I know too well. Over the years, always looking for a different challenge, I've written in virtually every genre *except* the Western. Finally I discovered a way to combine many of my favorite categories of fiction into one novel, which is when I started to develop a larger audience. In time, I suspect, Ed will find his own way to make his wide-ranging interests more a marketing asset than a liability. I, for one, can't wait to see what he'll give us in the years ahead.

296

One warning: considering how powerful Ed's prose can be, if he ever writes about a hog kill, his personal experience should lead to such pungent olfactory descriptions that readers all over the world will be hard-pressed not to void their most recent meals into the pages of that book. Don't worry, you'll be warned in advance if one of his novels has a hog-kill scene in it because, being the reader's friend, I will be sure to have an endorsement on the jacket, alerting you in language something like this: "A brilliant, dazzling, breath-taking novel, a work of sheer genius. Everyone should read Gorman—but in this case, only while wearing a protective rubber sheet or while sitting naked in a bathtub."

7. *The Lovely Gorman Home*
That fine spring day in Cedar Rapids, after visiting the Czech museum adjacent to the hog kill, we went to lunch at an all-you-can-eat buffet restaurant with as lavish a spread as I had ever seen. I ate a soda cracker.

After lunch we went to Ed and Carol's house, which was most tastefully furnished. The place was spotless, with beautiful polished-wood floors, and suffused with a friendly atmosphere.

A couple of minutes after we arrived, my eyes began to sting, then burn, then flood with tears. For a moment I thought I was overcome with emotion at being welcomed into my friends' home. Then my sinuses suddenly felt as if they had been filled with cement, my face began to swell, and my lips itched. I realized that I had either been caught in the beam of an extra-terrestrial deathray—or was in a house where a cat resided. As I had never previously encountered monsters from far worlds but *had* encountered cats to which I was allergic, I decided I could believe the Gormans when they repeatedly insisted that they were not harboring fiendish extra-terrestrials but merely felines.

I wish I could tell you that their house was positively crawling with scores of cats; an eccentricity like that would make them even more fun to write about. However, as I remember, there were only two. For some reason I am not allergic to every cat who crosses my path, only to about half those I meet, but I seemed to be allergic to both the Gorman cats. Neither creature looked like a feline from Hell, though they had a demonic effect on me, and in less than half an hour we had to move on.

When I stumbled out of the Gorman house, I was shockingly pale, sweating, and gasping for breath. My watering eyes were so bloodshot they appeared to be on fire, and the only sound I could squeeze out of my irritated vocal cords and swollen throat was a wretched gurgle rather like that issued by a nauseated wombat.

(I realized much later, the oddest thing about that moment was the reaction of the neighbors to my near-death paroxysms on the Gormans' front lawn. None of them exhibited the least surprise or concern. It was as if they had seen scores—perhaps hundreds—of people erupting from that house in far worse condition and had become enured to the drama. Maybe they *were* cats from Hell . . . which might explain why sometimes, instead of purring, they spoke rapid, intricately cadenced Latin.)

The Gormans, being two of the nicest people I've ever known, were excessively apologetic, as if somehow they were responsible for my stupid allergy. When I could breathe again, and when my eyes had stopped spurting blood, I found myself repeatedly assuring them that none of it was their fault, that they are *allowed* to have cats in the United States of America regardless of my allergy, and that they would not rot in Hell because of their choice of pets.

(Ed has a tendency to feel responsible for the world and to blame himself for things beyond his control—like floods in Sri Lanka and train wrecks in Uzbekistan. Like any good Catholic boy, he knows that he is guilty for all the sins of the world, a vile repository of shameless want and need and lust, who deserves far worse punishment than any plague God could deliver upon him. In his mind, having cats to which a guest has an allergy is just one small step below taking an Uzi out to the mall and blowing away a hundred Christmas shoppers.)

8. *A Thankfully Uneventful Trip to Iowa City, Iowa*

Anxious to get me away from his cats and to atone for what they had done to me, Ed suggested we take a ride from Cedar Rapids to Iowa City, where we could have a pleasant stroll through Prairie Light, a large and nationally known bookstore, then have an earlyish dinner (as Gerda and I had to rise at dawn to resume our journey to California). He assured us that Iowa City also boasted a feline slaughterhouse where we could go to compare the stink of cat-kill to that of a hog-kill.

Aside from a hair-raising ride due to the sheer contempt in which Ed holds those lane-dividing lines on public highways, our sidetrip to Iowa City was uneventful. Just good conversation—much of it book talk—and a nice dinner. I had another soda cracker. I was able to keep it down with little trouble. I was quite sure that, in a month or so, the memory of the hog-kill stench would have faded sufficiently to allow me to eat normally again, certainly before my weight had slipped much lower than ninety pounds.

9. *Ed Gorman, the Phone Company, and Me*

As I write this, it is nearly three years since our stay in Cedar Rapids and our two days with Ed and Carol. As both of us are to some degree workaholics and as neither of us, therefore, is much of a traveler, Ed and I have not yet managed to get together again face to face. We stay in touch by reading each other's books—and with the help of the telephone. Our conversations continue to be punctuated with a lot of laughter—a precious, vital medicine in this madhouse world. Here's a cute anecdote: sometimes at three in the morning, Ed calls up and, with a couple of handkerchiefs over the mouthpiece of his phone, distorts his voice and makes obscene threats, apparently because he's concerned about keeping my life interesting and full of color, and I am always touched by his genuine concern that I never become bored, by the fact that he would take the time and trouble to entertain me in such a fashion. He doesn't realize that I know the identity of the obscene caller, and he would surely be embarrassed to know that I am aware of his thoughtfulness. But you see, no matter how much he distorts his voice, those cats are in his study with him, and even long-distance my lips go numb and my eyes begin to bleed.